KILLER PIZZA
THE SLICE

GREG TAYLOR

SQUARE
FISH
FEIWEL AND FRIENDS
NEW YORK, NY

SQUARE
FISH

An Imprint of Macmillan

Square Fish and the Square Fish logo are trademarks of Macmillan and
are used by Feiwel and Friends under license from Macmillan.

Library of Congress Cataloging-in-Publication Data

Taylor, Greg,
Killer Pizza : the slice / Greg Taylor.
p. cm.
Summary: Having passed the tests to become Monster Combat Officers,
teens Toby, Annabel, and Strobe are sent on a secret mission to deliver to
the Monster Protection Program a beautiful fourteen-year-old monster who
wants to defect, regardless of the considerable dangers this poses.
ISBN: 978-1-250-00478-9
[1. Monsters—Fiction.   2. Adventure and adventurers—Fiction.   3. Horror stories.]
I. Title. PZ7.T21345Kil 2011   [Fic]—dc22
2010048928

Originally published in the United States by Feiwel and Friends
First Square Fish Edition: May 2012
Square Fish logo designed by Filomena Tuosto
Book designed by Barbara Grzeslo
mackids.com

10 9 8 7 6 5 4 3 2 1

LEXILE: 840L

PROLOGUE:
ESCAPE

A girl—backlit by a three-quarter moon, low in the cloudless sky—raced across a barren, fallow field. Before reaching the dense forest that surrounded the field, the girl stopped and looked back in the direction she had just traveled. A few precious moments ticked by, then the girl turned and continued on her way. In no time at all, she was swallowed up by the forest.

And the darkness.

Later, two men appeared in the field. The moon's harsh, brittle light clearly illuminated them as they came across the field. Dressed in plain, old-fashioned clothes, they could have stepped right out of the pages of history. Say, the American Midwest in the early 1900s. The men's contemporary jewelry and tattoos—a jarring and some-what disturbing fashion statement—spoiled the compari-son, however.

The lead man, distinguished by a tattoo in the shape of

a sideways cross on his forehead, stopped halfway across the field, knelt, and studied the ground. Footprints. Clearly visible in the dirt. The man nodded at the sight, stood, and buttoned his coat against the night air. His colleague did the same. Then the two went after the girl.

■ ■ ■

The tall, skeletal-looking man sat in a wooden rocking chair, staring at the flames in a nearby stone fireplace. The shadows cast by the flames, flickering across the man's hollowed-out face, resembled restless spirits, spirits that wanted to be anywhere else but this place, this room.

Outside, back clouds had turned day to twilight. Rain attacked the windows. Wind blew through the eaves, causing an odd, groaning sound. When there was a knock on the door, muffled by the sounds of the storm, the Tall Man didn't answer right away. Then, in an odd accent impossible to trace, he said, "Come in."

The strangely shaped door, much wider than a typical door, opened, and the two men who had gone after the girl entered. They hesitated for a moment, then crossed the room. They stood quietly as the Tall Man continued to rock in his chair. Finally, the rocking chair ceased its back and forth movements.

"We followed her tracks for over a hundred miles, sir. To the nearest town. We believe she has taken a southwestern route." It was the man with the cross tattoo on his forehead who spoke, his quirky accent even stronger than the Tall Man's.

The Tall Man nodded slowly. "A southwestern route . . ."

"Yes, sir."

"So what you're saying is, after several days tracking the girl, all you have brought back to me is the news she has taken a southwestern route."

"When the rain came, it was very difficult—"

"In other words . . . you allowed a child, a mere child, to elude you."

A heavy silence fell over the room. The two men shifted uneasily. When the Tall Man slowly turned in his chair, he wasn't looking at the men, but rather something behind them. The nod he gave was barely perceptible.

What happened next showed why it was not advisable to get on the Tall Man's bad side. Exactly *what* happened . . . well, it defied any logical explanation. The man with the forehead tattoo suddenly went rigid. His mouth opened wide, but no scream emerged. The other man stumbled back against the wall, his eyes locked on the horrific sight in front of him.

His partner's body was actually crumpling inward! It was as though every ounce of moisture was being sucked from his insides! But what could be causing this hideous attack? Other than the three men, no other living thing was visible in the room.

Within a minute, the man's body resembled a mummy. A mummy with hollow eye sockets, earrings dangling from wrinkled earlobes, and a shriveled-to-half-size tattoo on its forehead. When the body fell forward and hit the floor, the Tall Man studied it briefly, as though it were a laboratory specimen of some sort, then turned his attention to the other man.

"You may go."

The man looked like he didn't believe what the Tall Man had just told him. He glanced wildly in the direction of his deceased colleague, then back at the Tall Man.

"*Go*. Before I change my mind."

The man didn't need to be told a third time. He hurried from the room and pulled the door firmly shut behind him as he exited.

The Tall Man stood and walked closer to the fire. Holding out his hands to the heat, he shook his head sadly. "You know what they say, Lemuri. If you want something done, do it yourself."

Standing a moment longer by the fire, warming himself for the long journey ahead, the man turned and walked to a nearby hat stand. He lifted a heavy winter coat from the stand and shrugged it on. Over this, he put a long rain slicker. A wide-brimmed hat completed the Tall Man's travel outfit. Walking to the door, the man opened it and stood to one side, as though waiting for something . . . or someone.

Suddenly, a shadow moved across the room. Actually, it was more like the outline of a moving figure. The mysterious form appeared to have the supernatural ability to blend in with its surroundings!

When the monstrous, chameleon-like shape moved through the open doorway—its wide, hulking profile solving the mystery of the oddly shaped door—a fierce gust of wind blew into the room, accompanied by swirling leaves and a heavy dose of rain. The Tall Man followed his invisible companion out of the room and pulled the door shut behind him, leaving a quiet and serene room in his wake.

Whoever this girl was that the Tall Man was so intent on tracking down, it was clear she had better run as fast as her legs could carry her. The man and his bloodthirsty sidekick were obviously forces to be reckoned with.

And a million miles from ordinary.

PART ONE:
MONSTROPOLIS

1

"I give up. This is totally insane."

Jostled by waves of people walking briskly in dozens of directions, Toby Magill looked hopelessly lost. His friend Strobe, a tall teen wearing a black watch cap, regarded the teeming crowd with a bemused expression. "I think we need to go over there. Past that sign and down those stairs."

"We just came *up* those stairs."

"No, we didn't."

"Yes, we did."

"You sure?"

"That's the only thing I am sure of."

"In that case . . . this is totally insane!"

"Take it easy, you two. We can figure this out."

That's exactly what Annabel Oshiro was trying to do . . . figure out the New York subway system with only a map as her guide. As Annabel studied her map, Toby and Strobe continued to take in the intense scene that surrounded them. Compared to the trio's Ohio suburban community of Hidden Hills, New York City was like a rocket blast of sound and movement.

Hundreds of people navigated the huge underground area that was an intersection for dozens of subway destinations. A bewildering number of overhead signs pointed the various ways to red, blue, green, and yellow subway lines, not to mention subway trains identified by numerous numbers and letters . . . a unique underground language. To the uninitiated, it was like standing inside a gigantic 3-D puzzle that simply didn't fit together.

"It would have made a lot more sense for the big guy to send someone to pick us up at the airport," Strobe said, obviously annoyed at this slight.

Annabel looked up from her map, nodded when she found the sign she was looking for, then slid her map into a side pocket of her backpack. "I think Harvey means this as a test, Strobe. He wants us to figure out how to get to KP headquarters on our own. Which is *this* way."

"I'm done with tests," Strobe declared as he followed Annabel down a narrow stairway toward a subway platform teeming with people. "We passed our test. A little respect is in order here."

It had been almost four months since Annabel, Toby, and Strobe met when they began working at Killer Pizza, Hidden Hills' newest pizza place. What they discovered not long after the grand opening was that the Killer Pizza franchise offered something much more than award-winning pizzas.

"Just because we killed an ugly-as-sin monster, doesn't mean we're experts," Toby pointed out. "There're always gonna be more tests to pass."

It was after a typically busy day in the Killer Pizza kitchen that Harvey P. Major III, the owner of KP, had revealed to an astonished Toby, Annabel, and Strobe that his pizza chain was actually a front—a legitimate front, with award-winning pizzas and franchises all over the world—that put all of its profits into an underground organization of monster hunters. Even though Annabel and Toby were only fourteen—Strobe, fifteen—Harvey had asked the still-disbelieving trio to try out for his elite group.

"That's our train," Annabel called out, quickly bounding down the stairs. The trio pushed their way into the rush-hour horde that was cramming into the subway car. They made it inside just as the doors closed. Toby, the last one in, was jolted when the doors slammed into his backpack. He yanked away from the doors to free himself, then flew across the aisle and landed in the lap of a passenger dressed in a smartly tailored business suit.

"Sorry!" Toby said, pushing himself away from the startled woman. When the train jerked forward and accelerated down the track, Toby lost his balance and toppled over. Fortunately, Strobe was there to catch the flailing teen before he hit the floor.

"Please excuse the boy," Strobe told the woman with a smile. "This is his first trip to New York." Tersely readjusting her crumpled newspaper, the woman pointedly ignored Strobe. After pulling Toby away from the woman and down the aisle of the crowded subway car, Strobe indicated an overhead bar. "Grab hold of that, will you. And try not to embarrass us for the rest of the ride."

"The doors attacked me," Toby countered good-naturedly. "You saw it."

Standing nearby, Annabel shook her head in exasperation. "I can't take you two anywhere. I swear."

"That may be true, but I ask you this," Strobe said. "Where would you be without us, huh?"

The subway train plunged into a dark tunnel, leaving the well-lit platform behind. Hurtling through the endless night of the tunnel on the swaying, jerking train, Toby found himself thinking about Strobe's question, but from his point of view. Where would *he* be without

Strobe and Annabel? Toby looked around the packed subway car. Not here, in New York City, that's for sure.

Fact was, Toby's life had been rather mundane before he started working at the take-out pizza place located on a Hidden Hills dead-end street. Since his first day at Killer Pizza, however, life had become tons more interesting. And maybe a bit too exciting at times.

The train suddenly entered another brightly lit platform area.

"This is our exit, guys," Annabel announced.

Toby threw himself into the middle of the competing mobs of people jostling to get on and off the subway. A veteran now of three subway car departures since arriving in New York, Toby was actually starting to enjoy what felt like a thirty-second extreme-sports event. The object? Get on or off the subway car before the doors close!

Energetically elbowing his way toward the beckoning platform, Toby made it just as the doors closed behind him, this time avoiding the subway-door backpack grab. Toby nodded in satisfaction as he located his KP partners on the crowded platform. He was already getting better at navigating the wild energy that NYC was famous for.

"From here," Annabel was saying as Toby approached, her eyes locked on her all-important subway map, "we need to get to the Fifty-first Street downtown platform of the green line and . . ."

"Annabel?" Strobe interrupted. "Just lead the way, okay?"

"What a surprise, Strobe. You're actually willing to let me lead. A little advice? Keep me in sight or you just might get lost." Annabel gave Strobe a competitive nudge, then pushed her way through the crowd.

■ ■ ■

Toby smiled when he caught sight of an unusual triangular high-rise building through the trees. "Hey, check it out, guys. How cool is Killer Pizza's headquarters?"

From a certain angle, New York's Flatiron Building looked like a huge ship's bow, aiming for Madison Square Park. Crisscrossing the park, the trio was on a collision course with the New York landmark.

"Bet you didn't know it's considered one of the first skyscrapers ever built," Toby revealed. "It was finished in 1902—"

"Looks like where Peter Parker works in the Spider-Man movies," Annabel observed.

"It is. It's one of the most recognizable buildings in the city, and not just because of the Spider-Man movies. Know how it got its name? It's built on a lot that resembles a clothing iron."

"I think somebody did a little research for this trip."

"You bet I did. I mean, how exciting is this?"

"It's not that exciting," Strobe said, playing it cool, as usual. "You obviously don't get out much, do you, Tobe."

"Compared to you, no, of course not. You know what? I can't wait to see KP's culinary operations."

"Well, you're gonna have to wait," Strobe shot back. "We're not here to learn how to make better pizzas, after all."

That's exactly what the trio's parents thought their children were doing in New York. Attending a weekend training session for "promising young employees" of Killer Pizza. But the real purpose of the trip was an intensive tour of KP's underground Monster Combat Officer headquarters.

Emerging from the park, the trio joined a crowd that was waiting for the light to turn at a nearby crosswalk. Then they walked across Broadway to the epicenter of Killer Pizza's worldwide operations.

2

The lobby of the Flatiron Building gave no indication of what went on inside its walls. Toby and Strobe strolled around the perimeter of the lobby, checking out the place as Annabel walked over to a security guard sitting behind a kiosk.

"Hi. I'm Annabel Oshiro, with Toby Magill and Strobe . . ." Annabel caught herself. Nicknames wouldn't do at KP headquarters. "Gordon Tibbles. We're here to see Harvey Major."

The guard gave Annabel a deadpan once-over, then pointed to an area just above and behind his kiosk. "Look up there, please."

"Excuse me?"

"Up there."

Annabel looked up in the direction indicated by the guard.

"Your companions need to do the same," the guard said.

"Hey, guys. Over here."

By the time Toby and Strobe had gotten their pictures taken by the phantom camera above the kiosk, the guard had put a call into Harvey's office. "Seventh floor," the guard said, pointing to the nearby elevators. "Someone will be there to meet you."

It was Harvey Major III himself waiting for the trio when the elevator doors opened onto the seventh-floor landing. At first glance, Harvey looked very boyish, certainly younger than his twenty-one years. But on closer examination, one could see that he had the eyes of a much older man, eyes that had seen a lot in a relatively short amount of time. Harvey never smiled much, but the trio noticed a slight uptick at the corner of his mouth when they stepped from the elevator.

"Welcome to New York," Harvey said, shaking hands with each of his employees.

"What are we seeing first, Chief?" Strobe asked.

"Unfortunately, your tour has to be postponed. Temporarily."

"Why's that?" Annabel asked.

Harvey walked to another elevator and pressed the button. "There's something I need you to do for me."

"Like a job?" Strobe was definitely up for anything resembling a job. Very much the gung ho soldier when it came to the smell of battle—of the monster

17

variety—Strobe had been disappointed in the recent lack of supernatural activity back in Hidden Hills.

"Actually, it is," Harvey confirmed. "I need you to make a pickup for me."

"Pickup?" Toby asked. "What are we pickin' up?"

The elevator doors opened, and the trio followed Harvey into the elevator. "A dekayi is coming in from the monster side," Harvey revealed as the doors closed and the elevator started to move slowly downward.

The trio had studied for, and passed, an examination covering all types of creatures of the night, the final step to becoming official Monster Combat Officers, but they had never heard of a dekayi. As for "coming in from the monster side," they could only guess what that meant.

"It's a division we have here," Harvey explained. "MPP. Monster Protection Program."

"You're kidding me," Strobe said.

"No."

"You never told us anything about a monster protection program." Strobe didn't like how secretive Harvey could be about his operation.

"There was never any need to. Until now."

"Do a lot of monsters come in from the monster side?" Annabel asked.

"Not in droves. But it's still a very important division

here at Killer Pizza. Mostly they're monsters we've captured. Remember, a lot of our enemies don't start out as enemies. They were humans bitten by any number of creatures. But in this case, with the dekayi, contact was made with one of our Canadian MPP specialists. Our agent was on her way to New York with her charge, when . . ."

The elevator abruptly shuddered to a stop. The doors slowly opened. Harvey lead the trio out of the elevator and down a deserted basement hallway.

"When what?" Toby asked.

"As it turned out, the dekayi had been followed by some of her people. There was a skirmish near the Canadian-American border. My person was injured. She's in the hospital. The dekayi managed to escape and has been on her own ever since."

"How is your agent doing?" Annabel asked.

"Time will tell. At present she's still in intensive care."

The foursome fell silent after this somber news. They were approaching a large metal door at the end of the hall when Strobe broke the lull in the conversation. "What makes you think this dekayi defector can be trusted?"

"Excellent point. One always has to be wary of a deserter from the other side. Which is why, after making contact with this one, you will take her to an apartment where she'll stay until we can debrief her. We need to be absolutely certain the flight from her community is not just a ruse to gather information on our organization. Until then, she'll be kept far away from KP headquarters."

Arriving at the end of the hall, Harvey slid a plastic card through a slot next to the metal door and pushed his way into a large gym. Strobe smiled at the sight. The trio's secret training center in the basement beneath the Killer Pizza building back in Hidden Hills was more than adequate, but it was nothing compared to this. A full-size basketball court took up one half of the large room. The other half was filled with a maze of sleek-looking exercise machines.

"Now I know what it feels like coming to the bigs after playing in the minors," Strobe said. "There is definitely money in pizza, isn't there."

"Let me put it this way," Harvey replied. "The man who owns one of my rival pizza chains built an entire university in Florida. I built . . . this." Harvey stared across the gym with an indecipherable look in his eyes. Then he turned and led the trio through an open doorway and into a locker room that was easily ten times the size of the one back in Hidden Hills. As in the gym, there were no people in sight.

"Why's it so deserted?" Toby asked. "Where is everyone?" Toby had been expecting overdrive activity, something like the scenes in all of those movies in which the lead characters are led into the bustling headquarters of some secret organization or other.

"There may be money in pizza, but there's never enough money. Which means I'm chronically understaffed. I had to send a large crew to Thailand last week. Just this morning, Steve took another group to Mexico." Steve Rogers, Harvey's right-hand man, had helped train the trio back in Hidden Hills. "The rest of my New York people are spread out across the U.S., helping the MCOs of various KP outposts."

Toby frowned as Harvey led the trio down a long row of lockers. "Is this typical, all this monster activity?"

"No, this is an especially busy time for us. Leap years tend to be like that. Don't ask me why. But every seven years, things get much more active in the monster community. Always been like that, according to my grandfather." Harvey stopped and nodded at several lockers. "You'll find the necessary gear in here. Prepare a backpack. Then I'll take you to the weapons room. You'll be using the crossbow on this excursion."

Toby felt a familiar tingle of excitement—laced with anxiety—as he exchanged his backpack for a black KP field pack. Preparing for a possible rumble with monsters was a unique feeling—to put it mildly—one that Toby had learned to channel instead of allowing it to bring him to his knees, which is what had happened when he first started out in the KP program. As he and his partners filled their packs with the necessary items, Harvey relayed the few facts he knew about dekayi.

They were an ancient, secretive race. Unlike the guttata the trio had battled back in Hidden Hills—who, with their ability to morph between their human and monster personas, preferred to live among the human population—the dekayi lived in their own secluded communities. They raised their children very strictly. No television. No public schools. No contact with the outside world. The dekayi the trio were about to meet apparently felt that life in her colony had become too repressive. Not to mention weird. She wanted a clean break. A new life.

"So you don't know what the dekayi's specialty is, how they go about doing their monsterly deeds?" Strobe had selected his crossbow—the same collapsible, high-tech variation on an ancient weapon the trio had used back in Hidden Hills—and was concealing it in a side slot of his backpack.

"No. What I do know I got from my father. He made contact with one decades ago. A similar situation to this one. The dekayi escaped from his village, got in touch with my father. A meeting place was arranged. When my father arrived, no dekayi. He never heard from him again."

"So his people got to him."

"That's what was assumed."

"Ruthless group."

"It's clear they don't want anyone leaving their community, that's for sure."

The foursome were waiting for the elevator door to open when Harvey gave his final instructions. "From the subway, it's three blocks to Central Park, which is where you'll be meeting the dekayi. Here's a map. The meeting place and the apartment where you'll be taking this young woman are clearly marked."

"Sounds simple enough to me," Strobe said.

"One thing I've learned over the years dealing with monsters, Strobe. It's never simple. Count on it."

The trio slung their backpacks over their shoulders. With Harvey's warning as their exit line, they headed off for their meeting with the mysterious dekayi.

3

It was still light and the traffic still heavy when the trio emerged from the subway station. Annabel studied the street signs, then led the way to Central Park.

"Here we are," Annabel announced.

"Did you know that at more than fifty blocks long and almost eight hundred and fifty acres, Central Park is one of the largest urban parks in the world?"

Strobe rolled his eyes at the return of Toby's alter ego, the New York tour guide.

"Several lakes, a skating rink, a zoo, an opera shell, and a really cool-sounding monument called Cleopatra's Needle are all within its borders."

"Fascinating," Strobe commented drily as the trio walked across Fifth Avenue to the park. "But we're here for a rendezvous with a monster called a dekayi. That's all I need to know right now. So let's get to it."

Annabel and Toby gave each other a look, then followed Strobe as he headed down a nearby concrete path, one of many entrances into Central Park. The path soon arrived at a main road that crossed through the park. Formerly used for traffic of the vehicular variety, the road was now a throughway for bikers and joggers. After dodging their way across the street, Annabel consulted her map, then led the way to a path that twisted off through dense trees and heavy foliage. The trees and bushes that rose up on either side of the walkway obscured their view of the park and the city beyond.

Following Annabel, it felt to Toby as though they were heading farther and farther away from civilization. But then the trio came around an abrupt turn in the path, the trees and foliage on either side fell away, and a large lake was revealed.

"Wow, nice," Toby said.

It was as though they had stumbled upon a fairy-tale-like setting right smack in the middle of one of the most densely populated cities on earth. A large boathouse was off to their right. To the left, a stone bridge connected one side of the lake to the other. Trees along the twisting shoreline of the lake were reflected in the lake's surface. It was a beautifully pastoral and peaceful spot.

If Strobe was taken with the scenic beauty, he wasn't letting on. "Where do we need to go, Annabel?" he asked, getting right to it.

"Over there, to that gazebo." Annabel indicated a secluded part of the lake, an inlet where a dense wall of trees hugged the water's edge.

"Doesn't look like anybody's waiting for us yet," Toby observed.

"It could be hours before the dekayi arrives," Annabel replied. "She's been traveling exclusively at night since she and the KP agent were attacked. I think you were in the bathroom when Harvey told us that."

"Oh . . . okay. Hey, did you hear that?"

"What?" Annabel asked, tensing at the concerned tone in Toby's voice.

"That was my stomach, grumbling. I noticed a hot dog stand back near the entrance. I read in one of my tour guides they have really good dogs here in the Apple. I wouldn't mind checking them out."

"Not a bad idea," Strobe said. "I haven't had much of anything since breakfast. I'll take a dog."

"How can you two even think about eating right now?" Annabel asked. The rendezvous with the dekayi was making her more hyper than hungry.

"Hey, I'm running on empty here," Toby replied.

"Me, too," Strobe said. "Make it two dogs, Tobe. With everything."

"You got it. Annabel?"

"Nothing, thanks."

"I think you should eat something. All we've had since breakfast are candy bars and Cokes. We need some protein. Feed our brains. Keep 'em sharp."

Maybe Toby had a point, Annabel decided. "Okay. A dog. With mustard."

"I'll be right back."

"Toby? Take this." Annabel handed Toby the map.

"Good idea." Toby took the map and headed back down the path that had led the trio to the lake. Strobe and Annabel headed in the opposite direction, toward the gazebo.

■ ■ ■

"You Okay Strobe?"

Glancing sideways at Strobe as they sat side by side on the gazebo bench, Annabel had caught him frowning as he looked out across the lake. The light had slowly drained from the lake as night replaced day. One by one, the rowboats on the lake had returned to the boathouse, leaving the ducks and mallards to patrol the shoreline.

"Worried about Toby, huh," Annabel teased.

"Yeah, right. Leave it up to the dude to get lost. A lot of good all his research did."

"I think I got him pointed in the right direction the

last time he called. He'll find us soon enough." Annabel stood, walked to the edge of the gazebo, and leaned against the railing. Gazing at the panorama of the lake, framed in the distance by the twinkling New York skyline, Annabel smiled and shook her head. "Do you believe we're actually here? In Central Park, waiting for something called a dekayi to show up?"

"Not the most typical thing for a couple of high school kids to be up to. Especially during the school year."

Smiling at Strobe's response, Annabel's expression suddenly changed. She had noticed a shape in the woods beyond the gazebo. It was as though the figure had materialized out of thin air, its unexpected and sudden appearance causing a swift chill to run through her. Indicating the figure to Strobe, Annabel cautiously stepped outside the gazebo. Strobe joined her. The shape among the trees hadn't moved.

"Welcome to the Big Apple," Annabel offered. It was the sentence Harvey had given them to introduce themselves to the dekayi.

No response from the woods. Then, in an exotic accent entirely foreign to Annabel and Strobe . . . "Why do they call it that?"

It was the correct response. The figure stayed hidden in the darkness for a few more moments, then slowly approached the edge of the woods. When the dekayi became visible to Annabel and Strobe, they were surprised at what they saw.

The reflected illumination from the lake and a nearby streetlamp revealed a stunningly beautiful teenage girl. Coffee-colored skin. Perfect complexion. High cheekbones and deeply dark, soulful eyes. The girl looked like she would be right at home on a Paris fashion runway. Well, except for her cheap, ill-fitting thrift-shop ensemble of too-tight pants, an oversize T-shirt, and a black baseball cap.

"My name is Calanthe," the girl said, her eyes wary.

"I'm Annabel. This is Strobe."

"There is supposed to be someone else with you," Calanthe said, glancing around the dark landscape.

Calanthe's statement surprised Annabel. Obviously, she had been in touch with Harvey within the past few hours, since he had sent the trio out to meet her. According to their KP boss, the dekayi didn't have computers or phones. So what did Calanthe do? Use a pay phone? Or perhaps a cell the Canadian MPP specialist had given her.

Regardless of how Calanthe had contacted Harvey, Annabel was suddenly struck by the enormity of what this girl was doing. Namely, abandoning a culture she had grown up in, the only way of life she had ever known, for something very, very different.

"Yes, there is someone else with us," Annabel replied. "He went to get something to eat and got lost."

"I say we leave without him," Strobe said curtly. "He'll just have to find his way back to KP by himself."

"I agree that we should not stay here," Calanthe said. "Since arriving in New York . . . I believe my scent has been rediscovered."

"Your scent?" Eyeing the surrounding woods, Strobe slowly took out his crossbow and started to assemble it.

"Yes. I was certain I had lost my pursuers, but that does not seem to be the case."

"Well, then I'd say that's our cue to giddyup." But as Strobe started down the path that led away from the gazebo, Calanthe called after him, "No. This way." She was indicating the heavy foliage where she had emerged from the woods. "If we are in an open area, we will not be able to see if the rukh comes."

"Rukh?" Annabel echoed. "What is that?"

"My master's bodyguard. Former master, that is."

Annabel detected a fierce kind of pride in Calanthe's voice when she said "former master." It was like a declaration of independence.

"What kind of bodyguard are we talking about here?" Strobe asked as he backed up toward the woods.

"A very ancient demon. Invisible."

"Ouch."

"If we stay in among the trees, we will be able to hear and see if it comes. The rukh is very powerful, but it does not have the power to stop branches and bushes from moving when it walks among them."

Strobe looked down the path. There was nothing in sight. But then, if an invisible rukh was coming at them, there wouldn't be anything in sight, anyway. "Okay, we'll go through the woods then. I'll take the lead."

"I will lead," Calanthe said. "I have a better chance of sensing the demon if he comes."

This one's pretty feisty, Strobe thought as he followed Calanthe into the woods. Bringing up the rear, Annabel flipped her NVGs down over her eyes to be able to navigate through the dark woods. At this point, Annabel just wanted to get out of the park safely. When she was waiting with Strobe in the gazebo, she had studied the map Harvey had given her and knew exactly which paths they needed to take to get out of the park and which streets would lead them to the apartment that would be Calanthe's temporary New York residence.

But now all bets—and all memorized directions—were off. It was time to improvise. The threesome had been walking though the deep darkness of the woods for a few minutes when Calanthe suddenly stopped.

"Hear something?" Strobe asked. He hadn't detected any unusual sounds interrupting the typical nighttime soundtrack of the woods.

"Yes. The rukh is somewhere in front of us. The master is here as well."

Strobe detected a strong undercurrent of fear in Calanthe's voice when she mentioned the master. The rukh sounded scary enough, but there was obviously something about the master that intimidated Calanthe even more.

"We should go back to where we were." Without waiting for a response, Calanthe walked past Strobe and Annabel and headed back in the direction they had just come. Annabel exchanged a look with Strobe, then followed Calanthe. Now at rear guard, Strobe kept a watch behind them. Chirping crickets, muted voices in the park, traffic in the city streets wafted softly through the woods as they went. Such a peaceful sound, Strobe thought, which only made their situation seem that much more surreal.

Calanthe once again stopped in her tracks. Strobe immediately spotted what had caused her to halt their progress through the underbrush. At the point where they had entered the woods stood a very tall, very thin man, his silhouetted shape so exaggerated that it could have been a cartoonist's caricature of a tall, thin man.

"Is that the master dude?" Strobe said in a low voice.

When Calanthe nodded, Strobe didn't hesitate. Stepping to his right to get a clear, unblocked shot at the Tall Man, Strobe brought up his crossbow and locked on the figure through the weapon's powerful scope. He was about to fire when a sharp hissing sound cut through the muted sounds in the park. The sound stopped as quickly as it had begun.

What was that? Strobe wondered. Through his scope he found the answer. An arrow was embedded in the Tall Man's long, thin neck. The angle of the arrow indicated it had come from a different direction from theirs.

Strobe was about to send another arrow flying in the man's direction when Toby suddenly burst from the darkness, tackled the Tall Man, and took him down hard to the ground.

4

Only moments before—when he had finally made it back to the lake—Toby was concerned when he didn't see Annabel and Strobe in the gazebo across the dark water. Hurrying across the bridge, he had lost sight of the gazebo when the path briefly entered the woods before emerging at the shoreline about twenty yards from the wooden structure.

That's when Toby had spotted the Tall Man, standing at the edge of the woods. There was something so otherworldly about the figure, Toby was certain the man couldn't be human. He just knew it. Which meant that his friends could be in some very real danger. After quickly assembling his crossbow, Toby had aimed, shot his arrow, then charged and tackled the Tall Man.

Struggling now on the ground with the strangely elastic figure, Toby knew he should have nixed the tackling part of his attack. In spite of having an arrow lodged in his neck, his opponent was impossible to pin down and incredibly strong. Toby knew he had no chance against this man.

"NO! STAY AWAY FROM HIM!"

Toby thought he heard someone yell those words. A second later, he was grabbed by powerful hands and yanked brusquely away from the Tall Man. Good thing, too. The man's long legs were just about to clamp themselves around Toby's neck.

Toby was startled when he saw the beautiful, delicate-looking girl who had just lifted him from the ground as though he weighed no more than a few pounds. Before he could say anything to his remarkable rescuer . . .

"Yo, gang." This in a deadpan tone from Strobe. "Company on the way."

Turning in Strobe's direction, Toby couldn't believe what he saw. Looking like CGI movie magic, the bushes were seemingly parting by themselves as large, misshapen footprints appeared one after the other in the moist ground. Something invisible was pounding toward the group through the woods!

At the same time, a few feet away, the Tall Man's gasping, wheezing attempts to suck in oxygen signaled the damage that had been done by Toby's arrow. But in spite of the fact that he could barely breath, the Tall Man was slowly rising to his feet.

Annabel had seen enough. "This way!" she commanded, starting down the path that led away from the gazebo. But Calanthe clearly had another idea. She took off in the opposite direction, toward the lake. Seeing this, Annabel immediately changed course and followed Calanthe.

"What's that in the woods, man?" Toby asked, feeling an unpleasant lurching in his stomach.

Toby didn't get a reply to his question. Calanthe had already dove into the lake and disappeared under the black, sparkling surface with Annabel right behind her. Strobe had fired off a series of arrows in the direction of the rukh and was on his way to the lake.

The last thing Toby observed before following his partners was the sight of the Tall Man slowly pulling the arrow from his neck. If that wasn't enough to light a fire under him, the invisible rukh quickly closing in on him certainly was.

Taking the most direct line from where he stood to the lake, Toby charged toward the gazebo, came out on the other side, and crashed into the water, earning zero style points for his inelegant dive.

Swimming like a madman, Toby gradually closed the

gap between him and his KP partners. In the water beyond, there was no sign of Calanthe. "What goin' on here?" Toby gasped as he came abreast of Annabel. He was already laboring from power-stroking in his heavy clothes and the pack on his back. "Where'd that girl go, anyway?"

"I don't know," Annabel replied. She too was tiring from her nighttime swim. "She hasn't come up for air since she hit the water."

"Must be some kind of fish species," Strobe offered.

Glancing over his shoulder as he took a long stroke, Toby saw the rukh churning through the water toward them. Now that the creature was in the water, it wasn't as invisible as it had been in the woods. The water splashing around its body and rolling from its large torso gave a hint of the thing's ghastly shape.

"What I want to know is what kind of species that thing is behind us," Toby managed to sputter between quick intakes of breath.

It was obvious to the trio that they were in an extremely dire situation. They were rapidly losing stamina and speed with each stroke. The rukh, on the other hand, definitely wasn't. At this rate it could be on them within . . .

SPLASH!!!

Toby took in a mouthful of water as he lurched away from the figure that had just surfaced next to him. Relief replaced alarm when he saw that it wasn't the invisible rukh, but rather Calanthe.

"Keep going," Calanthe instructed, swimming effortlessly next to Toby. "I will try to drown the rukh."

"Calanthe, no," Annabel urged.

But Calanthe had already disappeared back underwater, her submerged, shimmering shape on a direct collision course with the creature.

"Calanthe!" Annabel yelled.

"Let her go," Strobe said, his voice strained and hoarse from the intense grind of his aquatic adventure.

Fortunately, Calanthe's intervention with the rukh turned out to be pivotal in the trio's ability to reach shore before being overtaken by the beast. One by one, they staggered from the water, then stood side by side to watch the battle that was raging under the surface of the lake. The site of the struggle was indicated by broiling, bursting bubbles on the surface of the water. Suddenly, the bubbles were obliterated by several massively violent percussive splashes. Then . . .

Nothing. The lake became eerily calm, a couple of circular, widening ripples the only indication that anything had occurred out there in dark depths.

"I can't see her, can you?" Toby asked.

Just then, there was a huge geyser-like eruption of water where the fight had taken place. Emerging from the watery blast were the telltale splashing strokes of the invisible rukh, once again heading toward the trio.

"No," Annabel said in disbelief. "She can't be . . ." Annabel's voice trailed off before she finished her sentence.

"Wait, no . . . *look*. There she is!" Toby pointed at a rippling underwater shape that had appeared a few yards from shore. Seconds later, Calanthe emerged from the lake.

Gasping at the sight of a savage gash on Calanthe's shoulder, Annabel splashed into the water to meet the girl as she walked to the shore. In spite of the fact that the cut was bleeding profusely down her arm, Calanthe barely acknowledged the injury. "I injured the rukh's leg. Which should have the effect of slowing it down."

Toby stared in wonder at Calanthe. Who *was* this girl who could lift him up like a sack of feathers, swim almost two football lengths underwater without taking a breath, and then do battle with some kind of invisible demon?

But then, Toby was no longer looking at Calanthe. That's because he had bent over and was violently throwing up. Strobe winced in disgust when he saw the remains of several barely digested hot dogs splattered at

Toby's feet. Toby spit a couple of times, wiped his mouth with the back of his hand, and straightened up with a grimace. "Whew!"

Just then a distinctive and rather unladylike bellow erupted from Calanthe. The dekayi teen had apparently found Toby's hot dog mishap to be funny! But when the trio looked at her in surprise, Calanthe's mirth had already disappeared. "We must go," she said, her determined expression firmly back in place.

"Wait a second," Strobe said. "Why not stay here and have it out with that thing?"

The rukh was steadily approaching the shore, but now at a slower pace. Either the creature was tiring or the injury inflicted by Calanthe had made an impact.

"Have it out. What does this mean?" Calanthe asked.

"Fight the thing. Kill it. Let's finish what you started."

"I do not recommend that. In the water, the rukh was not as powerful. That is why I lured it into the lake. But once it emerges onto land, it will be very difficult to kill." Calanthe was already heading into the woods as she spoke.

"There's your answer," Annabel said. "Let's go, you two."

Strobe and Toby hesitated before joining Annabel and Calanthe. A group of people stood on the far shore of the lake, shouting and pointing in their direction. The group's nocturnal swim and Calanthe's altercation with the invisible rukh had not gone unnoticed.

But it wasn't the people on the shore that Toby and Strobe were concerned about. The thing that held their attention was the sight of the Tall Man on the other side of the lake. Standing perfectly still inside the dark gazebo, he was staring out across the water in their direction.

"Okay, that guy's creepy," Strobe said.

"Yeah," Toby replied.

"I'd say we have a little adventure on our hands, Tobe."

Toby turned and double-timed it into the woods with Strobe. The rukh was now less than fifty yards from shore, eating up the distance with each massive stroke of its invisible limbs. On the other side of the lake, the Tall Man hadn't moved. He stood in the darkness of the gazebo, staring at the woods where Toby and Strobe had just disappeared.

Silent . . .

Still . . .

It was as though Calanthe's master was waiting for his monstrous sidekick to do the dirty work before making his final, chilling appearance.

5

"Harvey. SOS."

Following Calanthe through the woods, Annabel was on her cell to her KP boss. "I have no idea. Somewhere in Central Park . . . I will. Bye."

"Harvey sending the troops?" Strobe asked from somewhere in the pitch-black darkness behind Annabel.

"There are no troops to send, remember? But Harvey's on his way. I'll give him a call when I know where we are."

Bringing up the rear, Toby caught a glimpse of street-lights to his left through the dark thicket of trees. So had Calanthe, who immediately changed direction toward the lights, leading the trio on a brisk jog through the under-brush. There was no path to follow, which meant Toby had to duck and weave his way through the tangle of bushes and trees, his reward being several whacks in the face from branches Strobe released with a snap in front of him.

Toby was happy to see the streetlights getting steadily brighter. He had just heard the rukh behind him, crashing heavily through the woods in the group's direction. The creature was back in its natural habitat, and closing fast.

■ ■ ■

Even in a city where the unusual and bizarre often rated barely a raised eyebrow, Toby and his companions would have surely attracted some attention as they hopped over a stone wall that separated the sidewalk from the park, had there been people around to see them. But the area where they exited the park was light on pedestrian traffic. Even traffic of the vehicular kind was sparse.

Spotting a street sign on the other side of the avenue, Annabel headed toward it, running diagonally across the street. The rest of the group followed, dodging a couple of cars that honked loudly at the group as they sped by.

"Where's a cab when you need one?" Toby asked, huffing in his wet clothes and heavy backpack as he ran behind Strobe.

"I'd like to see you try that," Strobe shot back.

"If this isn't an emergency I don't know what is. Maybe we can hitch a ride outta here."

"Let me know when you flag something down."

Annabel was already on her cell to Harvey again

when Strobe and Toby reached the sidewalk. "Seventy-fifth and Central Park West . . . Right. We'll be there."

"What's up?" Strobe asked.

"Harvey said to keep moving. We don't want to wait here and be bait for that thing. Harvey'll call when he gets in the area."

"How long's that gonna take?"

"Not too long. He's already halfway up here."

Breathing deeply, Toby, Strobe, and Annabel looked like they could use a break before moving on. Calanthe, however, didn't appear to be even winded by her swim and jog through the woods. Staring intently across the street at the park, she held her body tightly coiled, like an athlete does just before blasting into action.

"All right. Let's go," Strobe said as he turned and started down Seventy-fifth Street. The foursome's quick footsteps echoed back at them from the brownstone buildings that lined both sides of the eerily dark and deserted street. Keeping a wary watch for the rukh as they ran, the group managed to reach the end of the quiet block without incident.

Seventy-fifth intersected with a much livelier thoroughfare, identified by an overhead street sign as COLUMBUS AVENUE. Clusters of people stood outside a number of restaurants as they waited to be seated. A nearby sidewalk café was crowded with diners. As the group half-jogged past the café, Calanthe suddenly reached out, grabbed a steak from a diner's plate, and gobbled it down without breaking stride.

"Hey! What the . . ." The startled diner whose dinner had just been poached jumped from his seat, looked around for his waiter, then started after Calanthe. But when he got a good look at the girl—with her ripped T-shirt, bloody arm, and three companions with water dripping from their black backpacks—the man decided to abandon that idea.

Jogging next to Toby, Strobe couldn't help but chuckle at Calanthe's sneaky cuisine attack. "This girl's a live one, man."

Just then Toby noticed something odd across the street. A man was staring with a perplexed frown up and down the street. "Hey! Everyone! Other sidewalk. Eight o'clock. The guy in the black hoodie. It looked like he was just shoved by something. Something invisible." The man was about twenty yards behind the group, which meant the rukh could already be directly opposite them.

The group was still checking out the man in the black hoodie when a startling sight erupted on the street nearby. A taxi slammed into something undetectable in the middle of the avenue and shuddered to an abrupt halt. The front of the vehicle crumpled inward, the hood flew up, and steam burst from the radiator.

For a brief, stunning moment, Toby thought he caught a glimpse of the monstrous rukh. It was as though the collision had caused the thing's chameleon-like ability to temporarily short-circuit. But then it was gone. Just like that, the rukh was once again unnoticeable in the thoroughfare.

"This way!" Annabel called out, instantly changing direction and running down an alley between two buildings. The alley was narrow and littered with trash, which forced the group to run in single file. Halfway down the alley, Toby heard a commotion behind him. Shooting a look over his shoulder, he witnessed the bizarre sight of trash cans flying every which way, as if they had just taken on a life of their own. A large wooden pallet lying in the middle of the alley was suddenly punctured, then magically jumped and flew down the alley, looking like some kind of zany Disney animated object. The sight would have been comical if the foursome's situation hadn't been so desperate. Stuck on the rukh's invisible foot, the pallet was quickly smashed to pieces by the creature's relentless charge.

By this time Annabel had reached a wider back alley that ran behind the Columbus Avenue buildings. Leading the group to her right, she skidded to a stop when she saw what was waiting for them at the entrance to the alley about fifty yards away.

The Tall Man.

"Fire escape!" Strobe called out, then he was running for it, and Annabel was right behind him; Calanthe and Toby were right behind Annabel.

Strobe leaped up, grabbed on to the bottom rung of the fire escape's hanging ladder, and pulled himself up and onto it. As he climbed upward, Annabel jumped and grasped the bottom rung and quickly followed him.

As she had already demonstrated, Calanthe was an astonishingly athletic girl. So Toby was not surprised to see her jump, grab the ladder, and follow Annabel and Strobe nimbly up the side of the brick building toward the first-floor landing.

Attempting to repeat Calanthe's actions, Toby leaped for the ladder. His hand brushed against the bottom ladder rung, but a firm grip eluded him. After losing contact with the ladder, Toby fell almost horizontally to the concrete alley below and hit the ground hard. Dazed by the jarring impact, he took a moment before getting to his feet.

The Tall Man was now walking toward Toby with a slow but spookily steady, assured gait. The rukh was somewhere behind him and closing fast. With no time to go back down the alley for another run at the ladder, Toby was trapped in a pincer-like attack.

A sudden crash behind Toby caused him to turn just

in time to see a large overflowing trash bin rise from the ground to a height of about ten feet. *Oh, no!* Toby thought, his eyes darting around the alley for a possible escape route. *That thing's gonna squash me under a ton of trash!*

"Take my hand!"

Toby looked up to see Calanthe reaching down for him. Taking a quick mental count of how many times this girl had come to his rescue within the last half hour, Toby leaped for her outstretched hand. In a flash Calanthe had grabbed him by the wrist, pulled him up and onto the ladder, and continued her climb up toward the first-floor landing.

Toby scrambled up the ladder behind Calanthe, at the same time keeping a concerned eye on the magically suspended-in-air trash bin below. He had no idea how far up the ladder he had to go to be out of the crazed creature's range. The first-floor landing, maybe? Hopefully, no farther than that.

Toby was almost to the landing when the bin— looking like a huge missile shot from an invisible cannon—blasted toward the fire escape and smashed into the ladder with a resounding *crash!* The jarring impact vibrated through the ladder and hit Toby's body like a massive electrical charge.

Somehow managing to hold on to the wildly swaying, screeching ladder, Toby desperately launched himself toward the first-floor landing just before the ladder ripped away from its mooring.

Fingertips on metal . . .

This time Toby's grip held. Dangling precariously from the metal platform, Toby mustered the energy to pull himself to safety.

"Toby!" Annabel yelled with concern from above.

Toby gave Annabel a thumbs-up, took a quick moment to catch his breath, then renewed his climb up the ladder. As he thumped heavily up the side of the building, he had to fight back the impulse to lose his backpack. The pack felt like a ton of bricks; the straps causing an intense, throbbing pain in Toby's shoulders. But Toby muscled through the pain and finally reached the tenth and final ladder.

Before joining his companions on the roof, Toby looked to the alley below. He had heard more and more voices as he climbed up the side of the building. There was a group of people mingling around the crumpled trash bin and twisted ladder. Some stared up at Toby with perplexed expressions. The rukh and Tall Man were nowhere to be seen. Which should have been reassuring, Toby thought, but actually only added to the tension.

Where were they?

As he took the final rungs to the roof, Toby suddenly caught sight of a foreboding figure waiting under a streetlamp at the far end of the alley. The Tall Man, staring right at him. The creepy figure once again caused Toby to shudder.

"Toby, what's wrong?" Annabel asked, looking down from the roof above.

Other than being chased by two monsters, one with teeth the size of my mom's biggest kitchen knives, everything's just fine, Annabel!

At least, that's what Toby thought he had seen back on Columbus, those teeth, when the rukh had become briefly visible. With a final glance at the Tall Man, Toby turned away from the spectral sight, forced the image of teeth the size of kitchen knives out of his head, and climbed the final steps to the roof.

6

Annabel was back on her cell, talking to Harvey. She watched as Strobe jumped down to the roof of the building next to the one they had just scaled. Calanthe went next, then Toby jumped, hit the roof, and fell forward from the momentum of the drop. After her quick discussion with her KP boss, Annabel joined the group on the roof below.

"Harvey wants us to continue across the roofs to the end of the block. Then down to street level. He should be there by then to meet us."

"You tell him what we're up against?" Strobe asked as the foursome continued their flight across the rooftops.

Annabel nodded.

"Did he ever hear of a rukh before?"

Another nod. This time in the negative.

Several minutes later, everyone was scaling a short ladder that led to another rooftop when a police siren suddenly erupted somewhere nearby, slicing through the muffled sounds of traffic coming from the streets below.

"Think those people in the alley called the cops?" Toby wondered.

"I hope not," Strobe replied. "That invisible freak'd pop the heads of the boys in blue before they knew what hit them."

"Lovely image. Thanks for that, Strobe."

By the time the four reached the last rooftop, they were totally spent by a chase that had taken them across a lake, through the Central Park woods, along several blocks of city streets, up a ten-story building, and across more than half a dozen rooftops. Even Calanthe looked tired.

"Last one," Annabel announced as she waited at the top of the final ladder. "It's all downhill from here."

Calanthe and Toby passed by Annabel as they made it to the top of the ladder. Strobe had been the first one to arrive at the roof and was heading for the doorway that would lead them to the interior stairway of the building. Annabel scanned the rooftops they had just crossed, looking for any sign of their pursuers. Nothing in sight.

"Locked!" Strobe announced, giving the door an extra yank just to be sure.

"The fire escape," Annabel said.

But before anyone could even take a step in that direction, all hell broke loose on the last rooftop of the last building the group would need to cross to get down to the meeting place with their KP boss.

The locked door suddenly burst clean off its hinges, slammed into Strobe, and sent him flying. In a flash, Calanthe was grabbed and dragged back in the direction they had just come. It was an odd and terrifying sight, Calanthe struggling wildly with the invisible rukh as it pulled her roughly across the gravel-topped roof.

Strobe instantly got up and charged after the creature, leaping and catching it just as it reached the ladder the group had scaled only moments before. Pulling out their crossbows, Annabel and Toby swiftly assembled them and snapped in the arrow cartridges. Clinging to the invisible rukh with one hand, Strobe was trying to get at the knife in the sheath on his forearm plate with the other.

Annabel and Toby quickly advanced on the creature, but were hesitant to take a shot. With Calanthe in the beast's grasp and Strobe riding the thing as if it were some kind of supernatural bronco, there were two people who might mistakenly take an arrow from their crossbows.

But then Strobe was no longer riding the creature. Just as he was about to plunge his knife into the thing's body, he was swatted to the rooftop's graveled surface by the rukh's invisible hand.

That's when Annabel took her shot. A hair-raising screech of surprise erupted from the rukh when Annabel's arrow sliced into its body. At the same time, the beast's cloak of invisibility lifted, giving Toby and Annabel a point-blank look at the hideous creature.

The thing had a monstrously squat, toad-like shape.

Smallish arms, resembling a human's.

Large, muscular dinosaur-like legs.

But it was the creature's face that drew Toby's and Annabel's attention just before they unleashed a barrage of arrows on the thing. Toby was right about the teeth. The rukh's face seemed to be nothing *but* teeth. Two small, brightly beady eyes were where a forehead would normally be. A nose orifice gaped obscenely between the eyes. But the creature's ugly, lipless mouth defined the rest of its face, the two rows of uneven, razor-sharp teeth dazzling in their size and destructive-looking power.

Taking advantage of the distraction caused by Annabel's arrow, Calanthe had managed to wriggle free of the rukh's grasp and was sprinting with Strobe toward the roof's open doorway. That's when Toby and Annabel opened fire on the creature.

Zapping in and out of view like a short-circuited neon sign, the rukh swatted at the rain of arrows, deflecting some as all the others found their mark. When their arrow cartridges were depleted, Annabel and Toby turned and ran to join Strobe and Calanthe.

SLAM!

The group couldn't believe their eyes when the rukh—looking like some kind of huge, otherworldly figure, the arrows jutting out weirdly in all directions from its body—suddenly appeared in the open doorway, blocking their exit from the rooftop. The creature had launched itself up and over them with one thrust of its powerful legs! The astonished quartet skidded to a stop, turned, and charged for the fire escape.

Strobe had a crossbow in hand and was ready to fire. "Keep going," he commanded, then he turned and planted himself between the rukh and his retreating companions. The creature had once again disappeared, but its position was betrayed by the arrows impaled in its body, not to mention the startling appearance of footsteps on the rooftop as one section of gravel after another was pulverized by the monster's huge feet.

Strobe emptied the contents of his arrow cartridge into the rukh, threw his crossbow aside, grabbed his knife, and waited for impact. But before he knew what had hit him, he was lying on the gravel, his chest exploding with pain from a vicious beast slap from the charging creature.

The rukh apparently wasn't interested in Strobe. It wanted Calanthe.

"Behind you!" Strobe yelled.

The creature's advancing footsteps suddenly disappeared. A second later, the beast zapped into view at the edge of the roof, cutting off the trio's escape route. Once again, the rukh had launched itself a good twenty-five yards up and over its prey without breaking stride.

Quickly sizing up their situation, Annabel called out, "The water tower. *Go*, Calanthe." Having never seen a water tower before, Calanthe followed Annabel's nod, then ran for the round structure perched atop four wooden legs, a common sight on New York City rooftops.

Preparing her crossbow for another attack, Annabel eyed the creature with a hatred Toby had never seen before. "We'll shoot that thing out of the air if it tries to jump over us, Toby."

But the rukh didn't have to jump over Annabel and Toby. As it had done with Strobe, it merely charged past the two MCOs, smashing them aside like a couple of lightweight human bowling pins.

Calanthe was already halfway up the ladder to a platform that ran around the perimeter of the water tower.

The rukh, now visible, suddenly slid to a stop. It appeared to be studying the situation—the primitive beast apparently had some gray matter in its brain—then charged one of the water tower's supporting legs.

CRACK!

The thick wooden leg bent from the rukh's attack, but held. As the creature backed up for another charge, Toby's eyes locked onto the metal door the rukh had smashed from its hinges. Arrows obviously couldn't stop the creature. Toby knew they had to come up with something else to save Calanthe, and fast.

On its second charge, the rukh pulverized what was left of the wooden leg. The water tower swayed, tilted precariously to one side, but didn't fall. Zeroing in on another tower leg, the rukh blasted toward it.

CRACK!

The rukh backed up and hit the leg with another brutal charge. It was about to go for a third shoulder slam, which would very likely collapse the tower, when . . .

"GO!"

While the rukh had been focused on bringing down the water tower, Toby had quickly pulled Strobe and Annabel into his desperate plan to bring down the rukh. It couldn't possibly work. The rukh was way too powerful. But with the element of surprise on their side . . .

The trio—holding the bent door in front of them like a flat metal battering ram—charged the rukh at Toby's single-word command. They slammed the door into its gut and pushed with all their collective might, forcing the creature toward the nearby roof edge.

Caught off guard, the surprised rukh screeched in rage. . . .

The trio gritted and pushed. . . .

The beast dug in its claws. . . .

Bent forward at a forty-five-degree angle, Toby, Annabel, and Strobe dug in with their rubber-soled shoes. . . .

The rukh snapped its enormous teeth at the trio, but was unable to connect with MCO flesh across the door/battering ram. Suddenly, the beast had been pushed right up against the low wall at the edge of the roof.

All this happened within split seconds. Heaving from the massive effort of shoving hundreds of pounds of monster flesh across the roof, the trio looked like they might collapse. But they had to finish their job, and fast, before the creature was able to regain the advantage in the life-and-death struggle.

With a final coordinated effort, they lunged at the rukh with their makeshift battering ram. Teetering backward from the blow, the beast clouted the metal door from the trio's grasp, appeared to regain its balance, then . . .

It went over the edge, uttering a high-pitched and weirdly human cry as it disappeared from sight.

Toby and Annabel fell to their knees, gasping for air. Strobe put his hands on his knees and stared at the ground as he breathed in deeply. A moment later, Calanthe appeared, ran to the edge of the roof, and looked over to the alley below.

"We kill that thing?" Strobe asked between intakes of air.

"I don't know."

One by one, the trio approached the edge of the roof. The rukh was lying in the middle of the alley, completely still. Then . . . one of its hands twitched. Then a foot. The monstrous creature rolled over and managed to slowly rise up on its two massive feet.

For a moment, it appeared the beast might topple over. But after steadying itself, the rukh looked up at the foursome with its small, mean, beady eyes.

It wouldn't have surprised Toby if the thing had made an attempt to leap up to the rooftop to resume the battle. But the creature was obviously hurt. Staring at the group, the rukh . . . slowly . . . vanished.

In a flash, Strobe was heading down the fire escape.

The rest of the group followed. When they got to the bottom landing, they dropped one by one from the hanging ladder to the pavement below. Strobe scanned the area, trying to determine which direction the rukh had gone.

"Where are you going?" Annabel asked when Strobe started off down the alley.

"To find that thing and kill it."

"I believe the rukh is going off to find a place to die." Saying this, Calanthe suddenly collapsed. Annabel was instantly by the girl's side, kneeling next to her and feeling for a pulse. Strobe immediately abandoned his search for the rukh and returned to the group.

"Is she okay?" Toby asked.

"She has a pulse, anyway."

"Maybe she just fainted."

"Do dekayi faint?" Strobe posited.

"I don't know," Annabel said. "We don't know anything about the dekayi. Without any kind of knowledge, how can we possibly help her?"

"Hey, check out her shoulder!" Toby knelt down next to Calanthe to get a closer look.

Calanthe's shoulder had clearly begun to heal itself. The skin surrounding the gash had taken on a strange, alien texture and color and was slowly coming together over Calanthe's wound.

"That's incredible," Toby said.

"Not to mention creepy," Strobe added. "Speaking of which, you two keep an eye on her, okay?"

"Don't go, Strobe," Annabel said. "We might need you."

"Harvey'll be here any second. Besides, I need to deal with that dude."

Toby and Annabel looked in the direction of Strobe's gaze. Standing on the other side of a nearby street the back alley intersected with was the Tall Man.

"I'm totally sick of this guy," Strobe said, then he was off after the dekayi. Toby and Annabel knew it was useless to call him back. Strobe had a mind of his own when it came to this sort of thing. *Thing* meaning just about everything.

Cradling Calanthe's head in her lap, Annabel looked down at the unconscious girl. Even though she was out cold, a frown still creased Calanthe's forehead. "This poor girl, Toby. Can you even begin to imagine what she's been through these past few days?"

"What about her entire life?" Toby was still checking out the supernatural healing session that was slowly making progress on Calanthe's shoulder. "The question is, if she doesn't die on us, can she make it in our world?"

A Jeepster Commando suddenly came around the

corner of the alley and bore down on Annabel and Toby. The two immediately recognized the vehicle. It was Harvey's official "field" car, the same one he had used back in Hidden Hills when he was training his new MCOs.

Toby felt a flood of relief when he saw the Commando. Harvey would be able to take over now and deal with this very weird situation. The unconscious female dekayi lying in the alley. The trio of official-looking people heading toward them from the direction of the collapsed fire escape ladder. The crippled water tower on the top of the building just behind them.

When Harvey got out of his Jeep, Toby stepped away from Calanthe to allow his boss to examine the patient. Harvey took a few moments to prod Calanthe's body gingerly with his fingertips. He put his ear to her chest, frowned, moved his ear down to her stomach, over to her left side, then right. After gently probing the area to the right of Calanthe's stomach, Harvey looked at Annabel. "It appears her heart is right here. Very interesting."

"Is she okay?" Annabel asked.

"I don't know. Let's get her in the back of the Commando."

"What about those guys?" Toby asked as he helped carry Calanthe to the Jeepster. One of the men was calling out to them as the trio approached.

"What about them?"

"I'm pretty sure they want to know why there's a smashed trash bin and a partially destroyed fire escape in the alley down there."

"Is that all? Let them wonder."

"What about the water tower on the top of this building?" Annabel asked when Harvey had closed the back door and the three were quickly getting into the car. "The rukh almost destroyed it. It might come down any second."

"That I'll deal with. Later. Where's Strobe?"

7

Strobe was deep into it, that's where.

He might have only been in Central Park, but it was as though he had entered a deep, dark jungle, nose to the ground and tracking a mysterious and dangerous species called the dekayi. The hunted had become the hunter. Strobe liked it better this way.

When Strobe had lived in Colorado, he had taken up the difficult and dangerous sport of rock climbing. What he discovered was that the start of each climb was the worst part. Fear and doubt threatened the entire enterprise. But after getting past the initial jitters, a zen-like focus had always come over Strobe, ironically when he was much higher up the cliff and the climb was in its most treacherous phase.

That's where Strobe was now, in his zen zone. After the explosive and completely crazed battle with the rukh, he was now able to concentrate solely on the Tall Man, who had led him back to where the whole adventure had begun. Strobe's senses were fine-tuned at this point, the sights and sounds of the park registering in the high-decible range.

Swish!

Strobe whirled at the sound of a branch brushing through the heavy night air and instantly headed in that direction. Catching a glimpse of the Tall Man as he moved away from him, he bent low and followed, his crossbow held at shoulder height and ready to fire. The dekayi had survived an arrow to his neck, so Strobe wanted a clear shot at his heart. (Of course, if he had stayed with Annabel and Toby a moment longer, Strobe would have known where a dekayi's heart was located.)

Narrowing the gap between him and his prey, Strobe's heartbeat quickened. This was the closest he had gotten to the Tall Man since the chase began. Suddenly, the dekayi stopped. So did Strobe, curious why the man had interrupted his steady progress through the woods. Perhaps, he thought he had lost his pursuer. Which is exactly what Strobe wanted the Tall Man to think. With his guard down, the dekayi would be especially vulnerable.

Slowly bringing up his crossbow, Strobe sighted through the scope and focused on the Tall Man's back.

Right . . . there. That's where Strobe figured the heart would be. He didn't hesitate when he had locked in on his target. He pressed the trigger and waited for the response.

Which was not what Strobe was expecting. He blinked, not sure what had just happened. In an instant, it looked as though the Tall Man had disappeared! Strobe heard his arrow thunk with a dull thud into a tree somewhere in the distance. Then he was running toward where the Tall Man had been only moments before, quickly reaching the spot and looking around the woods in dismay.

"I *had* him," Strobe said angrily. Turning 360 degrees as he studied the woods, Strobe tried to detect anything that would betray the Tall Man's escape route. Which turned out to be pretty easy.

Spotting something on the ground through his NVGs, Strobe cautiously approached the site, his crossbow at the ready. Kicking first one, then another shoe aside, Strobe followed the path suggested by the discarded apparel. He frowned when he saw what was just beyond them in the underbrush. The Tall Man's hat. His rain slicker. His heavy coat. A little farther along . . . the man's old-fashioned trousers. Then his shirt. Finally, underwear.

The discarded clothing meant one of two things. Either the Tall Man had stripped and was running through the woods nude. Or he had changed, transformed into something else. Strobe was pretty sure the dekayi hadn't become a streaker. Running around in Central Park totally naked wasn't the best way to lose someone who was chasing you.

Just then Strobe heard a sharp, high-pitched, and very hair-raising sound in the woods beyond. The sound was otherworldly, alien, unlike anything Strobe had ever heard before. It was also difficult to gauge where the sound had come from. Strobe's immediate impulse was to track the sound. But a faint inner voice warned . . . *Don't do it.*

When Strobe heard a repeat of the strange and terrifying sound, he reluctantly backed off in the direction he had just come. His inner voice appeared to be winning out. But then Strobe stopped and reconsidered his decision to retreat from the dark, pathless woods.

Hissssssss!!!

The eerie sound was much closer this time. Whatever the Tall Man had become, he was coming for Strobe, that much was clear. That did it for Strobe. He turned and headed for a street lamp that illuminated a concrete path about fifty yards away. Shouldering aside branches as he made his way toward the light, Strobe hated the feeling of cutting and running. He was a fighter at heart, but he also knew it was unwise to take on the unknown. Better to live to fight another day than take a chance like that.

Reaching the path, Strobe stopped to take a look behind him. "Later, dude." With that parting promise, Strobe took off down the walkway, toward the lights of the city.

8

After making his way back to KP headquarters, Strobe found Toby and Annabel in the locker room. In the time it had taken Strobe to track the Tall Man and then return to the Flatiron Building, his partners had showered, changed into clean clothes, and were now waiting to hear how Calanthe was doing. The last report they had received from Harvey was . . . no change. Calanthe was still unconscious, her shoulder still undergoing its mysterious healing process.

"What happened with you, Strobe?" Toby asked after he and Annabel brought their partner up to date on Calanthe's condition.

"Tracked the guy back to Central Park, had him in my scope, then . . . just like that, he disappeared. Changed."

"Changed? Into what?"

"Don't know. Didn't stick around to find out."

"That's not like you," Annabel said.

"Yeah, well . . . if you'd heard the sound that guy made you probably would have done the same."

Just then Harvey entered the locker room. "Strobe. Good to see you're back. Any luck?"

Strobe shook his head no.

"How's Calanthe?" Annabel asked.

"Still out. Her heart rate appears to be steady, anyway."

"I'm happy to hear that. When I took her pulse in the alley, it was very odd, very irregular."

"Actually, I think that's the way a dekayi's blood is pumped. Two quick beats. Then a slow one. I don't think it's irregular."

"So at this point, there's nothing you can do to help her?"

"Not really. I don't want to experiment and possibly do some harm. So I'm just going to keep an eye on her. And wait. You three look exhausted. Why don't I show you to your dorm rooms."

The trio didn't argue with Harvey's suggestion that it might be time to shut it down for the night. Keyed up as they were from their high-charged nighttime romp and brutal battle with the rukh, they knew it was time to give their depleted bodies a rest. A short while later, when three heads hit three pillows, Toby, Annabel, and Strobe fell into a deep sleep.

■ ■ ■

They were up early.

No alarm clock was needed. The trio naturally woke, got dressed, and met in the hallway outside their dorm rooms. Harvey had pointed out a cafeteria the night before—or "mess hall" as he called it—and that's where they went.

A man wearing a white chef's jacket was behind a cafeteria-style counter, cooking up something that smelled gloriously mouthwatering. Harvey was in a corner booth, hands cupped around a huge mug of coffee, his posture and blank expression betraying an all-nighter. When he saw his three MCOs, he nodded toward the counter. "Grab a tray, get something to eat. Then we'll talk."

After the trio had complied with Harvey's order and were sitting in the booth with their breakfast, Harvey relayed what had happened overnight. Which turned out to be not much of anything.

"I think what might be happening here is Calanthe has entered a kind of coma, a hibernation state," Harvey surmised. "Perhaps this is what dekayi do when they've been injured. Calanthe's shoulder has not completely healed. So, until it has, until she is completely healthy, she sleeps. That's my best guess, anyway."

"What happens in the meantime?" Strobe asked. "With us, I mean."

"There's no sense in you staying for the rest of the weekend. Steve was supposed to be your host, give you the grand tour. But he's still off in Mexico, and now I'm going to be tied up with Calanthe and other business matters."

"Why can't we stay?" Annabel asked. "I don't really care about the tour. I'd just like to see how things turn out with Calanthe."

"Which could take a while," Harvey countered. "It's better you go. I have you booked on a plane for this afternoon."

"But you'll let us know the second anything happens with her, right?"

"Of course."

"Where's the company doc, by the way?" Toby asked. "Shouldn't he be here, helping you out with Calanthe?"

"He's out in the field, with everyone else."

"You are stretched pretty thin, aren't you, Chief?" Strobe observed.

"To the limit."

■ ■ ■

Toby, Annabel, and Strobe didn't have to take the subway to the airport. Harvey drove them in his Jeepster Commando. When he pulled up at the curb, he swung around so that he could see Toby and Strobe in the backseat, as well as Annabel, who was riding shotgun.

"I want you all to know how impressed I am with what you accomplished last night. You went up against a totally unknown species, and you managed to save that girl. No matter what happens to her, you've given her a chance at a new life. Remember that."

Annabel, Toby, and Strobe nodded somberly, then gathered up their backpacks and got out of the vehicle. After giving their KP boss a parting wave, they headed off to catch the plane that would take them back to Hidden Hills, back to their much more predictable and sedate everyday lives.

PART TWO:
LIFESTYLES
OF THE REAL
AND
OTHERWORLDLY

1

From his position behind the counter, Toby could see the flickering black-and-white images of the giant spider—smashing into a house with awesomely destructive force—on the building across the street from Killer Pizza.

It was Saturday night, and there was a large crowd outside the KP building watching *Tarantula*, the fourth movie to be shown as part of Killer Pizza's Monster Mash-up Saturday-night event. Some of the crowd were sitting on folding chairs they had brought for the occasion, some were lying or sitting on sleeping bags spread out on the dead-end street and sidewalk, others stood in groups on the outskirts of the crowd.

It had been Toby's brainstorm to project movies on the building opposite KP on Saturday nights. Immediately seizing on his Monster Mash-up idea, Harvey had placed Toby in charge of running the event. This had meant that in addition to such things as creating an advertising campaign and securing a projector to show the DVD movies, Toby was the one who selected the films to be shown on the white wall of the wholesale appliance store.

Toby had been surprised at how quickly M/M had caught on. He thought a few people would show up, anyway. But right from the start the crowds had gathered outside the KP window. Not being a big fan of the super-intense *Saw* kind of horror movies, Toby's main criteria for M/M was that the films had to be *fun*. He assumed that his relatively tame selection of classic horror, fifties' sci-fi and Japanese creature features wouldn't appeal to the majority of Hidden Hills teens. But there they were, out there every Saturday night, along with a younger crowd and an increasing amount of adults.

"Hello? Anyone in there?"

Toby shifted his eyes from *Tarantula* to a surly-looking teen, someone he vaguely recognized as a Triple H classmate. "Sorry. What did you say you wanted?"

"Creature Double Feature with sausage, pepperoni, and Canadian bacon."

"You're a meat man," Toby said with a smile, which was met by a deadpan look from the guy. *Never joke around with a hungry person!* Toby reminded himself. "It'll be up in fifteen minutes."

Entering the kitchen, Toby immediately started in on the Creature Double Feature. He had to jockey for counter space with Strobe and Annabel, who were in constant motion as they juggled a bewildering array of pizza and side-dish orders between them. After shoving several Monstrosities into the oven, Strobe elbowed Toby aside brusquely on his return to the counter.

"Hey, watch it, man," Toby said, annoyed that Strobe's nudge had caused him to spill half of the tomato sauce from his ladle onto the counter.

"I'll watch it, all right."

Oh, boy, here we go, Toby thought. He knew from experience how quickly Strobe's moods could change. Just a little while before, the guy had seemed in a perfectly okay frame of mind. "What's the matter, Strobe, can't take the heat?"

"You and your Monster Mash-up idea." Strobe was flattening out a thin layer of dough for an order of Mummy Wraps.

"Yeah . . . what about it?"

"We're only about three times busier than we were before this thing started. And we were busy enough as it was." After applying the Mummy Wrap innards, Strobe twisted the dough around the small mound of ingredients and shaped the wrap until it resembled a mummy lying in its sarcophagus.

"Hey, I can't help it if you don't appreciate the difference between a Ray Harryhausen or a Wah Chang special effect. If you did, you might actually look forward to our little Saturday evenings together. Besides, I thought it was a good thing for a business to be busy. *Busi*ness. Busy? Get it?" Toby's lame pun received zero reaction from Strobe.

"Hang in there, Strobe," Annabel said. "A few more weeks, and it'll be too cold to show movies outside at night." Tossing a large doughy pie high into the air, Annabel caught it and slapped it onto the flour-dusty counter. "This is the fifth Dragon Breath I've made tonight," she told Toby with a smile.

Toby nodded modestly. The Dragon Breath pizza had been his creation, and it had proved to be a popular item on the KP menu.

"If I were you, I'd talk to Harvey about getting a piece of the action on that one," Strobe suggested.

Annabel rolled her eyes at Strobe's comment as she picked out the spicy ingredients for the Dragon Breath. "It's always about the money with you, Strobe."

"Just because you . . ."

"Don't start."

"I'm just sayin'. When you got it, you don't have to worry about it."

"What makes you think I have it? I'm getting the same salary as you are."

"Touché, Annabel," Toby said.

Strobe let the topic drop. He knew he shouldn't get

into Annabel's home life. She and her dad hadn't been getting along very well lately, mainly because her wealthy, autocratic father—who had very firm plans for his daughter's future—regarded Annabel's decision to work at a lowly pizza shop for minimum wage instead of at one of his business supply stores as an irritating form of teenage rebellion. Which, in some ways, it was.

So Strobe just concentrated on his Monstrosities and Vampire Stakes and Frankensausages, and the trio continued with their nonstop pizza making—punctuated by occasional conversation—for the next hour, then called it a night when the late-shift crew arrived. Being minors, Toby, Annabel, and Strobe could only work until nine o'clock.

The trio were now free of any kitchen duties until the following weekend. At Harvey's request, they had agreed to work at Killer Pizza on Friday and Saturday nights. A new manager—unaware of the secret underground basement in the KP building, where Toby, Annabel, and Strobe continued to train a couple of times during the week—had been hired by Harvey and was running the day-to-day operations of the place.

"Well . . . night, you two," Annabel said after she and her two coworkers had pushed through the front door of the KP building. Toby and Strobe waved so long to Annabel, then watched as she walked off through the crowd.

"Gonna stay for the rest of the movie?" Toby asked Strobe after Annabel had gotten on her bike and disappeared around the far corner of Industrial Avenue.

"I think I have about a million better things to do. Don't tell me . . . you are."

"Of course."

"I thought you already watched this masterpiece."

"I did." Good, bad, or ugly, Toby watched every movie he was considering for Monster Mash-up all the way through. "Your point being?"

"You know how it turns out. Why watch it again?"

"What kind of question is that? If you like something . . . a movie, book, recipe . . . it's fun to experience it all over again."

"I don't see the fun in that, man. It's like spinning your wheels. I want the new experience."

"Yeah, well . . ." Toby shrugged. "Just another thing that makes us different."

Strobe slapped Toby on the shoulder. "Later." Toby nodded a good-bye, then picked out a spot to watch the climax of the movie. An all-out battle to defeat the gigantic tarantula was underway on the building across the street.

The irony of selecting creature features for M/M while he continued to train to fight the real thing wasn't lost on

Toby. Just another interesting wrinkle in his new MCO life, is the way Toby looked at it. Besides, after his wild experience in New York, Toby was happy to deal with monsters of the cinematic variety. At least for the time being.

■ ■ ■

After the movie was over, Toby stored the DVD projector in KP's back room, spent a few moments chatting with the late-shift kitchen staff, then went home to a typical Saturday night scene.

His sister Stacey and her rambunctious group of friends were in the family room, laughing and screeching over one another as they watched music videos and laid waste to a prodigious supply of snacks provided by Toby's mother.

Speaking of whom, Mrs. Magill was on the phone in the living room, talking to either one of her local PTA pals or her long-distance mother or brother or sister. Toby was amazed at how much time his mom could spend on the phone. By contrast, he rarely saw his dad anywhere near a phone. He was the only person Toby knew who didn't own a cell.

"Hey, Dad," Toby said after opening the hallway door that led to the garage. He knew that's where his dad would be, in his little workshop space at the far end of the garage, restoring another dilapidated jukebox he had found in the green sheet or at a swap meet or one of the estate sales he loved to attend.

"Hey, there, Toby. How'd it go tonight?"

"Good."

"We on for tomorrow?"

"Of course."

A late morning/early afternoon Sunday ritual had recently been established at the Magill household. A Sunday brunch, just for Toby and his father, who had developed a keen interest in his son's culinary ambitions.

"What are we having tomorrow?" Mr. Magill's voice was muffled, having asked the question while lying on his back, his head stuck inside the jukebox.

"You know that's a secret."

"Just a hint."

"Okay, for just one of the dishes."

"Well, that's better than none."

"Can you spell *chocolate*?"

"Oh, man, you just hit me where I live!"

Toby smiled as he shut the hallway door. Going upstairs, he headed straight for his bedroom. Like any teen fortunate enough to have his own room, Toby's was his sanctuary. Stocked with all the necessary items near and dear to teendom—computer, video games, the proper posters on the walls, graphic novels, a few action figures left over from his nerdy younger years—Toby's room also contained his ready-for-combat black KP field pack, *Monsters of the World* textbook, and last but not least, his crossbow.

All MCO items were carefully hidden, of course. For the most part, Toby's mother and father observed the bedroom off-limits rule typically enjoyed by teenagers, but Stacey was a notorious, *numero-uno* pain-in-the-butt snoop.

Firmly closing his door, Toby went to his desk and opened a side drawer. This is where he kept his recipe notebook. Filled with ideas for new dishes, Toby wanted to tweak his latest concoction, which was one of the dishes he would be trying out on his dad the following day.

Toby noodled around with the recipe—taking an occasional break to thumb through a pile of Hidden Hills Library cookbooks he had taken out for inspiration and ideas—but his concentration was constantly being interrupted by thoughts of Calanthe.

Annabel had relayed to Toby and Strobe earlier in the evening there was nothing new to report regarding the girl's condition. It had already been a week since their return from New York, and Calanthe was still in her mysterious coma-like state.

Which Toby found pretty depressing. Truth was, a day hadn't passed since the trio's return from New York that he hadn't thought about the girl they had saved from the monstrous rukh. It was Calanthe's eyes, more than anything, that had a hold on Toby. There was something about them, something dark and mysterious, that had gripped his imagination and wouldn't let go.

Toby suddenly yawned, the long busy day finally catching up with him. He took off his glasses and flopped backward onto his bed. He lay there for a moment, then reached out for his notebook. There was one last thing he needed to check out. When he put his glasses back on, it was a pair of eyes that came into focus.

Yeah, maybe there was a little bit of an obsession going on here, Toby had to admit to himself. After all, he had sketched Calanthe's eyes on the page opposite the original recipe he had come up with for a Sweet Tooth Pizza. Turning the notebook to better catch the light, Toby stared at his version of Calanthe's eyes. Dark. Haunted. Mysterious. At the same time that Toby scrutinized his drawing . . .

Five hundred miles to the east of Hidden Hills, at 175 Fifth Avenue in New York City, in the basement headquarters of Killer Pizza's MCO operations . . .

Calanthe's eyes finally opened.

2

OMPHHH!

Before he could react, Toby was knocked sideways by a shoulder slam from a kid walking past him in the crowded Hidden Hills High hallway. Toby knew it was forbidden to glare or say anything to the guy, an obvious upperclassman, so he just kept going. Being a lowly freshman at Triple H meant Toby was a clear target for abuse, which he had learned to grin and bear. Fighting monsters was one thing, but being the new kid in a new school? Watch out!

On guard against another possible body blow, Toby weaved through the stream of students coming at him like something in a really intense video game. The lunchtime bell had just rung, eliciting an explosive response from the students, happy to have some freedom after being cooped up in one classroom after another since early morning.

Toby was on his way to the gym. Annabel had asked him to meet her there at lunchtime. She needed to talk to him about something. The topic? When Toby had asked, Annabel mysteriously declined to give him so much as a hint of what it was she wanted to discuss with him and Strobe. Toby was more than happy to meet with Annabel and Strobe. He rarely saw either of them during a typical school day.

When Toby entered the gym, a group of students were playing basketball at one end of the court. Their lunchtime game was being supervised by a teacher dressed in too-short shorts and the official Triple H sports T-shirt. (GO, JAGUARS!) Strobe sat at the other end of the court, halfway up the bleachers, reading a book. As Toby approached, he recognized Strobe's book by its tattered cover. It was *Monsters of the World*.

"Think it's a good idea to have that here at school?" Toby asked as he sat on a bleacher near Strobe.

"Why? What's the problem?"

"Isn't it obvious? Last I heard, we're part of a secret organization."

"Toby," Strobe said, in a tone one would use on a child. "If someone was to pick up this book . . . say, I left it here by mistake . . . what do you figure they would think it was?"

Toby considered the question. "Probably a book that had been discovered in the fiction section of a used bookstore somewhere."

"Exactly."

Strobe turned his attention back to *MOTW*. It did have the well-worn look of a tome Strobe might have found in a local secondhand bookstore.

"What are you reading about, anyway?" Toby asked.

"I'll tell you what I'm not reading about. Dekayi. Harvey wasn't kidding when he said he didn't know much about them. They rate a brief mention in the appendix, but that's it. As for the rukh? Doesn't even get a mention."

"You know what's kind of cool? Harvey'll be able to use that information we gave him about the dekayi and rukh for the new edition of the book he's been working on."

Harvey had asked the trio to write down everything they could remember about the dekayi and rukh before he took them out to JFK.

"Which none of us will get credit for," Strobe predicted.

Just then Annabel appeared from the door opposite Toby and Strobe and walked across the court toward them.

"Hey! Only athletic shoes on the court!" the teacher

overseeing the basketball game boomed, punctuating his order with an intimidating glare as Annabel quickly changed course and skirted the perimeter of the court to get to her KP coworkers.

"Idiot," Strobe said, glaring back at the teacher. "The things people get themselves in a twist over."

Toby smiled. He knew what Strobe meant. Considering what they had just been through in New York, a few scuffs on a hardwood basketball court from street shoes didn't seem all that important.

"Any idea what Annabel wants to talk to us about?" Toby asked as she approached.

"Nope. Didn't tell me a thing. Just said, 'Be there!'"

When Annabel arrived at the bleachers she settled on a seat below her KP partners. Looking up at Toby and Strobe, Annabel wore an expression that was a mixture of . . . well, it was hard to guess what her expression signaled, what it was she was about to tell them.

"So what's up, Annabel?" Strobe asked. "The suspense boils over."

"Well, I have good news, bad news, and potentially exciting news."

"In that order?"

"Yes, in that order. For starters? Calanthe has come out of her coma, or whatever it was she was in. Harvey said she appears to have weathered the ordeal as well as he could have hoped and seems to be in good health."

"That's fantastic." Toby was relieved, hearing this.

"So what's the bad news?" Strobe asked.

"Harvey said Calanthe doesn't want to have anything to do with him or anyone else at Killer Pizza."

"That's weird," Strobe replied. "I thought she wanted to come to KP. Does Harvey have any idea why she's acting like this?"

"Yes. He thinks Calanthe might be suffering a kind of post-traumatic stress syndrome. It took a lot for her to escape from her village, and now she's feeling the after-effects. Combine that with the shock of the new. This is something Calanthe obviously wanted, a new life, but now that she has it . . . it's freaking her out. It's so totally different from the world she grew up in, she doesn't know how to deal with it."

"I still don't get why she isn't letting Harvey and the gang help her," Toby said. "Like Strobe said, that's kind of strange."

"Well, this is the interesting part. Harvey believes that maybe Calanthe has imprinted on us."

"Imprinted?"

"It's what baby chicks do when they come out of their shell. The first thing they see . . . they think it's their mother. It's called imprinting. We were the first people Calanthe met when she entered her new world. According to Harvey, from the little he's been able to get Calanthe to open up to him, we're the ones she wants to be with."

Strobe laughed. "So we're the mother hens. Let me guess, the chief wants us to come back to New York to help jump-start the girl, get her up and running in her new world."

"Actually, no. What Harvey suggested is that Calanthe come here, to Hidden Hills."

Strobe and Toby were too surprised by Annabel's answer to immediately say anything. "And this would be the potentially exciting news?" Toby ventured.

Annabel nodded. "Harvey would set things up to make Calanthe look like a foreign exchange student. He'd give her a passport, prepare the foreign exchange program's papers . . ."

"Wait, wait, hold on a second . . . back up here." Strobe didn't look very excited about Annabel's potentially exciting news. "What you're saying is that Harvey wants us to take care of Calanthe? This much I can tell you. I didn't sign up for the KP program to become a Monster Protection Program specialist."

"Don't overreact, Strobe. We wouldn't become MPP

specialists. This is a temporary thing, just until Calanthe becomes oriented to her new life. Think about how exciting this could be."

"Where would Calanthe stay?" Toby asked.

Strobe shot his KP partner a nasty look. With a question like that, it sounded as though Toby might actually be considering this.

"If we decide to accept Harvey's proposal to become Calanthe's mentors, I'll ask my parents if she could stay with me."

"And you think they'd go along with that?" Strobe looked skeptical.

"There's only one way to find out. What do you say, guys? Calanthe needs us. She's all alone in her new world. Think about how that must feel. I really think we can help her."

Toby didn't hesitate with his answer. "I'm in."

Annabel gave Toby a grateful smile, then turned her attention to the holdout. "C'mon, Strobe, you can do this. I know you'd be a great mentor to Calanthe."

Strobe knew there was absolutely no way he could wriggle out of this one. Not if he ever wanted Annabel to speak to him again. "You two heard it from me first. We're going to come to regret this."

"No, we won't," Annabel insisted.

Strobe hesitated, then nodded reluctantly. Annabel responded to the group's collective decision to bring Calanthe to Hidden Hills by giving her KP mates a hug and a kiss on the cheek.

"If you'd done that in the first place, I might not have played so hard to get," Strobe deadpanned. Slinging his backpack over his shoulder, he got up and headed for the exit. Annabel and Toby fell right in next to him. This time, instead of skirting the basketball court . . .

Annabel and her two partners went straight across it, pushed through the double-exit doors, and disappeared into the hallway beyond. The entire way to the door, the trio had ignored the bellowing warnings from the red-faced teacher, who finally abandoned his students' basketball game to chase down the belligerent rule breakers.

3

"I need you to record everything you can find out about the dekayi's habits and lifestyle. Where they live. Where they're from. Their legends, religion. Nothing is too trivial, understand?"

"Calanthe didn't give you *any* of that stuff?" Strobe asked. He, Annabel, and Toby were in Annabel's bedroom, gathered around her computer having a teleconference with Harvey. Almost a week had gone by since the trio had agreed to take on the Calanthe assignment.

"No, she didn't. Calanthe was very distrustful of my entire staff."

Sitting closest to the computer, Annabel was frowning as she tapped a notepad with her pen. "Don't you think it's a good idea to get Calanthe settled in here first? Make sure she's comfortable in her new home before we start grilling her about her home life?"

Harvey's expression was stern. "I'm afraid getting

Calanthe comfortable in her new world could take some time, Annabel. Meanwhile, the more we know about the dekayi, the better we'll be able to protect Calanthe. And the sooner we know it, the better."

Annabel managed a slight nod in response to Harvey's answer.

"Okay, that's it for now. Calanthe should be arriving in Hidden Hills very soon. Good luck. And don't hesitate to call if you have any questions."

"Hey, before you go, Chief?" Strobe said. "The three of us got detention a few days ago. Can you take care of that for us?"

Harvey's answer was a deadpan look, followed by the sudden disappearance of his image from the computer screen. Strobe shrugged nonchalantly. "Figured it wouldn't hurt to ask. The guy's reach is pretty impressive, after all." When Strobe stepped aside to allow Annabel to get up from her chair, he couldn't help but notice her concerned expression. "What's wrong with you, Annabel?"

"I feel misled by Harvey. He said he wanted us to help Calanthe adapt to her new life. It sounds to me like he's more interested in her as a specimen to be studied."

"It's probably a bit of both."

"Well, I can tell you this. Calanthe's going to be living in my house. That makes me in charge of this operation."

"Whoa, listen to the girl!" Strobe said with a smile, which was not returned by Annabel.

"You know what that just felt like?" Toby said. "The three angels getting their assignment from Charlie."

"Last I heard, the angels were three women, dude."

"You know what I mean."

"I do. We now have our assignment. Let's go greet our girl."

■ ■ ■

A half hour later, the trio was still waiting on Annabel's front porch for their girl to arrive. Even though Halloween was more than a week away, the houses on Annabel's street—including hers—were already extravagantly decorated for the holiday.

Leaning up against the side of Annabel's house, Toby was checking something out on his iPhone. "I still can't believe Calanthe didn't want to take a plane."

"What's not to believe?" Annabel replied. "She's never been on a plane before. Just imagine how much that could freak her out. I'm not sure if Calanthe's ever been in a car."

"She must have, at least to get to New York." On watch for the car that would deliver Calanthe to Annabel's doorstep, Strobe stood in the driveway, casually scanning the street.

"I've been meaning to ask, Annabel, how'd you persuade your parents to do this?" Toby walked over to the porch bench and sat next to Annabel. "I was pretty surprised when you told us they were going along with it."

"It wasn't easy. I had to do a little negotiating, mainly with my father."

"Yeah? What'd that entail?"

"Well, I was going to tell you guys eventually."

That got Toby's and Strobe's attention.

"I told my dad I would quit my evil KP job."

"That's a joke, right?"

"No, it's not. For the time being, I'm going to become Daddy's good little girl. Peace will reign in the household. I wouldn't want it any other way with Calanthe here. She deserves that."

Annabel had genuinely surprised her kitchen cohorts. "But what are we gonna do without you?" Toby asked plaintively. "We'll have to break in a new coworker."

"Either that or work a two-man shift."

"Don't have a breakdown, Tobe," Strobe said. "We'll deal."

"Here she is," Annabel said suddenly. A black sedan had appeared and was approaching the house. Gathering in the driveway near the porch, the trio resembled formal greeters waiting to welcome a traveling dignitary of some sort.

When the car pulled into the driveway and braked to a stop, everyone was surprised to see Steve Rogers get out. "Hello, all," Steve said with his usual warm smile. Always the sympathetic counterpart to the brusque, intense Harvey, Steve had been a very welcome presence during the trio's exhaustive nose-to-the-grindstone tryout to become Killer Pizza MCOs.

"Steve, how'd you get roped into this assignment?" Strobe received a sharp nudge from Annabel for his question.

"I volunteered. After getting back from my south-of-the-border adventure, a nice relaxing drive to Ohio was just what I needed."

"Yeah? What'd you have to deal with down there?" Strobe received another jab from Annabel. "What's with you, girl? Stop it!"

"Now's not the time to be asking Steve about what kind of monsters he battled in Mexico!" Annabel hissed.

Steve had come around the car and now opened the passenger door for Calanthe. From where he stood in the driveway, Toby could see the outline of Calanthe's figure in the dark interior of the car. She hadn't yet made a move to get out the car. It was as though she was afraid to emerge into the light of day. When Calanthe finally did slide out of her seat, Toby experienced sharply conflicting feelings about what he saw.

The last time he had seen Calanthe, her hair had been matted and dirty from her swim through the Central Park lake. Now her hair shone brightly, the beautiful thick black curls falling to her shoulders. Instead of her former eye-catching (not in a good way) thrift-shop wardrobe, Calanthe now wore a red hoodie sweatshirt, black T-shirt, blue jeans, and Converse sneakers. Even though she had a lot to learn about the modern world, Calanthe could definitely pass as a typical teen right now, which meant she would fit right in at Triple H.

That was the good news.

The bad was Calanthe's entire demeanor. Quickly taking in the surrounding neighborhood, Calanthe's eyes had a nervous, edgy look to them. She held her body stiffly, as though fearing something terrible, something unexpected might happen at any moment. To Toby, Calanthe looked . . . *depleted* was the word that came to him. She looked beyond exhausted. Hers was a condition that wasn't just physical. It seemed to Toby that it went all the way to her soul.

We have a lot of work to do here! was Toby's concerned thought as Annabel approached Calanthe to welcome her with a hug. But as Annabel attempted to wrap her arms around her new houseguest, Calanthe instantly backed off.

"I don't believe that's a dekayi custom," Steve said softly.

"Oh . . . sorry, Calanthe."

There was an awkward silence before Steve interrupted the moment by taking a brand-new suitcase from the backseat and handing it to Strobe. "Sorry to leave so quickly, but I'm needed back in New York."

"You're not staying?" Annabel asked, surprised at Steve's instant departure. "Don't you at least want something to eat before you go?"

"I'm good, thank you, Annabel. Calanthe? It was very nice to meet you. I wish you all the luck in your new home. I know these three will take very good care of you."

Calanthe responded to Steve's words with a barely perceptible nod. Steve got back into the car and started the engine. "Okay, bye all. As I'm sure Harvey already told you, don't hesitate to call if you need anything."

"Those were his exact words," Strobe replied.

After the three MCOs said their good-byes and Steve's car disappeared down the street, Annabel led Calanthe toward her front door. "My parents wanted me to tell you they're very sorry they couldn't be here for your arrival, Calanthe. It's a busy day for them at work. You'll meet them this evening."

"Parents?"

"Yes, my mother and father."

Calanthe's expression was blank.

"You . . . do know what parents are, don't you?" Annabel asked with a cautious laugh.

Calanthe shook her head. "No, I do not know what that word means."

The trio was stunned at Calanthe's response.

"Oooookay," Strobe said. "Definitely something to add to the Calanthe talking-point list." Strobe exchanged a look with Annabel and Toby, then followed them into the house and up the long stairway to the second floor. On the way up, Strobe hoisted Calanthe's suitcase with a shake of his head. It was so light!

Calanthe's one sad little suitcase was a perfect metaphor for her entry into her new life, Strobe realized. She had practically nothing to start out with. No knowledge of the customs and details of her strange new world, such as welcoming hugs and airplanes and . . . parents? Did the dekayi have no parents? What could that possibly mean?

When Annabel reached the top of the stairs, she

continued along the mezzanine that overlooked the foyer below and entered a skylit hallway. She stopped at a doorway near the end of the hall and turned to Calanthe. "This is your bedroom," she said with an encouraging smile.

With that, Calanthe entered her bedroom . . . and her new world.

4

The rukh was motionless.

The creature was not dead, but rather in a state not unlike the one Calanthe had recently experienced. After its fall from the New York rooftop, the thing had searched out an isolated place—not to die, as Calanthe had surmised—but to recover from its serious injuries. It had not gone back to the dekayi community to heal. That was a distance too far to travel. Instead, the beast had found the perfect spot, not far from the alley it had slammed into with such ferocious force.

The rats in the subterranean tunnel where the rukh currently resided gave the creature wide berth. The hulking, invisible form resting in a recess near the ceiling of the tunnel set off an ancient reaction in the underground rodent population, a violently explosive nervous-system response that cried . . . *stay away*!

So the rukh rested comfortably and undisturbed in

its hideaway beneath the bustling New York metropolis. It would not move until it had healed. It would not eat until it had healed. What it would do, once its strength had returned, was go back on the hunt. The primitive creature knew there was unfinished business to tend to. It had been given a scent, and it would not stop until it had followed the distinctive, one-of-a-kind odor to its source. No matter how many twists, turns, or detours might be thrown at the beast, it would go on and on and on . . .

Until the girl was found.

5

The day after Calanthe's arrival in Hidden Hills, Toby and Strobe returned to Annabel's house. When Toby rang the doorbell, it was Mr. Oshiro who opened the door. Dressed in an expensive sport shirt and khaki slacks, he looked like he might have just come back from the golf course. "Annabel's upstairs with Calanthe," Mr. Oshiro said after giving Toby and Strobe a cool once-over.

Stepping into the large foyer, Toby gave Annabel's father a respectful nod and a smile. Mr. Oshiro looked past Toby at Strobe, who had followed Toby into the house. Judging from the older man's expression, the scruffy-looking Strobe wasn't the type of person who normally visited Annabel.

"How's Calanthe settling in here at the Oshiro household, Mr. O?" Strobe asked.

Toby winced at his friend's casual greeting.

"I haven't spent much time with our new houseguest," Mr. Oshiro replied. "She only just arrived yesterday."

After seeing Calanthe to her room the day before, the trio had held a quick meeting without Calanthe in Annabel's bedroom, where it had been decided that Toby and Strobe would come back the next day after their workout session at KP. It was obvious the traumatized teen needed some time to adjust to her new surroundings before the trio began their "official" sessions with the girl.

"Annabel did tell you that Toby and I have volunteered to help Calanthe adjust to her new school, did she not?"

Mr. Oshiro was staring at Strobe's muddy, frayed combat boots in a way that suggested he'd never seen anything quite like the teen's footwear in his entire life. "Annabel's mother mentioned something about that to me. I'm not sure what kind of help Calanthe needs. The girl is from Port Said, Egypt, after all. It's not as though she's coming in from the wilds of the Sahara or someplace of that nature and needs a total . . . makeover, I believe you kids call it."

If you only knew, Toby thought. Catching Strobe's eye, he indicated they should head upstairs. But Strobe showed no inclination of terminating his conversation with Mr. Oshiro just yet.

"Hosting a foreign exchange student can be very time consuming, Mr. O. We just wanted to take some of the pressure off Annabel. And FYI, Calanthe will be attending classes with Toby. We were all concerned she wouldn't be able to keep up with the honors classes your brilliant daughter is taking. That's why Toby's involved."

Thank's for that, Strobe. Let's shine a spotlight on how much of an underachiever I am! Grabbing Strobe by the sleeve, Toby pulled him toward the staircase before he could do any more damage. "Nice to see you, Mr. Oshiro."

After the two had gone up the stairs and were out of earshot of Mr. Oshiro, Toby shot Strobe an annoyed look. "What was all that back there?"

"What . . ." Strobe asked innocently.

"You know *what*. You were baiting the guy. Calling him 'Mr. O.' Talking about why we're coming over here. That's called too much information, okay?"

"I disagree. Better to have it right out in the open, talk about it, instead of skulking around. That'd only make this whole setup even more suspect than it might already be."

"Okay, I'll give you that. But please stop calling him Mr. O, will you?"

"That *was* just to bait him," Strobe said with a smile.

"Why would you do something like that?"

"Maybe I didn't dig the guy's vibes."

"What was wrong with his vibes?"

"From what Annabel told us, her dad's happy she quit Killer Pizza, right? I get the impression the dude thinks we're excess baggage his daughter should toss aside, as well."

Toby frowned. This was a sensitive subject. He didn't want to believe that Strobe was right. But maybe he was. It could be that Annabel's dad didn't want her associating with the two of them anymore. They were from the "other side of the burb," after all.

"Besides, I just like to annoy grown-ups from time to time."

"From time to time, Strobe?"

Just then Annabel appeared from Calanthe's room at the end of the hall. Toby was surprised at how happy she looked. "How's she doing?" Toby asked in a low voice as he and Strobe met Annabel in the hallway.

Annabel smiled and crossed her fingers. "Really good, actually."

"Get out. Seriously?" Definitely not what Toby was expecting to hear.

"Yeah, she totally surprised me this morning. She slept for over twelve hours last night, which I think she really needed. Harvey said she wasn't sleeping very well in New York, and it's like she was this completely differ-ent person when she woke up." Annabel had turned and was leading Toby and Strobe back down the hall. "I think Harvey might be right about this whole imprinting thing. Now that Calanthe's here . . . settled down a bit . . . it's like she's come home or something. It's a pretty impressive transformation."

"That's great news, Annabel."

"Isn't it, though?" Annabel stopped outside Calanthe's door. "By the way, you don't have to whisper. She can't hear you."

"Why, is she taking a nap?"

"No. She's in iPod land."

"Hey, no fair," Strobe said sternly. "We should have all had input into what Calanthe listens to first."

"It's my house. I get to pick what Calanthe listens to." Annabel gave Strobe a "take that" look as she entered Calanthe's room. Following Annabel, Toby and Strobe were greeted by the sight of Calanthe sitting cross-legged on the floor, staring out the window, and moving her head slowly, somewhat cautiously, to whatever song was currently pumping into her brain. She was facing away from the trio and hadn't noticed them enter.

"She doesn't seem to like chairs, by the way," Annabel said.

"What's that supposed to mean?" Toby asked.

"Maybe they don't have them where she comes from. A lot of cultures don't. But she hasn't sat on her chair since she arrived."

"Didn't she have dinner with you and your parents last night?"

"No, she ate here in her room. She was asleep before my parents came home. But she did sit at the kitchen table for breakfast with everyone this morning."

"How'd that go?"

"Not too bad."

"She didn't grab any food off your parents' plates, did she?" Strobe asked.

Annabel smiled. "No, I had a little talk with her before breakfast about table etiquette. She did fine. Didn't say much, just nodded a lot when my parents talked to her. She looked a bit uncomfortable, but that's okay. She's a shy foreign exchange student, after all."

"Doesn't like chairs," Strobe mused. "Just shows how much we need to discover about this girl's culture. I'd say it's time we got started." Circling around Calanthe to get in her field of view, Strobe gave her a big smile. Calanthe stared at Strobe for a moment, then slowly took out her earbuds.

"Hi, Calanthe. What are you listening to?"

Calanthe looked spacey from her first-time iPod experience. "Music."

"Yes, I know. Music. But what *song* are you listening to?"

Calanthe frowned. "I don't know."

"Strobe. Enough of this," Annabel insisted.

"You're right. We'll deal with this music situation later. First things first. You know what time it is, Calanthe?"

Calanthe shook her head no.

"High school boot-camp time!"

Calanthe's expression signaled she had no clue what that meant. "Boot camp . . ." she repeated.

"It's an expression we have. You're going to school tomorrow, right? You have a lot to learn. *Boot camp* means learning a lot in a little amount of time."

"Don't put too much pressure on her, Strobe," Toby said drily.

"Do we have to go somewhere for this boot camp?"

"No, Calanthe," Annabel said as she stepped between her and Strobe. "We're going to have boot camp right here. In this room. *Your* room."

Toby swiveled the computer chair around, sat down, and gave Calanthe an encouraging smile. "Don't worry, you'll catch on really fast. Before you know it, Calanthe, you'll be hummin' along, acting just like a typical Triple H student."

"'Catch on.' 'Humming along.' These are additional expressions of yours, yes?"

The trio exchanged looks. They had never thought about how many taken-for-granted expressions a person uses every single day. Tons of them, really.

"On the other hand, maybe she won't catch on really fast," Strobe whispered behind his hand to Toby.

Hearing that, Annabel gave Strobe a withering look. "Once class is underway, misbehaving students will definitely be dismissed. Could you get the door, please, Toby?"

Toby crossed the room and closed the bedroom door. Then he, Annabel, and Strobe settled in for their first official high school boot-camp session with Calanthe.

6

"Awesome, Calanthe! High five!"

Calanthe regarded Strobe's open hand, held up high. "Slap my hand with your hand. Like this." Strobe slapped his right hand with his left to illustrate what he meant. Calanthe responded with a sharp slap to Strobe's palm.

"Okay, that hurt. You don't have to hit so hard. A *high five* means good job. Well done."

"'Good job,'" Calanthe repeated.

"Yeah, you did absolutely great, Calanthe," Toby said. He meant it, too. Calanthe had soaked in everything the group had thrown at her over the past few hours and given it right back to them. Clearly on the upper end of the smarty scale, Calanthe had combined intense concentration with a seriousness of purpose that had impressed her three teachers.

"Okay, I say we move on from current teen vernacular and slang," Annabel said as she went to Calanthe's closet and pulled out a backpack.

"Aw, c'mon. This is the fun part," Strobe complained.

"And *this* . . . is an iconic part of every high school student's attire. Here, let me fit you, Calanthe."

Calanthe had been sitting on her bed during her slang quiz. When she stood, Annabel slid her arms through the two backpack straps and adjusted them to fit Calanthe's height.

"What is this for?"

"Books."

"Lots of books," Strobe said.

"A backbreaking amount of books," Toby added for punctuation. "Although I doubt you'll have any trouble with the weight."

"What are all the books for?"

"There's one, sometimes more, for every subject." Satisfied with how the pack fit Calanthe, Annabel stood back and nodded. "You'll have a locker to store your books in. Do you have lockers where you come from?"

"No. What is that?"

"Toby will show you when we go to school tomorrow. He'll help you with your combination and any other questions you might have."

"What do you mean by *combination*?"

"I'll explain on Monday," Toby said.

"You do know that you have to sit in a chair for your classes, right?" Strobe asked.

"No, I did not."

Strobe wheeled the computer chair over to her. "Here, try it out."

When Calanthe sat, she looked uncomfortable in her chair.

"Don't worry, you'll get used to it," Strobe said dismissively.

"What I'd like to do now is go through what you can expect during a typical school day," Annabel said. "From getting up first thing in the morning until the final bell of the day."

"Ten to one you don't have bells at your school, right?" Strobe guessed.

"No, I don't know what you mean by 'final bell.'"

"Bells ring all the time at our school," Toby explained. "An annoying amount of bell ringing, if you ask me. So many bells . . ."

"Okay, all right, Toby. I'll get to the bells. But first . . . getting up in the morning. I don't know how early you normally get up, Calanthe, but I'm going to have to set your alarm for six o'clock."

"How ridiculously early is that?" Strobe interjected.

"Tell me about it," Toby replied. "I was thinking about that just the other day. When was that decided? Who pinpointed seven thirty as the perfect time to start a school day?"

"I don't know, but I wouldn't mind having a word with the genius who did."

"Guys, I think we should—"

"I forget where I read this," Toby said, ignoring Annabel's attempt to get the group back to the business at hand. "But did you know that some schools are experimenting with a starting time of around nine, nine thirty? Turns out the students aren't as tired, *surprise*, and do better overall than—"

"Okay, enough of this." Annabel was obviously irritated at Toby's and Strobe's continuing conversation about the proper time to begin a school day.

"Right. Sorry," Toby said.

"Where was I?"

"Alarm," Strobe said.

"Right. I'm going to set your alarm for six o'clock, Calanthe."

"Six o'clock. That is a measurement of time, yes?"

Strobe laughed. "Do you believe the depth of knowledge this girl knows absolutely nothing about?"

"Okay, out! Both of you."

Toby looked genuinely surprised by Annabel's command.

"You two obviously need a break. I'll continue one on one with Calanthe."

Toby looked over at Strobe, hands held out in a

"What'd I do?" gesture, then he and Strobe got up and headed for the bedroom door.

"Just so I don't have to go downstairs and hang out with your dad," Strobe said.

"You know where my room is. Go amuse yourself on the computer or something."

"The computer! We haven't even started in on Calanthe with that one. I can't wait to see what fun that's gonna be." Strobe just managed to duck out of the way of Calanthe's new backpack, which Annabel had chucked at him. With dead-on accuracy.

7

"**It is in the middle of a vast forest. The nearest town** is very far away. The village has been there many, many years. It is inhabited by perhaps a hundred, hundred and fifty people. We live very simply. We have our own livestock. Grow all our own food. We do not have what you call fast food."

Calanthe was surprised when everyone smiled at her last comment. She didn't think she had said anything amusing. After the group had completed their long and tiring day of HS boot camp, they had taken a dinner break, then Calanthe was asked to talk a bit about her village. Whatever she wanted to tell the trio was fine. No pressure. This wasn't a grilling session.

"We do not have . . . this." Calanthe turned a bedside lamp on and off and back on.

"Electricity," Toby said.

Calanthe nodded. "We have no automobiles. No . . . tall buildings like in New York."

"New York must have been really weird for you."

"Yes, the tall buildings freaked me out."

"Excellent, girl," Strobe said. "Okay, so we get what your village is kinda like. But what are you, anyway? What makes you different from us humans? That guy who followed you to New York? He turned into *some*thing that night."

"I don't want to get into that right now, Strobe." Annabel's tone was firm. She absolutely would not allow this conversation to go there.

"Why not?" Strobe replied.

"I have a question, Calanthe," Toby said, wanting to help Annabel steer things in another direction. "When you arrived here yesterday, you didn't know what Annabel meant when she said parents. You don't have parents where you come from? A mother? Father?"

"I don't know what those words mean. *Mother. Father*."

"Well, I don't want to get into the mechanics of it or anything, but a mother is the person who gives birth to a child."

"Oh, I see. Yes, I know all about that."

"So . . . who raised you? Who brought you up?"

"My village did. My earliest memory is of being in a large room with about ten children of my own age. We were tended to by the some of the women of the village. When we were older, we were moved to another building. And another large room."

"So you're an orphan," Strobe said. Calanthe gave Strobe a questioning look. "That's someone who doesn't have a mother or father. Either the parents have died or the child was given up."

"What does *given up* mean?"

"The parents didn't want the child for some reason or other."

"That's one way you're not like an orphan," Annabel broke in. "It doesn't sound like your parents didn't want you. This is just the way the children are raised in your village."

Hearing about the way Calanthe had been raised, Annabel suddenly felt—for the first time, really—a strong sense of responsibility for her new houseguest. Not only was she, Toby, and Strobe acting as surrogate parents for Calanthe in her new world, it turned out they were Calanthe's first true guardians, period.

"You know what? I think that's enough for today, guys." Annabel had noticed Calanthe's eyes droop, the weight of the day finally taking its toll.

"Okey-doke." Strobe hopped off the desk he had been sitting on. "Shall we, Tobe?"

Toby held his hand up to say so long to Calanthe. "This is how we say good-bye." Calanthe imitated Toby's good-bye wave. "You were really impressive today, Calanthe. Seriously, I don't know how you managed to soak all that in and actually remember it all."

Calanthe waved again as Toby and Strobe left the room.

"I'll be right back," Annabel said.

As Annabel walked with Toby and Strobe downstairs and outside to the street, arrangements were made for the following day. Where to meet before, during, and after school.

"I really think she's gonna be okay," Strobe said. "I wouldn't have believed that yesterday, but—"

"Yeah, that girl's sharp as a tack," Toby added.

"There's just so much more she needs to learn," Annabel said.

"And she will." Strobe's breath was visible in the cold October night air as he talked. "The good news is she's already got more on the ball than some of the imbeciles I have to sit next to at school."

Annabel smiled, said so long to Toby and Strobe, then returned to her house. She was shivering from the short time she had spent outside without her jacket.

"Want some hot chocolate, Calanthe?" Annabel asked as she came into her bedroom. Calanthe was not sitting on the bed, where she had been when the trio left the room. In the time it had taken Annabel to go outside with the guys, Calanthe had taken her thick comforter from the bed, placed it on the floor, and was sound asleep on top of it. In her clothes. With no pillow for head support.

Annabel shook her head at the sight. Going to the closet, she took a blanket from the top shelf. After placing it over Calanthe, Annabel paused by the door, her hand on the light switch. Calanthe's chest expanded and contracted in an odd cadence. One long breath. Then two short ones. Her breathing was in the same rhythm as her abnormal heartbeat. Abnormal for humans, anyway.

Annabel turned off Calanthe's light and went to her bedroom. After helping prepare Calanthe for her first day of school, it was time for Annabel to do some schoolwork of her own. She had to read a big chunk of *The Turn of the Screw* for her English class. Lying in bed, reading the Henry James classic, Annabel wasn't sure if it was the subtle creepiness of the book or the whole Calanthe situation that was causing her to feel uneasy.

Probably both, Annabel surmised. One reflecting off the other. For in spite of how well Calanthe had responded to her HS boot camp, Annabel still felt nervous about the girl's upcoming first day of school. Actually, it was more than that.

In the same way that Calanthe didn't know much about her new world, there was so much they didn't know about the world Calanthe had come from. What little Calanthe had revealed about her village was enough of a picture to suggest just how weird her upbringing had been. And it was certainly enough to make Annabel uneasy about what else was to come, what other odd and disturbing customs Calanthe would disclose about the dekayi world.

Knowing it was useless to try to concentrate on her book, Annabel placed it on the nightstand and reached for the lamp switch. Her tossing and turning began as soon as the light was out. There was way too much on Annabel's mind for her to fall asleep anytime soon.

Among the many thoughts and images that flitted through Annabel's head was Strobe's question that she had prevented Calanthe from answering.

"What are you, anyway? What makes you different from us humans?"

Or, as Strobe had put it when they were being briefed by Harvey in New York, how did the dekayi go about doing their monsterly deeds?

8

In Calanthe's former village, in a large, mostly empty meeting hall, an important discussion was underway. The Tall Man, who had returned to his village the previous week, was with his three village elders. The group sat on rough canvas-covered cushions, in a circle on the floor. It was the elders who had asked for this meeting, to convey their concern about the Calanthe situation.

"I mean no disrespect, sir, but how can you be certain the rukh survived its fall from the rooftop?" It was the youngest of the elders who had asked the Tall Man the question.

"In all the years I have led this community, have I ever failed any of you?"

"No, you have not."

"Then you must trust me when I say . . . the rukh survived. I can sense it."

The Tall Man had spent several days and nights in

New York City—both to heal from his wound and to wait for the rukh's return—then had made the trek back to his village when the rukh failed to make an appearance. A purplish round scar on the Tall Man's neck was the only lasting sign of his skirmish with Toby, Annabel, and Strobe.

"But don't you think it prudent for *us* to be doing something to bring Calanthe back to us?" It was another of the elders who had posed the question. "I'm concerned that if we wait for the rukh to do the task . . . well, there is very little time left, sir."

"I am quite aware of how little time there is." The Tall Man's reply was delivered with a sharper tone, something that did not escape the attention of the elders.

In a deferential gesture, the youngest elder bowed slightly to the Tall Man before he spoke. "These people in the city, sir. You say they were fighters of some sort. Who's to say Calanthe will not reveal to them where we live?"

"She very well may attempt to do that. But Calanthe does not know the exact location of our village. Up until her escape she had never set one foot outside the boundaries of our village."

"I still do not understand why she felt it necessary to leave us." It was the oldest of the three elders who had spoken, the disappointment obvious in his voice. "What could she possibly want from the Beyond that we could not provide her?"

"There are more than a few mysteries in this world. But on this particular issue, let me reassure you. No matter what it takes, Calanthe will be returned to our village. The Day of Days will not occur without her in attendance."

From the expressions of the three elders, the Day of Days was something very important, very crucial. The senior elder stared gravely at the Tall Man, then indicated to the other two elders that it was time to leave. The Tall Man did not leave with them. After they had gone, he stood and began to walk the length of the large room.

Illuminated by torches attached to a series of wooden pillars, the room appeared to be a meeting hall of some sort. Rows of cushions faced a stage-like proscenium. This is where the Tall Man was headed. As he got closer to the stage, something that had been obscured by shadow from where he had spoken to the elders slowly became visible.

It was a large wooden statue of a serpent. Serpent-*like* would be a better description, in that the creature had two rows of stunted legs—with webbed, clawed feet—running along its sinewy length. The long shape twisted ominously across the back wall of the stage, almost to the top of the high ceiling.

The Tall Man stared at the statue for a moment, then he began to speak. The foreign words he used sounded age-old, as though they had come from the beginning of time. The language, and the way the Tall Man spoke them, matched the thing he was speaking to. Ancient, mysterious. And very sinister.

Suddenly, the Tall Man's words stopped. That's because his head was disappearing into his body! So were his arms and legs. At the same time, his torso was growing and morphing into something that looked very much like the statue he had been speaking to.

When the Tall Man's gruesome transformation was complete, the thing he had become half crawled, half slithered to the statue, moving in and out of the contours of the wooden figure as it went upward.

A very strange kind of ritual seemed to be taking place here. A meeting of the minds, so to speak. Whatever it was the Tall Man was "discussing" with his wooden-idol counterpart, one thing was certain. Annabel's tossing and turning back in Hidden Hills was justified, her concerns warranted. The Tall Man had promised his elders that Calanthe would be returned to the village for the Day of Days, and the intimidating dekayi leader looked like the type of monster who always delivered on his promises.

9

Annabel woke with a start.

"Calanthe! What's wrong?"

Calanthe stood at the bottom of Annabel's bed, still in the clothes she had slept in. "Nothing. I simply awoke before I heard the alarm."

"Oh . . . Okay." Annabel squinted at her bedside clock. "Wow, it's not even five o'clock yet. You must be a little nervous about your first day of school, huh? A bit excited, maybe?"

"No, I am not nervous. I am used to getting up even earlier than this."

"You are?"

"Yes. The children in my age group milk the cows and clean out the stalls every morning."

"Yikes. That's . . ." Annabel put her hand up in front of her mouth to stifle a yawn. "You know what, Calanthe? I wouldn't mind sleeping another hour, if that's okay with you."

"Of course. I will wait for you in my room."

Annabel watched Calanthe as she headed out of her room. "On second thought, maybe we could use the extra time to get ready."

When Calanthe stopped and looked back into the dark room, Annabel thought she detected a brief luminous glow in the girl's dark eyes. Then it was gone.

"I don't wish for you to get up early on my account," Calanthe said.

"No. This is good. Let's see what I've got in my closet for you to wear." Annabel turned on a light and opened her closet.

"I'm not wearing this?"

"No, Calanthe. You've been wearing those clothes long enough. And BTW?"

"Initials for *by the way* . . ."

Annabel smiled and nodded when Calanthe properly identified BTW. "You don't wear the same thing to school every day."

"I don't?"

"No. Unless you go to a private school. Private-school kids have to wear uniforms."

"What is a uniform?"

"For the most part? Pretty ugly."

■ ■ ■

Walking next to Calanthe down the crowded hall, Toby was well aware of what a head turner the girl was. Annabel had picked out a simple but eye-catching outfit for Calanthe to wear on her first day of school. Black turtleneck, black miniskirt, black leggings, tall black boots. A red hairband held Calanthe's hair away from her face, allowing her regal profile optimum visibility. The hairband and two red earrings accented the ensemble with just the right touch of bright color.

Like a wave down the hall, the heads of the kids in the hallway swiveled as Calanthe walked past. The girl was blessed with a powerful double-barreled "it" factor—exotic beauty *and* the new girl.

"Here we are," Toby said, taking Calanthe by the arm and steering her through a swarm of students toward a nearby classroom. "First class of the day. English. Any questions before we go in?"

"No."

"Sure?"

"Yes."

Looking at Calanthe, Toby had a feeling he was more nervous about her first day at school than she was. "I do have one tip before we step through that door. Until you're feeling more comfortable here, at school? Don't feel like you have to say anything in class, raise your hand or anything like that. Some kids get all the way through school without raising their hand once. That's one of my goals, actually."

Calanthe frowned, thought for a moment about what Toby just told her, then turned and walked into the classroom.

■ ■ ■

"Everyone? Your attention, please. I'd like to welcome Calanthe Sanura, our new foreign exchange student. Calanthe is from Port Said, Egypt. She will be with us for the rest of the year."

The students in the classroom turned around to look at Calanthe. She and Toby had been the first to arrive for English and had been given two seats next to each other near the back of the room by the teacher. Calanthe gazed calmly back at the faces of the students staring at her. It appeared to Toby that she was studying her classmates . . . their expressions, what they were wearing, their hairstyles, the girls' jewelry and makeup. The girl was intensely interested in everything around her, that much was clear.

I totally like this girl, Toby thought as he watched Calanthe. *She's just so . . . cool. And calm.*

There was something else about Calanthe, which Toby had tried to capture in his drawing of her eyes: her dark, haunted quality. It was all part of Calanthe's intriguing personality, which continued to unfold as something unique and unpredictable.

■ ■ ■

After three morning classes and a study hall, Toby and Calanthe made their way to the cafeteria for lunch.

"What is that?" Calanthe asked, pointing to one of the lunch selections on the other side of the glass partition.

"We call that mystery meat. Which means you should probably stay away from it."

Calanthe nodded at Toby's assessment of one of the main course offerings, then moved on past it. "What about this?"

"That's pizza. But don't touch it. I can make you a lot better pizza than this stuff." Toby led Calanthe away from the offending cheese pizza slices. "Ah, here we go. Can't go wrong with this." Toby grabbed a piece of baked apple crumble, placed it on Calanthe's tray, then took one for himself. "Hey, there's Annabel."

After the two had finished loading up their trays, they walked across the cafeteria to Annabel's table, where she had saved them a couple of seats.

"How's it going, you two?" Annabel asked. She was smiling when she asked the question, but Toby thought her smile looked forced, a cover-up for her underlying concern about what the answer might be.

"Fantastic," Toby replied.

"Yeah?" Annabel looked genuinely surprised at Toby's response.

"Absolutely. Let me tell you, Calanthe's catching on so fast she'll be helping me with my homework by the end of the week."

"I don't believe that's going to happen," Calanthe said modestly.

"Now that I think about it, I hope it doesn't either. That'd be pretty embarrassing."

Annabel smiled, happy to hear the easygoing banter between Toby and Calanthe. It actually appeared that things were going okay on Calanthe's first day of school.

Toby and Annabel noticed that Calanthe was staring at her miniature milk carton with a concentrated frown, apparently unsure how to open it.

"That's a little different from milking the cows, huh, Calanthe?" Annabel said.

"Here, let me show you," Toby offered.

"No, I want to figure it out myself."

"That's what she's been doing all day, Annabel. Trying to figure everything out for herself."

"That's the best way to learn," Annabel replied.

"And I do want to learn everything," Calanthe said after she had mastered the carton and taken a sip of milk though her straw. Which seemed to delight her, this being the first time Calanthe had ever used a straw. "I want to know everything about how you live here, in your world."

"And you will," Annabel said.

Looking at Annabel, Toby could see in her expression the growing affection that she was feeling for Calanthe. It seemed to Toby that she—more so than he or Strobe— was really beginning to take the "mother hen" moniker to heart.

10

Three hours later Toby and Calanthe were in geometry, the last class of the day.

For Toby, the entire day had turned out to be energizing in a way he could have never foreseen. He and Annabel both thought Calanthe might be intimidated by the intense newness of her environment, with the dangerous possibility of her reaching OVERLOAD before getting on the bus at day's end, thanks to all of the hyperstimulation.

But Calanthe hadn't reached OVERLOAD. Not only that, but her questions had never stopped coming. Everything Toby took for granted during a typical school day had come under Calanthe's microscope.

What does *this* mean? Why are those people doing *that*? What does a *pep rally* mean? Instead of tiring of Calanthe's questions, Toby found himself looking forward to them. Calanthe had forced him to gaze at his world through her eyes, which had turned out to be a pretty fascinating experience. What an interesting creature the human animal was, when you really thought about it.

BRRIIIIIIIIIINNGG!!!

An explosion of energy rocketed through the classroom when the end-of-the-school-day bell rang. Students grabbed their backpacks and jumped for the door. Toby and Calanthe stayed right where they were as the hyper teens jostled and nudged one another and filed out of the room, chattering and laughing all the way. Even after everyone had left the room, including the teacher, Toby and Calanthe stayed seated.

"Well, what do you think, Calanthe?"

Calanthe didn't answer at first. She seemed to be soaking in the silence of the room.

"What do I think?"

"Yeah, your first day of school. What are your impressions?"

"I think . . . the students are very excitable."

Toby laughed. "Yeah, they tend to be, I guess. Especially compared to what you're probably used to."

"It is very subdued where I come from. We are never allowed to act . . . boisterous like this. We would be severely disciplined if we did."

"Well, you don't have to worry about anyone disciplining you here. You did great today, Calanthe. You really did. You totally aced it."

Calanthe's expression asked for an explanation of *aced it*.

"The grading system Annabel talked about yester-day? A, B, C, D? If you get an A in a subject, that means you aced it."

"So that means good. 'Aced it.'"

"More than good."

Toby held his hand up for a high five. Calanthe reached over and hit Toby's hand, the resulting smack echoing off the blackboards.

"Okay, that's still a little too hard."

■ ■ ■

"Where's our girl?"

Using the bleacher seats as steps, Strobe approached Toby and Annabel, who sat in the front row of the bleach-ers overlooking the football field. It was the prearranged spot for them to all meet after school.

"Well, where is she?" Strobe repeated as he sat next to Annabel.

Toby pointed toward the ground. Strobe frowned, looked down, and saw Calanthe lying on the concrete in the dark, shaded area beneath the bleachers.

Strobe laughed. "What's goin' on? What's she doing down there?"

"Sleeping," Annabel said.

"Sleeping . . ."

Annabel nodded.

"Let me get this straight. After attending her first day at Triple H, Calanthe decided to take a nap on the hard concrete beneath the bleachers."

"The day finally caught up to her," Toby said. "She's totally exhausted, man."

"Have either of you checked her pulse lately?"

"Poor girl," Annabel said as she looked down at the sleeping Calanthe.

"How'd she do today?" Strobe asked.

"Great," Toby said. "Like I told her at the end of the day, she totally aced it."

"Excellent. How long we gonna let her stay down there? We're gonna miss our buses."

"I'm going to call my mom in a little to bring us home," Annabel said. "You can go now if you want, Strobe."

"I think I will. We gettin' together tonight?"

"I say we give Calanthe the night off. We'll do our next boot-camp session tomorrow."

"She looks like a little girl down there," Strobe observed. "A clueless little girl. Like there's nothing wrong in her world."

"Right now, there isn't," Annabel said. "She's here, with us. Safe and sound."

The trio stared at Calanthe for a moment, then Strobe nodded. "Okay, then. See you all tomorrow."

Strobe waved as he went up the bleachers. Toby and Annabel stayed where they were, sitting protectively on the bleachers above Calanthe. It wasn't long after Strobe had left when Toby noticed something.

"Annabel, check it out." Toby was staring down at Calanthe. After Annabel's eyes had adjusted to the darkness below the bleachers, she was alarmed to see that Calanthe's body had begun to jerk sporadically. It appeared the girl was in the grip of a nightmare. Toby had already grabbed his backpack and was heading down the steps to the track that ran around the football field. Annabel quickly followed him.

The two had to duck their heads to get under the first couple of rows of bleachers, but were able to straighten up as they approached Calanthe. She was still under the spell of her nightmare; her sudden movements accompanied by an occasional burst of indecipherable language. Annabel and Toby knelt down on either side of Calanthe.

"Should we wake her up?" Toby asked.

Annabel didn't answer. She was staring in alarm at Calanthe's face, neck, hands.

Toby was speechless when he saw what Annabel was looking at. Calanthe's skin was slowly becoming translucent and revealing her underlying muscles, veins, and arteries!

Fumbling to get his cell out of his coat pocket, Toby quickly took several pictures of Calanthe's face and hands. Just in time, too. As suddenly as it had begun, Calanthe's attack, or whatever it was, was over. Her skin was back to normal. But Calanthe was still in the midst of her nightmare. When she started to talk in her sleep, Annabel leaned down close to her lips.

"What's she saying?" Toby asked.

Annabel shook her head. She wasn't sure. But then she looked up at Toby.

"What? What is it?"

"I think she said . . ." Annabel listened again. "Slice."

"What?"

"That's what it sounded like. *Slice*."

"Slice. Anything else?"

"That's all I could make out." Annabel looked at Calanthe with concern. "Probably just talking nonsense. She's dreaming, after all."

After a few more disturbing verbal outbreaks, Calanthe's nightmare appeared to be over. She had returned to her child-like, peaceful sleeping state.

"Whew!" Toby sat back on his haunches with a relieved sigh.

"Yeah, this is a bit exhausting, isn't it?"

"Kind of makes you wonder what's next, doesn't it?"

"Yes, it does."

Toby and Annabel fell silent as they kept a wary watch on Calanthe.

"Sometimes?" Annabel said. "When I look at Calanthe? Like right now?"

"Yeah?"

"Well, this might sound weird, but sometimes Calanthe reminds me of some of the characters in the books I've been reading for English."

"What books have you been reading?"

"*Wuthering Heights. The House of Mirth.* I just started *Turn of the Screw.*"

"Never read them."

"The main characters are these . . . well, they're doomed heroines, really. You can just sense that things aren't going to turn out well for them." Annabel's eyes suddenly widened in dismay. "I can't believe I just said that. Forget I even mentioned it, okay, Toby?"

"No, it's okay, Annabel. I think I know what you mean." As soon as Annabel had compared Calanthe to the heroines in her book assignments, Toby knew she had hit on the thing he had tried to capture in his notebook drawing. There was that certain something in Calanthe's eyes—it had haunted Toby from the moment he met her—that gave Calanthe the aura of a tragic heroine.

"You'll never tell her I said that."

"Of course not."

"And I didn't really mean it, you know? Because the thing is, a tragic heroine always has a character flaw that causes her downfall, right? And Calanthe doesn't have a flaw like that, she really doesn't, and—"

"Annabel . . . Annabel. Everything's gonna be okay."

Suddenly, Calanthe stirred. When she opened her eyes, she didn't seem to know where she was. Instantly panicking, she jumped to her feet and backed away from Annabel and Toby.

"Calanthe . . . it's us." Annabel held out her hands toward Calanthe in a "calm down" gesture.

Calanthe looked wildly back and forth at Annabel and Toby.

"You just had a little nightmare," Toby said. "Everything's fine now."

Calanthe continued to back away from Toby and Annabel. After her bruising nightmare, she clearly needed a moment to reorient herself to her new world. Her new life. A couple of deep breaths later, the breaths matching her odd heartbeat cadence, and Calanthe appeared to be back to normal.

"Okay?" Annabel asked.

Calanthe thought for a moment about Annabel's question. Then she said, "Yes. I am here, with you. I am okay."

What a relief, Toby thought. *'Cause just a minute ago you looked like a live version of one of those see-through bodies I saw on my museum field trip last year!*

11

It was the dead of night.

Compared to the buzz of activity during the daylight and evening hours, New York's Central Park Zoo was oddly dream-like at three A.M. in the morning. The majority of the animals in the zoo kept daylight hours and slept during the night, just like the humans who took care of them. Some, however, such as the two-toed sloth, came alive in the dark. It was their time to cut loose, so to speak.

But on this night, all of the animals seemed to be up and about.

"What's *wrong* with these guys?" the night guard grumbled to himself as he walked into the Central Garden area of the zoo. The animals were clearly agitated. The snow monkeys' screeches echoed from the Temperate Territory. The parrots were going nuts inside the Tropic Building. Even the polar bears were getting into the act. The guard had never heard the roars coming from the direction of the Polar Circle in all the time he'd worked at the zoo.

"It's not even a full moon." The three or four days before, during, and after a full moon definitely had an effect on the animals. But nothing like this. Nowhere near like this.

The guard snapped on his flashlight as he approached the large outdoor tank that housed the three California sea lions. The sides of the tank were constructed of glass to enable visitors to watch the sea lions as they frolicked underwater. The underwater lights having been turned off hours before, the tank was now a dark, hulking silhouette in the night. The guard swept his flashlight across the rocky island in the middle of the water. No sign of the sea lions.

"All right, all right already!" the guard yelled in irritation. "Calm down, will ya!" All of the screeching and yipping was getting to him. If anything, it had increased in volume. The guard explored the nooks and crannies of the rocky island that served as the sea lions' home with his flashlight. Nothing.

That was just so strange. Where could the sea lions have gone? The guard hadn't heard anything about them being taken. . . .

"*What's that?*" the guard cried out, whirling in the direction of the strange sound he had just heard over his shoulder. His flashlight beam stabbed at the dark, illuminating nothing but the empty path that led back in the direction he had just come. The bushes on either side of the path started snapping back and forth as a sudden night wind kicked in.

The guard was starting to get pretty spooked. He had the unnerving feeling that the entire park was coming alive around him. The animals' frenzied cries. The dancing shadows from the windblown bushes. The sense that *something was nearby*. He could feel that something. But what? What was it? He couldn't see anything!

Then . . .

With another startled cry of surprise, the guard yanked the gun from his holster and held it next to the flashlight as he focused on a spot to his left where he had seen a sudden movement. His eyes widened in fear and he backed off when he saw a ghost-like form materialize from the darkness and start toward him.

What on earth is that? the guard wondered, alarm and panic threatening to short-circuit his already shaky nervous system.

But wait . . . *where* was it? Like a magic trick, the shadowy form seemed to have suddenly disappeared.

"AAAAHHHHGHHH!!!"

The guard's scream, an eruption from the pit of his stomach, burst out of him when an invisible force slapped him clear off his feet. The gun flew from the guard's hand and skittered across the concrete path when he hit the ground. Desperately crawling after the gun, the guard looked around wildly for whatever it was that had just attacked him.

Then something hit the lagoon with a loud splash. The guard looked over his shoulder to see . . . well, he wasn't sure *what* he was seeing. Something was churning across the water, but the concussive splashing was the only thing visible to the guard.

This isn't happening, the guard thought feverishly. But it was. Whatever the thing was in the lagoon, it was invisible!

As the animals continued to screech and bellow and warn one another about the horrible thing that was among them, the guard—still on his hands and knees on the ground—felt like his brain wasn't working properly. His thoughts were jumbled, jagged, as though his synapses were trying to connect but simply couldn't. The guard was able to perceive that something extraordinary was happening, something that would be very difficult to explain when he made the call to his superior back at his office.

But as he got to his feet to head in that direction, the guard felt himself convulse, a delayed reaction to the mysterious attack he'd just experienced. He threw up violently, his coughing, rasping gags joining right in with the animals' cries and screeches.

Meanwhile, the rukh had already exited the zoo. Having finally awoken from its healing sleep, the zoo had been the creature's first pit stop, a little nourishment for the journey ahead. Now there was one thing on the rukh's mind, and one thing only.

The girl's scent.

Pointing the way to Hidden Hills.

12

"You just drag this mouse...and click. See?"

Calanthe stared in fascination as she watched the result of Toby's click on the mouse, which was the YouTube Web site popping into view on the computer screen. To say Calanthe was speechless would be an understatement. The Internet neophyte had not said a single word since her very first computer session had begun a half hour before.

"You know what, guys?" Annabel said, looking with concern at Calanthe. "I think we should have held off on the computer part of today's boot camp. Calanthe's looking a bit spacey to me." Calanthe didn't appear to have heard a single word Annabel said, confirming Annabel's assessment that she had hit her limit.

Two days had passed since Calanthe's momentous first day at Triple H, the climax of which had been her strange transformation under the school bleachers.

Calanthe had gone right to bed after dinner those first two nights and slept for twelve straight hours, just as she had on her first night in Hidden Hills. Toby and Annabel had decided not to discuss Calanthe's nightmare with her or show her the pictures of her strangely translucent skin. All that could wait for another time.

On Calanthe's third day at HHH, however, she appeared to be getting stronger and more capable of handling the amped-up stimulation high school life was throwing at her. So the trio had held a second boot-camp session for Calanthe after school, covering yet more slang and other important aspects of high school life. Calanthe had blown right through her session, no problem, so the group had decided to throw in a quick computer lesson to wrap things up for the evening.

"Maybe you're right, Annabel," Strobe said, smiling at Calanthe's blank, spaced-out expression. "A couple of YouTube music videos might put her over the edge. But I do want to show Calanthe something before we sign off."

Strobe nudged Toby off his seat and took control of the computer. Calanthe focused on Strobe's fingers as they flew across the keyboard. When he hit RETURN, a Web site called Earth Maps appeared on the screen.

"You have maps where you come from, right?" Strobe

asked Calanthe. Staring at the computer screen, Calanthe didn't respond to Strobe's question.

"See what I mean?" Annabel said. "She's totally out of it."

"Okay, okay. But trust me, this'll be a good way to end the day. A geography lesson. It's *educational*." Strobe moved so that he was between Calanthe and the computer screen. "Earth to Calanthe . . ."

Calanthe shifted so that she could see the computer, but then focused on Strobe when he once again interrupted her field of vision. "You have maps where you come from, right?" Strobe asked.

Calanthe thought for a moment, then shook her head.

"Get out. You've never seen a map?"

"Yes, I have seen a map," Calanthe replied slowly, as though it took some effort to recall the image. "The person I met in Canada gave one to me."

"Okay, well, what you're about to see is nothing like the map that person gave you."

Calanthe watched Strobe type a few words on the keyboard. When he hit RETURN, the screen morphed into a picture of the earth, a beautiful blue-and-white orb hanging in black space. "This is where we live, right? It's called earth. Now, get ready for a really cool ride."

With Strobe at the controls, the all-seeing camera in

the sky suddenly dove toward the earth. Within seconds the United States filled the screen. "This is the United States . . ."

Strobe took the camera across the U.S. toward the states of Pennsylvania, New Jersey, and New York. "This is the northeastern United States . . ."

The camera singled out the state of New York. "And this is where we met, in Central Park in New York City." With an exciting visual flourish, the camera plunged into New York City and . . . presto!

Close-up of the lake in Central Park.

Totally enthralled by Strobe's dramatic global tour, Calanthe smiled. "How did you? . . ."

"Okay, now check this out—" Strobe interrupted. Calanthe studied what Strobe was doing with his fingers as he led the camera up and away from New York, across Pennsylvania and . . .

Whooosh!

Close-up of Hidden Hills, Ohio.

"This is where we are now. This is our hometown of Hidden Hills."

Calanthe shook her head in amazement. She couldn't believe what she had just seen!

"Okay, now a little background on your new friends."

Calanthe's eyes darted from Strobe's fingers to the

computer screen as the camera flew across the United States. "This is the Pacific Ocean," Strobe said as the camera left land behind and blasted across the water. "And this . . . is where Annabel's ancestors come from." Strobe froze the image high over the country of Japan. "It's called Japan."

Calanthe stared at the screen, then looked at Annabel. Annabel nodded. "My father was born there. He moved to the United States when he was around our age, actually. He met my mother here, in the U.S."

"See, isn't this fun?" Strobe said. "Tobe? Would you like to show Calanthe where your people are from?"

"Sure."

Strobe made way for Toby to sit at the computer. Within seconds, the camera was flying around the world and zeroing in on the British Isles. Its final destination . . .

Scotland.

"My dad's dad was born in Newcomnick, Scotland," Toby announced, freezing the camera on a close-up of a small Scottish village.

"I thought you might have some Scot in you," Annabel said.

"That wouldn't be because I flush red as a beet every time I'm nervous or embarrassed, would it? I'm not sure where my mom's from. But my dad . . . yeah, he wears the kilt from time to time."

"A kilt?" Calanthe asked as she reached over for the mouse that Toby had abandoned when he swiveled around to talk to Annabel.

"That's a dress," Strobe said.

"It's not a dress, you imbecile," Toby said derisively.

"A skirt, then."

"It is not a skirt."

"Of course it is."

"Scottish men do not wear skirts. They wear *kilts*."

"They look like skirts to me. They're open at the bottom. They ain't pants, that's for sure."

"Boys . . ." Annabel interrupted.

"Yeah, well, my ancestors could whip your ancestors, whatever they are, skirts and all."

"How lame a comeback was that? Seriously. Please show me you can do better than that, Tobe."

"Oh, boys . . ."

"While I'm searchin' for something, chew on this. At least I don't think a kilt is a skirt!"

Strobe had seen a dictionary on a nearby bookshelf and was quickly paging through it. He smiled when he found what he was looking for. "Kilt . . ." Strobe read gleefully. "A pleated *skirt* reaching to the knees, especially the tartan skirt worn sometimes by men of the Scottish Highlands!"

Strobe raised his arms in triumph.

"*Guys!* You need to check this out."

Strobe grinned at Toby, Toby glared defiantly back at Strobe—trying to preserve some shred of dignity from his humiliating defeat—then they both looked at Annabel, who nodded toward Calanthe. The image on the screen was no longer of the Scottish town of Newcomnick. The camera had returned to the northern part of the United States.

"Calanthe didn't do that, did she?" Strobe asked.

Annabel nodded.

"Wow," Toby said. "That's really impressive, Calanthe."

Calanthe didn't seem to be listening to Toby. Instead, she was concentrating on moving and clicking the mouse.

"I knew this girl was sharp, but this is beyond beyond," Strobe observed as he and Annabel and Toby watched Calanthe move the focus of the image on the screen from the northwest U.S. to the Canadian province of Quebec. The POV of the camera took a sudden nosedive toward a large expanse of forest.

A large lake became visible as the camera moved closer and closer to the earth, finally freezing on a close-up shot of the fall-colored trees, brilliant in their red and orange and yellow hues.

The trio was silent as they stared at the computer. Calanthe stayed rooted where she was, then she slowly spun around in her chair. Looking at Annabel, Toby and Strobe, in turn, she said . . .

"Home."

13

"You had it all planned out, didn't you? That's why you did the Earth Map thing. To get Calanthe to show us where her village was."

Walking with Strobe down the crowded school hallway, Annabel waited for Strobe's response. Strobe took a sudden right across the hall and stopped at a locker.

"I don't know what the big deal is," Strobe said as he exchanged his morning books for his afternoon ones. "It's important to know where Calanthe's from, right?"

"So you admit it. You didn't do Earth Maps for educational reasons. You wanted to trick Calanthe into showing us where she used to live."

"Listen, Annabel, there's something you should know about. I was talking to Harvey yesterday. Before our bootcamp session with Calanthe?"

"Why were you talking to Harvey? Why weren't we all on the line with him?"

"Harvey thinks you're too protective of Calanthe. I

agree with him. This nightmare Calanthe had the other day? The skin episode? You never said a word about that to her, did you?"

"If you had been there, you might have second thoughts about saying anything—"

"No, I wouldn't. This is exactly what I'm talking about. I would have shown her those pictures Toby took and asked her what it was all about. That girl is stronger than you think she is."

"Is she? How can you know that, for sure? I'm with Calanthe practically around the clock, remember. And I can tell you, sometimes when I look at her, she seems so vulnerable to me."

Strobe closed his locker door and started off down the hall. Following him, Annabel had to use two steps to every one of Strobe's to keep up with his long, lanky gait.

"So what did Harvey want to talk to you about?"

"He got word about an incident at the Central Park Zoo a couple nights ago. The news media will never get hold of this one. It's totally hush-hush."

"What happened?"

"From the intel Harvey got, he thinks the rukh made an after-midnight visit to the zoo. He didn't tell his source that, but that's what he thinks went down."

"Why the rukh?"

Strobe explained what the guard at the zoo had reported about his terrifying nighttime smackdown. "Remember when we first met Calanthe? In Central Park? She said that she thought the rukh had rediscovered her scent. Her *scent*, Annabel."

The two had arrived at the top of a stairway. Strobe was going one way, Annabel another. "It's like that thing is some kind of supernatural bloodhound. It managed to track Calanthe from the wilds of Canada to New York City. Why not from New York City to here?"

Annabel frowned at this news. "Is Harvey sure the rukh survived? That it's alive?"

"He can't be positive, but he thinks it's a good bet that's what hopped over the fence at the zoo. We've seen the range that thing has when it comes to the big jump."

"So what can we do about all this?"

"The best defense is always a good offense. I'm flying to Montreal tomorrow morning, meeting up with a group of MCOs, and heading off to find Calanthe's village."

Annabel was so surprised at Strobe's revelation that she wasn't sure how to respond.

"It's a fact-finding mission. Harvey doesn't like being so ignorant about a monster species, especially one so close to home. It's possible the rukh has gone back to its village. If so, we'll deal with it."

"But what if the rukh *is* alive? What if it's heading right here and—"

"Plan B is we grab a dekayi or two up there," Strobe revealed. "It might be helpful to have a couple of these dudes. Get some info out of them. Use 'em as hostages, maybe, a bargaining chip to wrangle Calanthe's freedom, if it comes to that."

"I can't believe this. . . ."

"Don't freak, okay, Annabel? We're gonna deal with this. But first things first. I need to talk to Calanthe before I leave tomorrow. We can't just babysit her anymore. It's time to get down to it. The more I know about what to expect up there, the better."

Annabel gave Strobe a reluctant nod. "Why don't you come over after dinner tonight."

"Okay. I'll be there around sevenish?"

Annabel nodded. "Are you sure *you* have to go up there?"

"C'mon, Annabel. You know I wouldn't miss this for the world. Besides, I know more about the dekayi than the dudes I'm going up there with. That kind of puts me in charge of the operation, is the way I look at it."

"How are you pulling this off, anyway? What did you tell your mom?"

"She thinks I'm going to New York. Harvey gave her

161

a call, said I made such an impression on Killer Pizza executives during my weekend training session that they want me back for an extended weeklong immersion class for future Killer Pizza managers."

"And she bought that?"

"You gotta understand, my mom's been through a lot with me. She's thrilled I'm apparently doing well in a business that's, shall we say . . . legal. So she's more than happy to have me miss a week of school for this."

"Just be careful, huh?"

"Always."

■ ■ ■

As Strobe's airplane approached the Montréal–Pierre Elliott Trudeau International Airport at 8:36 the following morning, he found himself once again thinking about the scene at Annabel's house the night before. Calanthe had given Strobe, Toby, and Annabel detail after detail about the dekayi species.

The revelation that the dekayi were descended from an ancient race of serpent people hadn't come as much of a surprise, nor the fact that their serpent alter ego's bite was extremely poisonous. But when Calanthe had told the trio about how a dekayi serpent could swallow a person whole . . . well, that caught Strobe's attention. He'd have to be on the lookout for that neat little trick.

Calanthe had relayed other details about the dekayi,

one of the most interesting being the physical change they called the Altering. This was the momentous event that delivered a teenage dekayi to adulthood, after which they possessed the ability to transform into their serpent alter ego. The Altering had not yet come to Calanthe, but she expected it to very soon.

As Strobe's plane touched down and taxied to the terminal, he pushed aside all thougts about Calanthe and looked out the window. He was confident that he had done all he could to prepare for this mission. He was ready to go.

After being subjected to a customs search, Strobe was met by three Killer Pizza MCOs. Thanks to Harvey's contacts, the MCOs had been able to bypass their customs search, which is why they had been able to bring along a KP backpack for Strobe, stocked with all the necessary items for battle that Strobe hadn't been able to pack.

The MCOs led Strobe to another, smaller terminal. They had flown from New York in a private KP plane, which would also be taking the quartet to a landing strip in the forest area that Calanthe had pointed out to Strobe, Annabel, and Toby. From there, a helicopter would take them on a tour of the area. And hopefully to the village where Calanthe once lived.

Strobe was pleasantly nervous as he followed the

MCOs out onto the tarmac, where the Cessna 206H six-seater was idling and waiting for them to board. This is what really thrilled Strobe. The hunt, the promise of battle. This is what he had signed up for when he had agreed to enter the KP Academy training program.

Yep, this is more like it, Strobe thought as he walked up the steps of the airplane behind the other MCOs. As far as he was concerned, he was one of them now. He was their equal. And he was ready for whatever they would find out there in the woods.

■ ■ ■

The forest was an unbroken swath of maple and oak trees, brilliantly red, orange, and yellow in their fall colors. Leaning out of the helicopter, Strobe studied the area below through a set of high-powered binoculars.

"Couldn't your little snake-girl be more precise about where to find her village? I mean, what'd she say again? It's somewhere in this area, like, sort of?"

Not for the first time, Strobe felt like giving Holt, the sarcastic MCO, a hard jab to the ribs. Obviously unhappy that Strobe had been invited on this trip, the guy had been riding him ever since they left Montreal a few hours earlier.

"I guess you weren't paying attention when I explained the first time," Strobe yelled edgily over his shoulder at Holt. "The girl left her village in the dead of night. It was the first time she'd ever been outside of the place."

"Yeah . . . so?"

"So sue her for not being able to remember the name of the first town she passed through. She gave me an excellent idea of where to look for her village. It's down there somewhere, and we're gonna find it."

"Yeah, if the storm doesn't hit first. We only have till tomorrow to track this place down, you know. That's direct from Harvey. He needs us back in the Apple by tomorrow night."

Eyeing the line of dark clouds that had appeared on the eastern horizon, Strobe was definitely worried about the approaching storm. The forecast was for snow. If the cold front hit before they had zeroed in on Calanthe's village, that could very well shut down the aerial proceedings until the following morning.

So the time was now, or return at daybreak for a second and final search. Definitely a "now" kind of guy, Strobe scoured the forest below through his binoculars, determined to find his needle in the haystack.

14

As Strobe was airborne up in the Canadian wilds, Calanthe was at school, at her locker, taking out a couple of books and putting them into her backpack. Toby had hit the restroom before the two headed off to history class.

"Hey, there."

The greeting had come from behind Calanthe. Looking over her shoulder, she saw a tall, preppy teen approach her, a huge smile on his face. Calanthe wasn't sure if his words had been directed to her or not, so she looked around to see if there was someone else nearby.

"No, I'm talking to you," the guy said with an amused laugh. Amping up his dazzling smile even higher, he added, "My name's Adam."

Adam held out his hand. Calanthe looked at the hand for a moment, then reached out and shook it.

"And your name is?"

"Calanthe."

"That's a beautiful name. Where are you from, Calanthe?"

"Egypt."

"*Egypt*. That's way cool."

Calanthe studied Adam curiously. This was the first time anyone had come up to her and introduced himself.

"So you're a foreign exchange student, huh?"

Calanthe nodded. Her eyes shifted from Adam, down the hall, and back again. She was wondering where Toby was.

"You know what, Calanthe? I'm really glad we met. Actually, I've been meaning to introduce myself since the first day I saw you."

Adam was obviously expecting a response from Calanthe. When he didn't get one, he said, "Right, well . . . the *reason* I've been meaning to introduce myself is 'cause I was wondering if you would like to go to the dance next Friday with me."

"No."

Calanthe had just seen, not Toby, but Annabel appear in the crowd of students, walking in her direction. Without another word to Adam, she walked off down the hall to meet Annabel.

Adam looked completely shocked and a bit puzzled

by Calanthe's one-word dismissal of his invitation to go to the dance. Shaking his head in wonder at Calanthe's odd behavior, he followed her confidently down the hall.

"Hi, Calanthe," Annabel said as Calanthe walked up to her. "Where's Toby?"

"He said he had to go to the bathroom."

"Well, let's go find him."

"Hold up a sec," Adam said, big smile back in place as he planted himself in front of Annabel and Calanthe. "So . . . what was that, Calanthe, a playing-hard-to-get kinda thing?"

Annabel looked at Calanthe with a frown.

"No," Calanthe replied, returning Adam's somewhat-threatening smile with a cool, calm look.

It wasn't hard for Annabel to guess what was going on. Her immediate instinct was to get Calanthe away from Adam, quickly, so she returned Adam's smile and said, "If you'll excuse us, we need to get to fifth period."

"And you are?" Adam asked.

"Annabel Oshiro."

"No, I mean, *what* are you?"

Annabel wasn't sure what Adam meant.

"Let me answer the question for you. You're a freshman, right?"

Okay, this guy's an idiot, Annabel thought. "I am a

freshman, yes." Annabel tried to hit just the right tone of humility. She had not yet experienced any bullying from upperclassmen since starting at Triple H, but knew that Toby had.

"So let me ask you something. What makes you think you can talk to a senior like that?"

Annabel frowned. "I wasn't aware that I was talking to you with any kind of—"

"I just need to have a little discussion with your friend here, Calanthe," Adam said, cutting off Annabel. "Then you and I can deal with the more important stuff." Calanthe stared curiously at Adam as he turned his attention back to Annabel. It was hard to read in her expression just how she felt about the unpleasant little scene that was developing in the middle of the hallway.

"This is what I suggest," Adam said in a threatening tone as he stepped closer to Annabel. "Since you seem to be so concerned about getting to your fifth-period class, why don't you go on ahead, and I'll walk Calanthe to her class. That way she and I can finish what we started before you came along and so rudely interrupted . . . *OOOOOWWWWW!!!*"

Annabel wasn't sure at first why Adam was suddenly grimacing in pain, but then she saw Calanthe's hand on his bicep. The pressure Calanthe was able to apply with just one hand had caused Adam to literally sink to his knees.

"Calanthe, that's enough!" When Calanthe didn't respond to Annabel's command, Annabel grabbed her hand and pried it away from Adam's arm. Still on his knees, Adam stared in disbelief at the foreign exchange student from Egypt.

"What was *that* all about?! Look at my arm, man!"

Adam had rolled up his shirt sleeve. Indeed, his arm had already started to swell and turn black and blue.

"I'm totally reportin' you to the principal, girl. You'll be on the next plane to Egypt so fast you won't know what hit you."

"Go to the nurse, get a little ice on that, you'll be fine," Annabel said dismissively. "As for the principal, I'd rethink that if I were you. Do you really want more people to know that a girl half your size brought you to your knees by just grabbing your arm?"

Adam looked around at the crowd that had instantly gathered to watch the odd spectacle of one of Triple H's main studs in obvious agony as he knelt on the linoleum hall, clutching his injured arm. Wanting to get Calanthe away from the unintended spotlight that had been suddenly beamed on their little scene, Annabel led her off down the hall.

"Well, Calanthe," Annabel said when they were out of earshot from the growing crowd behind them. "That was very interesting."

"I did not like the way he was talking to you."

"And I appreciate that you came to my defense, but we need to talk about how we're going to deal with this kind of situation if it comes up again in the future. Okay?"

"You are protecting me from harm from my people, yes? Strobe is in Canada at this very moment, doing just that. I wish to do the same for you."

"The point here is that you can't be attacking boys at school like that. There are rules against that sort of thing. I mean, surely you have similar rules at your village."

"It depends. Sometimes altercations between our people result in a fight to the death."

"Wait. What did you just say?"

Annabel couldn't believe what Calanthe had just told her. Before she was able to ask any more questions about this alarmingly brutal dekayi custom, Toby appeared from a nearby bathroom and walked over to them.

"Hey, you two. What are you doing in our neck of the woods, Annabel?" Toby frowned when he noticed the gathering down the hall. Adam had just emerged from the crowd, still clutching his injured arm, still looking dazed and confused about what had just happened. "What's goin' on down there?"

"I'll explain later," Annabel said as the warning bell clanged loudly, signaling a few minutes until the start of fifth period. Toby watched Adam and the dispersing crowd a couple of classrooms away for a moment, shrugged, then turned and followed his two girls.

15

The snow was thick and heavy and had instantly turned day to twilight. As soon as it had started, the helicopter had banked away from the expanse of forest and returned to the airport. The search for the dekayi village was suspended until the following morning.

Strobe sat brooding in his motel room. Holt and the other two MCOs had headed out for a night on the town—what little town there was—leaving "the minor" behind. As much as Strobe wanted to be one of the gang, he knew he wasn't. He wasn't the MCOs equal. His life experiences might have caused him to grow up faster than his contemporaries, his height might have put him eye to eye with guys twice his age, but Strobe was still only fifteen years old. Which made him someone who was caught between two worlds. A kid/grown-up.

Strobe clicked off the television, put on his jacket, and went outside. The snow was still falling, blanketing everything in a heavy white cover and muffling the sounds of the chains on the cars driving past and the jukebox thumping out an unrecognizable country song in the motel diner.

Strobe didn't know where he was going. He just needed to walk. Somewhere. Anywhere. Actually, Strobe had done quite a bit of this type of not-really-going-anywhere kind of walking in the various towns and cities he and his mom had lived in over the past few years. The walks helped calm him down when he was in one of his moods.

Since coming to Hidden Hills, however, Strobe hadn't taken as many of these aimless walks. That was because of Annabel and Toby, more than anything. Strobe's two MCO partners/kitchen mates had managed the difficult feat of smoothing him out a bit. Making him feel a little less transient and more . . . connected to something.

Thinking of Toby and Annabel as he trudged through the snow, and particularly the recent high school boot camp with Calanthe, Strobe smiled. His crew back in Hidden Hills was a heck of a lot more fun to be with than the MCOs he was stuck with on this mission, that was for sure.

A big rig suddenly blasted past Strobe, spraying him with sludge and causing him to step away from the side of the road. Standing in the deep snow, Strobe looked at the hazy lights of the empty main street of town, the direction he had been heading. Instead of continuing on to town, Strobe turned around and started following his footprints back to the motel.

It was probably a good idea to go through his field backpack one more time, Strobe thought, make sure everything was in its proper place, all weapons were working flawlessly. He needed to be totally prepared for whatever he might discover in the woods bright and early the following morning.

Besides, Strobe didn't feel like walking just to walk anymore. That feeling had suddenly passed. Maybe it was because Strobe knew he had a place to go back to after this mission in the Canadian wilds was over.

16

Toby woke in an instant.

He lay perfectly still, listening for the sound that had jolted him awake. All was silent, then . . .

Yes, there it was again. Something had hit his window. Definitely. Toby slid out of bed and cautiously approached the window. When he pulled down the bottom slate of the shutter and peeked outside, he couldn't believe what he saw in the middle of his backyard.

Calanthe.

Seeing Toby at the window, she held up her hand in a hello gesture. Toby responded by holding up his index finger, then wondered if Calanthe knew that meant he'd be outside in a minute or so. Probably not.

So Toby quickly dressed and headed downstairs. Since becoming an MCO he had developed superior sneaking-out-in-the-middle-of-the-night abilities, so he wasn't concerned that he might get caught. But what about Calanthe? How had she managed to slink out of the Oshiro household at two o'clock in the morning without anyone noticing? Stepping onto his back porch, Toby spotted Calanthe's silhouette at the edge of the neighbor's yard. As he approached her, she turned and disappeared into the woods. Following Calanthe, Toby felt a strange kind of thrill. He'd been woken up by a wildly unpredictable girl in the middle of the night who was leading him . . . where? What did Calanthe want to see him about?

Toby had no idea, and he didn't really care. At some point he would discover what this after-midnight excursion was all about. In the meantime, he was kind of loving the surprise of Calanthe's nighttime visit, the suspense of it.

It took about a ten-minute jog through the woods before Calanthe revealed their destination, a railroad bridge that passed over the stream Toby and Calanthe had been following. Calanthe led Toby under the bridge, stopped directly beneath the trestle, and leaned up against the rock wall.

When Toby joined her, the two stood side by side, staring silently into the darkness. Toby thought maybe Calanthe was allowing him to catch his breath before revealing what she wanted to see him about. He didn't want to break the moment by asking any questions. He was perfectly okay just standing next to Calanthe under the bridge, surrounded by the still and silent woods.

Some time passed before Calanthe finally spoke. When she did, her opening line was a good one. "I'd like to tell you a story . . ."

■ ■ ■

A spellbinding story it was.

It was about a secret cave near Calanthe's village that she would sneak out to visit in the middle of the night. It was a place only a few villagers knew about. Anyone who dared go there was well aware that if it was ever discovered that they had left their beds after curfew, they would be dealt with very severely.

To Calanthe, the risk had always been worth it. The cave was a magical place, after all, with illustrations painted on the walls by villagers of generations past, who had dared to even contemplate what was referred to in the village as the Beyond. The primitive paintings were of automobiles and airplanes and tall buildings. Of people dressed in bright, exciting clothes. Of televisions and exotic musical instruments such as drum sets and electric guitars.

The illustrations had been inspired by rumors of

such things, passed down by a few rebel villagers who had reportedly discovered magazines left behind in the woods by the rare Outsider who had hiked and camped within walking range of the village. Whenever Calanthe felt herself slipping into the mind-set imposed on her by the village elders, she would take the risk, sneak out in the middle of the night—always when the moon was hidden in the nighttime sky—and make her way to the cave.

There she was able to remind herself that there actually *was* a different world beyond her borders. It was a place she knew she would run away to some day. When the time was right. When she was ready. Calanthe had finally been ready just the previous month. And now here she was . . . in the world she had only been able to dream about for as long as she could remember.

"What was it that made you realize that you were ready?" Toby asked, taking advantage of a pause in Calanthe's story to ask the question.

"Do you know why I brought you here?"

Toby shook his head, unconcerned that Calanthe had ignored his question.

"This place reminds me a little of the cave where I would go, with all the drawings and markings."

Calanthe stood back to look at the graffiti that covered

the walls under the bridge. "I don't know what these markings mean, exactly, which makes them mysterious in a way that the drawings in my cave were mysterious."

"When did you discover this bridge, Calanthe?"

"The second night after I arrived in Hidden Hills."

"You haven't been sneaking out every night, have you?"

Calanthe nodded.

"And here Annabel thought you were sleeping for twelve hours straight."

Calanthe smiled. "I did the first night. I didn't think Annabel would like me to be doing this, which is why I haven't told her. I do feel the need to be out here, however. I like it."

"I guess when you've lived your whole life in the woods . . . it must get into your blood, huh?"

Calanthe's expression showed she didn't get the expression "into your blood."

"It's like . . . the woods, nature . . . it's inside you now. It's become a part of you."

Calanthe thought about that, then nodded.

"Is there anything else about your village you miss? I mean, it sounds like a pretty intense place, overall."

"There were some good things. Your world seems very frantic by comparison. I'm not sure if I like that part of it. But mainly you could say growing up in my village was similar to what the rukh does to its victims."

Toby was surprised at Calanthe's statement. "What does the rukh do to its victims?"

"I have only heard of this, never seen it. But I have heard that the rukh sucks the insides out of the thing that it is attacking, leaving behind just the skin and bones."

"That's quite a trick."

"In my village it is forbidden to have any thoughts that are unusual or original or different from what we are taught to think. It is as though the outlawed thoughts are sucked right out of us by the elder villagers, until that kind of thinking, those kinds of taboo thoughts, don't even occur anymore."

Calanthe fell silent. Toby had the feeling she had said what she brought him to the bridge to say, so he let the silence continue. Besides, he wanted to ponder what Calanthe had just told him. It was pretty scary, the notion of an adult population controlling their children's thoughts and actions, in any way possible. It wasn't only in Calanthe's village that this kind of thing occurred, Toby knew. But Calanthe's experience was *beyond* beyond, as Strobe would say.

"You know what?" Toby said, finally breaking the silence. "I'm really glad you got out of that place."

Calanthe smiled. "Yes, I have experienced much in the little time I have been in your world."

"You can say that again."

"I have experienced much in the little time I have been in your world."

"Actually, Calanthe, that's just an expression. When someone says you can say that again? You don't have to say the same thing—"

Calanthe had broken into a smile, which is what had stopped Toby in the middle of his sentence. "Wait, are you goofin' on me? Did you know what I meant when I said that?"

Calanthe's expression was a little playful, a little mysterious. When she turned and headed off into the darkness, Toby smiled and shook his head. He was about to follow Calanthe when something on the stone wall under the bridge caught his eye. Among the graffiti—some of it painted, some etched into the stone—was a freshly carved addition. It read, simply . . .

CALANTHE.

17

Finally! **Strobe thought with relief.**

He had just caught sight of something other than endless snowcapped forest, which was all he had been looking at through his binoculars for the past three hours. The MCOs' search hadn't begun until early afternoon, the snow not letting up until then. Strobe was elated that he had finally done what he had set out to do. . . . He had found Calanthe's village. Just in the nick of time, too, seeing as it would be dark before long, night coming much earlier this far north.

"Over there!" Strobe yelled to the pilot, pointing out a small break in the forest, several miles off. "See it?"

When the helicopter got closer to the break, Strobe was able to confirm that he had discovered fallow crop fields, right in the middle of thousands of acres of forest. If it was the dekayi's farmland, the village itself was hidden from sight under the thick canopy of snow-covered trees that completely surrounded and boxed in the fields. Before they had reached the open ground, Strobe yelled out to the pilot, "We go down here!"

"Back off, Tibbles!" Holt commanded. "I say where we go down. And when." Strobe had just interrupted Holt's afternoon nap with his direction to the pilot. Holt looked around for his binoculars, found them under his seat, then adjusted the lenses to study the crop fields in the distance.

"We go down here!" Holt yelled, returning Strobe's glare with a jaunty grin. "Okay, fellas! Look lively! Time to rock 'n' roll!"

Strobe and the other MCOs pulled on their backpacks and positioned themselves next to the open side door of the helicopter.

"Harris, you're first. Then Dixon. Watch these two closely, Tibbles. You might learn something. We don't want you to fall off the rope and crash into the trees, do we?"

Strobe waited until Harris and Dixon had descended from the copter and were heading toward the forest below before easing out of the copter door and sliding down the rope.

"Back off a bit, then hang for us," Holt yelled to the pilot. "I'll call when we're comin' out." Holt hitched himself to the rope, then jumped out of the helicopter. In no time at all, the entire MCO crew had disappeared into the forest below.

■ ■ ■

Scanning the woods as he walked behind his three MCO mates, Strobe was struck by how quiet it was. It was also darker on the ground than it had been up in the helicopter, which gave Strobe the feeling that the surrounding forest was closing in on him.

Holt was leading the group. They were in single file, each scanning a particular area of the forest. "There it is," Strobe heard Holt whisper up ahead. Turning away from his rear watch, Strobe saw the shapes of several wooden buildings through the maze of trees. When the other MCOs fanned out and selected a tree to shield themselves from view, Strobe followed their lead. He took his binoculars from his backpack and studied the buildings in the distance.

No sign of any people. No sound interrupting the stillness of the forest. No smoke from the rough-hewn, stone chimneys.

Strange.

"Harris, Dixon . . . ," Holt said. "Follow me. Tibbles . . . stay here and watch our backs."

Strobe felt the rage rising from the pit of his stomach. "I'm not stayin' here!"

Holt fixed Strobe with a glare. "You'll stay here, or pay the consequences."

"And what might that be?"

"Ignoring an officer's command in the field will get your butt tossed from the program. Actually, I dare you to ignore my command. Go ahead, do it! Get your butt tossed. I'd love it. I never thought Harvey should let teenagers into the program, anyway."

There you have it, Strobe thought as the three MCOs turned and walked stealthily off into the encroaching darkness. *The guy hates me just because I'm a teenager.* Strobe knew that Holt would continue to ride him until he did something that could very well get him thrown out of the KP ranks. So he decided right then and there he wasn't going to give Holt the pleasure. He would toe the line, in spite of how difficult that was for him, starting right now.

Slipping on his NVGs, Strobe made certain his crossbow was loaded and ready, then settled in for his rearguard assignment. Until he heard otherwise, he was determined to steadfastly keep a watch out for any unusual movement in the deep, dark woods of the Canadian wilderness.

18

"Two Monstrosities!"

Halley—the person Toby had picked to take Strobe's place for his Saturday-night shift—looked out of control as she placed the order form on the revolving wheel. Her eyes were wide and harried, her face flushed. Studying Halley with concern, Toby noticed that her white apron displayed yet another red pizza-sauce design. Over the past few hours, Halley's apron had been a constantly changing canvas, featuring one zany abstract image after another.

"You know what, Halley? Take ten minutes."

Halley looked at Toby blankly. "Sure?"

"Definitely. Matter of fact, take fifteen."

"Whew. Thanks, Toby."

As she left the kitchen, Halley passed a sleepy-eyed teen who was pulling several pizzas from the oven. *At least Ron doesn't freak out like this girl,* Toby thought as he got to work on Halley's order. *He's no Annabel, though, that's for sure.* Ron had been Toby's choice to replace Annabel.

When Toby heard the *Jaws* theme thump ominously from a speaker at the front of the shop—it was the official KP greeting that alternated with a loud, ghoulish laugh and a high-pitched scream whenever someone entered the Killer Pizza shop—he went to deal with the new customers. Who happened to be Annabel and Calanthe.

"Your expression says it all," Annabel said with a smile.

"Tell me about it. Any news from Strobe?"

Annabel shook her head.

"Guess that means he either found the village or he's on his way back to Hidden Hills."

"I can't tell you how many times I wanted to give him a call."

"I'm sure he'll call if he has any news. Hey, what can I get you two?"

"Actually, we stopped by to see if you needed any help."

"You serious?"

"Yeah, I feel bad, deserting you like this. It was okay when Strobe was with you, but . . ."

Toby had already pulled up the section of counter next to the cash register, allowing Annabel and Calanthe to enter into the kitchen.

"This might be kind of boring for you, Calanthe." Toby brought a stool from the area behind the counter into the kitchen for Calanthe to sit on.

"No, I wanted to come."

As it turned out, Calanthe was intrigued by the entire Killer Pizza operation. The hectic activity in the kitchen. The endless stream of people coming through the front door, young and old alike. The movie illuminating the wall on the other side of the street, this being Monster Mash-up night.

After observing the action for a while, Calanthe offered to help out. Toby thought about that for a moment, then placed Calanthe at the front counter to take orders. As she had shown numerous times before, Calanthe was a quick study, and that was certainly the case with her first Killer Pizza shift. She handled the nonstop activity like a pro, never once getting flustered.

When the shift was over, Toby rewarded Calanthe with something he had promised her in the school cafeteria. Her very first taste of pizza—*real* pizza— which was something the dekayi certainly didn't possess on their menu.

"I like it," Calanthe announced, after quickly devouring her pizza slice.

"I can tell," Toby observed.

"What do you call this kind of pizza?"

"A Fangtastic Hawaiian."

"It is very good. I would like another piece, please."

"We call them slices. It's a slice of pizza."

"Well, whatever you call them, hit me!"

When Toby turned back to Calanthe after retrieving another pizza slice, she was staring straight ahead with a slight frown on her face.

"Calanthe?"

Calanthe didn't answer. She appeared to be somewhere else all of a sudden.

"Calanthe? Everything okay?"

Calanthe gave Toby a blank look. Toby rotated the pizza slice under Calanthe's nose, a culinary variation on smelling salts. When the aroma hit home, Calanthe's eyes lost their faraway look. "For me?"

"Yes, for you."

Calanthe smiled, took the pizza, and bit into it. Wherever the girl had been for those few moments, she was back. And enjoying her pizza, which was gone as fast as the first slice.

"Can I try the Monstrosity next?"

■ ■ ■

Walking his bike up Hazel Street alongside Annabel and Calanthe, Toby was approaching his house when he asked, "So what do you two want to do now? The night is still young." Toby looked exhilarated and happy, just being with Annabel and Calanthe. He wanted to keep the evening going.

"I don't know what you're doing," Annabel replied, "but Calanthe and I are going home, where I will be introducing her to one of the classic teen girl pastimes."

"Which would be?"

"The slumber party."

"Sounds great. Can I come?"

"Yeah, right."

"C'mon!"

"No boys at girls' slumber parties. Unless of course they sneak out in the middle of the night and crash 'em. But from what I heard, you already had your sneaking-out adventure last night."

That stopped Toby in his tracks. He looked from Calanthe to Annabel, then back at Calanthe. "Yes, I decided it was time to tell Annabel about my noctural excursions."

"And I'm glad you did, Calanthe. Because obviously Toby wasn't going to tell me." Annabel arched an eyebrow at Toby, then started off down the street, giving Calanthe a tug on the shirtsleeve.

"Hey, wait a second. I didn't think it was my place to tell you. If I had, that would have betrayed a confidence."

Annabel responded by giving Toby a wave over her shoulder.

"Good night, Toby," Calanthe called back. "See you tomorrow."

Toby watched the two girls walk off down the street, then strolled across his lawn, kicking absentmindedly at the leaves strewn across the grass as he went. Arriving at the front porch, Toby suddenly stopped, as though something had just occurred to him. He turned and stared off into the night. Not in the direction that Annabel and Calanthe had just gone, but rather northward, far beyond the two girls.

I wonder how Strobe is doing up there? Toby thought. He pondered his question for a moment, a slight frown on his face, then propped his bike up against the side of his house and went inside.

19

Strobe was still keeping watch in the woods. He was
cold and getting increasingly annoyed. It had been almost
an hour since Holt and the other MCOs had gone off to
check out the village. Strobe was on the verge of abandoning his position to head to the village to find out what
was keeping them so long. As he looked through his binoculars at the nearby village, Strobe suddenly heard a
sinister hissing sound cut through the silence that had
permeated the woods ever since he had entered them.

Whirling toward the sound, Strobe was just in time
to see the tail end of a large serpent-like creature disappear behind a nearby tree. Strobe's heart slammed into
high gear at the sight of the monster.

That was one huge snake!

Another high-pitched hiss sliced through the woods,
this one from another direction from the first. Then *another*, from yet another direction. The three monstrous

serpents sounded alike, but they each had their own distinctive accent, their own personality. Which was more disturbing to Strobe, somehow, than if they had all sounded exactly the same.

Strobe knew what was happening. He was being surrounded, and the three dekayi were communicating with one another via their weird high-hissing language. Without another thought, Strobe took off through the woods in the direction of the village.

He quickly reached the outskirts of the complex and took a path between two single-story wooden buildings. From what Strobe could tell, the village appeared to be arranged in a circular pattern. The houses he had just run past were part of a large circle that surrounded another circle of slightly larger buildings. Strobe ran past this second ring to find a third ring of buildings.

The strangely designed village appeared to be deserted. Either that or the dekayi were hiding out in their dark homes. Whichever, the place was totally creeping Strobe out.

It wasn't just how deserted it was. It was knowing how completely bizarre the inhabitants were that lived here, thanks to Calanthe's descriptions of her people and their habits. The main question on Strobe's mind as he ran through the village was . . .

Where had Holt and the other MCOs disappeared to?

Staying in the dense shadows of the buildings as he ran, Strobe saw the reflected flickering light of a torch, illuminating a narrow walkway up ahead. Slowing to walk, Strobe moved cautiously toward the light. When he turned the corner, the sight that greeted him was absolutely horrifying.

Strobe lurched back into the shadows and brought up his crossbow into a ready position. There were no dekayi in sight, but the thing that had caused Strobe's violent reaction was . . .

Actually, Strobe had to study the sight through his crossbow's infrared scope to figure out exactly what he was looking at. One thing was obvious. Dixon—hands tied behind his back—was hanging upside down by his ankles from the top of a post that held a flickering torch.

The truly terrifying part of the scenario, however, and the thing that Strobe was studying through his scope, was that Dixon appeared to be encased in some sort of slimy cocoon. The thick, translucent, black-tinged ooze was moving along his body, collecting at his head and dripping to the walkway below.

As Strobe watched, Dixon's body rotated slowly and his face swung into view. Strobe was relieved to see that

Dixon was alive. But when the MCO's wide-open eyes met Strobe's, they conveyed just how completely out-of-his-head terrified he was. Dixon was sending Strobe a single, desperate message. *Get me out of here!*

Suddenly, Strobe heard the dekayi that had been following him, their hissing voices echoing between the buildings. He pulled down his phone mouthpiece, flicked on the walkie-talkie that hung from his belt, and ordered the helicopter pilot to head immediately to the crop fields.

Then he ran across the walkway to Dixon. He hadn't been able to detect from the shadows where he'd been standing that the post Dixon hung from was covered with the same disgusting muck that encased him, making it impossible to climb. Exactly what Strobe had intended to do to cut the MCO down.

Shoving his knife back into its sheath, Strobe stepped away from the post and brought up his crossbow. "I'm gonna have to shoot you down, Dixon. Get ready for impact." But Strobe never got off a shot at the rope holding Dixon to the post.

"Aaaaaaggghhhhh!!!"

Strobe shouted out in alarm as a thick blob of the black-tinged ooze splattered his hand. It had come from somewhere above and behind him. As Strobe retreated back into the shadows of the nearest building, he lost his grip on the crossbow and dropped it. Just then the hissing of the three dekayi became louder, more immediate. Seconds later, they were visible in the torchlight that illuminated the walkway, slithering and crawling toward Strobe.

Strobe felt a chill of pure terror when he saw the odd-legged serpents. One of them was on the walkway. The other two were on the sides of the buildings that formed a wall along either side of the walkway, the feet of their stunted legs making a sucking sound as they crawled along the walls.

Strobe willed himself to keep it together. Not an easy thing to do, with the trio of bizarre-looking serpents slithering toward him. A hiss from above indicated there was also a dekayi on the roof overhead. Strobe was pretty sure that's where the black-tinged ooze had come from. It was the dekayi's spit! Which, as Strobe now knew, had the ability to completely numb a person's hand within thirty seconds.

You gotta get out of here, and fast!

Just before Strobe made a break for it, he exchanged a look with Dixon. *I'll be back for you!* That's the message Strobe sent, hoping that it translated. Then he grabbed his crossbow with his left hand, the one that still had feeling in it, and sprinted down the walkway toward the center of town.

The walkway turned to the right. Then left. Another left. Another right.

Strobe had no idea where he was going. He just wanted to put as much distance between him and the advancing dekayi as possible. At the final turn before reaching the center of the village, Strobe skidded to a stop and slammed back up against the side of a building.

There, on another torch-lit pole, hung Harris. The chilling sight of Harris, encased in the same gelatinous cocoon—made Strobe feel weak. He actually felt himself buckle, then forced himself to stand up straight.

The unseen dekayi were getting closer every second. Strobe could tell by the sound of them, a sound he'd never heard before, except maybe in his nightmares. The slithering/crawling. The high-pitched hissing. It was like a bizarre, aural tidal wave, building in intensity as it bore down on him.

The center of town was in sight at the end of the walkway. With a final glance at Harris, Strobe ran toward it. Approaching the square, Strobe had the sinking feeling that the dekayi *wanted* him to go there. That he'd been led right into a trap. When he broke into the square, his eyes went immediately to a wooden stage at the far side of the open area.

What Strobe saw on that stage brought him up short. From a pole set in the center of the platform, hung Holt, upside down. He wasn't covered in the black-tinged ooze, however. Not yet. But he was in the grip of a huge serpent, its body wrapped around him from top to bottom. The serpent's head hovered above Holt's feet, which were bound and hanging from the post crossbar overhead. The creature's tongue flicked in and out. Its large sharp fangs were bared.

Strobe started for the stage, bringing up his crossbow into a shooting position as he went. It was awkward, having to use his left finger on the trigger instead of his right, but his hand was still paralyzed by the disgusting dekayi slimeball. Strobe was halfway to the stage when the serpent's body suddenly constricted, instantly increasing the pressure on Holt.

"NOOOOOOOOOO!!!!"

Holt's face contorted into a grotesque mask as he screamed in torment. It looked as though his body might actually burst from the serpent's vice-like grip. Strobe immediately stopped in his tracks and lowered his crossbow. The dekayi responded by relaxing its grip.

Face-off. One that Strobe knew he couldn't win.

"Go, Tibbles. Get out if you can. Bring help!" When Holt spoke, it was with extreme effort. It sounded to Strobe as though Holt knew these might be the last words he would ever utter.

By now the other dekayi had arrived at the edge of

the square, their signature hissing language now joined by another sound, the whir of the approaching helicopter's blades. Strobe glanced quickly at the buildings that surrounded the square, chose one, and sprinted toward it. Shooting a look at Holt over his shoulder, he immediately wished he hadn't.

The serpent was vomiting the gelatinous black-tinged ooze up and down Holt's body, instantly paralyzing the MCO. With that disgusting and disturbing image searing through his brain, Strobe dropped his shoulder when he was a few feet away from the door of the building and plowed into it, blasting the door open.

Strobe was desperate at this point to escape a similar fate as Holt and the rest of the MCOs. He felt feverish and sick and hyper with adrenaline at the thought. And he knew he would not let that happen. He would die first. It was after Strobe had slammed the door shut and moved farther into the dark building . . .

That he saw what was waiting for him.

20

"Usually there are more than two girls for a slumber party. This is more what you'd call a sleepover."

A thousand miles might have separated Annabel's home and Calanthe's former village, but considering what was going on in the two places, they might as well have been on different *planets*. Completely clueless of what was happening to Strobe, Annabel and Calanthe had just settled on Annabel's queen-size bed with their bowls of snacks and drinks. Calanthe nodded gravely at what Annabel had just told her, as though she had learned some ancient wisdom about teen life in the human world. Which, in a way, she had.

"What happens during these slumber parties? Sleep-overs?" Calanthe had a serious expression on her face as she asked the question.

"Lots of music." Annabel indicated the amplified iPod that was playing a rousing pop-rock song. "Lots of snacks." Annabel held up her bowl of popcorn and indicated Calanthe's bowl of chips. "And most important, lots of talk."

"Talk?"

"About anything and everything. Stupid things. Important things. Whatever comes to mind." Annabel lay down on her stomach, feet up in the air and crossed at the ankles behind her, and started munching on her popcorn.

"What would you like to talk about?" Calanthe asked, remaining in her cross-legged position at the head of the bed.

"Oh, I don't know. Why don't you tell me a little more about your village."

"What would you like to know?"

"Did you ever do anything like this? Just sit around at night? Talk?"

"Never by ourselves."

"You mean there was always an adult supervising you?"

"Yes."

"That's ridiculous."

"That's what I came to believe."

"When, Calanthe? When did you start to become so . . . different from all the other villagers?"

Calanthe didn't have to think about her answer. "It was the night of the Sleeping that changed me."

"The Sleeping?"

"It is a ritual in our village. All the children, when they reach the age of three, are taken out into the forest and left there, all by themselves."

"They do this when you're only three?" Annabel asked.

"Yes. Each child is required to stay in the forest overnight, then make their way back to the village the following morning. With no help or guidance. The Sleeping is meant to teach the children to not be afraid of the forest."

"Either that or make you terrified of going into the woods for the rest of your lives. Obviously you made it back. What about the ones who got lost?"

"We never saw them again."

Annabel's mouth dropped in amazement. "I can't believe it. Three-year-olds left to die out in the woods? Fights to the death? I'm amazed you made it through all that. What a totally weird place you came from."

"Yes, but as I said, it was the Sleeping that changed me. It was that night, while I was wandering in the dark looking for a place to stay, that I found the cave that I told you and Toby about. When I entered the cave, I couldn't see a thing, it was so dark. I stumbled along for a while, feeling with my hands for direction, and finally made it to the center of the cave. There I discovered some flints and brush to start a fire with. It was then that I knew others had been there before me. They had left the flints and branches for when they returned. It took me a long time to start a flame, but when I finally did . . . as the fire became larger and larger . . . the pictures on the walls slowly became visible. It was as though a veil had been lifted from my eyes."

"That's actually a really beautiful story, Calanthe."

No reply from Calanthe. From the expression on her face, it appeared that she had returned to that cave, was once again looking at those pictures, being transformed by them. Then the moment passed, and Calanthe was back in the here and now.

"So . . . are you sure you were only three when this happened?"

Calanthe nodded.

"How old are you now, anyway? I never did ask you that."

"Almost four."

Annabel laughed. "Almost four? What does that mean?"

"It means I have lived for almost four sections."

"Okay, obviously your calendar is a little different from ours."

"It is? How old are you?"

"Fourteen. I'm fourteen years old."

"That's what you call your sections. Years."

"Yes." Annabel hopped off her bed, went to her desk and came back with a desk diary. "Let's figure this out. I'll show you what I mean by years. You can explain your sections."

Annabel lay down on the bed next to Calanthe and opened her desk diary. "OK, here's a calendar for one year. Twelve months in a year. See? Twenty-eight to thirty-one days per month. One day is twenty-four hours long."

Calanthe studied the calendar with a concentrated frown. "This is very complicated."

"How do you measure your . . ." Annabel thought about how to put this. "Time. I mean, what is a section?"

"It has to do with the seasons. The number of seasons that pass. A section is four planting seasons, come and gone."

"Okay, it sounds like one of your sections equals four of our years. If you've lived for almost four sections, that means you're around fifteen, sixteen years old."

"What is that?" Calanthe asked. Annabel had paged through her calender to the current week. Calanthe was indicating the October 31 square, which had an image of a ghost floating over the word *Halloween*.

"That's Halloween. It's a holiday we have. We get dressed up in scary costumes, kids mostly, some adults, and go around from house to house in the neighborhood to get a bunch of candy."

Calanthe frowned.

"I know. Weird, huh?"

"If we had a calendar like this, there would be a symbol of a circle, with a jagged line through it. It would be around this time of year."

"Really? What does the symbol mean?"

"It stands for a holiday of ours as well, our most sacred one. It's called the Day of Days."

"What do you do on that holiday? What do you celebrate?"

"We thank our gods for our bountiful crops and pray for deliverance through the coming winter. It's a very old ceremony, from the beginning of our days. It's very festive. The children are allowed more freedom than usual, which is nice. It's a day to look forward to."

Annabel nodded. Over the years she'd read in her history books about such ceremonies celebrated by ancient, agricultural societies.

"Out of all the children," Calanthe continued, "I was

chosen to be the hostess for the Day of Days this year. It is a very big honor."

"Wow. You must have been excited."

"No, I was not." Calanthe's expression was a mask, not giving away or expressing any emotion. "Toby asked me the other night when it was that I felt I was ready to leave my village. I had wanted to leave for a very long time. But I was afraid. I didn't think that I could actually make it. When I was chosen to be the hostess for this year's celebration, that was the sign I was looking for."

Annabel frowned. "Why was that?"

Calanthe didn't answer right away. When she did, it was as though she was reciting scripture of some sort. "After sunset on the Day of Days, a large bonfire is built. The entire village gathers for a final ceremony. The name of the ceremony is difficult to translate from our original language. The best I can do is . . . the Slice."

Annabel's heart quickened. *Slice*. That's what she thought she'd heard Calanthe say that day under the bleachers.

Calanthe made an attempt at a smile. "That's slightly humorous, yes? Tonight, I had my first slice of pizza. In both cases, the definition is the same. To separate from the whole."

Annabel didn't like the turn Calanthe's story had taken. She didn't have to wait long to hear the ending.

"At the end of the ceremony," Calanthe continued, "in order to assure that our gods continue to smile on us throughout the winter and the spring, an offering is made."

No, Annabel thought. *Don't say what I think you're going to say.*

"Each year, it is the hostess for the Day of Days who is offered up to our gods."

Annabel closed her eyes, as though that might somehow blot out what she just heard. "You were actually going to be sacrificed, Calanthe?"

"Yes."

"That's totally insane."

"I am hoping, once this year's Day of Days has come and gone, that my people will forget about me. That I will be left alone to live with you. In peace."

"So, that's the main reason they came after you. To bring you back for the Day of Days."

Calanthe nodded. "I know they will continue to look for me until then. It is not a random thing, the person who is chosen for this honor. It is a divine choice. That's what my people believe. And this year, I am the one."

"Whew." Annabel realized that her mouth was really dry. "I need something to drink before we talk about this anymore. How about you, Calanthe?"

"Some juice would be nice."

Annabel nodded and was about to go get their drinks when Calanthe suddenly grabbed her wrist. "What are you? . . . Calanthe! No! That hurts!"

But Calanthe did not let go. Annabel gasped from the pain of Calanthe's grip. "Please, Calanthe . . ." After several desperate attempts, Annabel managed to wrench her arm away from Calanthe. She slid off the bed and backed away across the room, her eyes opening wide at what she was seeing. Just like the day under the bleachers, Calanthe's skin was becoming translucent, slowly revealing her underlying veins, arteries, and muscles.

"Calanthe! Can you hear me?"

Apparently not. Calanthe wasn't dreaming this time, but she was in the grip of something very powerful. It was as though she had become possessed by another entity. The attack was already causing Calanthe to sweat profusely. Her hair was matted to her forehead. Her T-shirt and baggy pajama bottoms were soaked through.

Annabel was certain that she was witnessing the Altering, the transformation Calanthe had told them about just before Strobe left for Canada. But why now?

Had Calanthe's revelation of the Day of Days precipitated the attack? Just as that thought occurred to Annabel, Calanthe suddenly came off the bed and seized her by the throat!

The pressure was so great, so fast, that Annabel couldn't breathe. Or speak. She grasped Calanthe's hand with both of hers to try to free herself. But it was no use. Calanthe's grip was overpowering. And excruciatingly painful. Any strength Annabel had left was quickly dissipating. She felt herself blacking out.

And then . . .

The attack disappeared as quickly as it had arrived.

Annabel felt Calanthe's deadly grip loosen. As soon as it did, Annabel inhaled huge gulps of air. She tried to focus on Calanthe, but all she could see were explosions of bright lights against a black background. Slowly . . . the bursts of light faded.

When Annabel's vision had finally cleared enough to be able to see Calanthe, the girl was staring down at her with a horrified look on her face. Calanthe knew what she had done to Annabel. Worse yet, what she had almost done. She stood and slowly backed away from Annabel. Then she turned and ran from the room.

Annabel tried to call out to Calanthe, but all that came out was a hoarse whisper. She tried to get up but fell back with a wince. She was extremely weak from Calanthe's assault. Forcing herself to crawl to her desk, fighting back nausea, Annabel grabbed her cell phone. Then she punched in Toby's number and waited for him to answer her call for help.

21

Things might have turned bad all of a sudden in Hidden Hills, but they were far worse for Strobe up in the dekayi village. After breaking into the building at the edge of the village square, Strobe had immediately felt that he wasn't alone in the darkly lit meeting hall.

He was right.

After moving farther into the hall, Strobe was able to make out at least eight serpent-like creatures, hovering in the shadows in the far corners, just out of reach of the light cast from the torches mounted on the wooden pillars.

Strobe immediately began edging his way toward the front of the hall. He was feeling dizzy at this point, the unbeatable numbers of dekayi only adding to the sensation that everything around him was swirling into a deadly tailspin. As much as he tried, he couldn't for the life of him figure out how to get out of his nightmarish trap.

The front door of the hall suddenly burst open, and the three dekayi that had been following Strobe pushed their way inside, their serpentine heads immediately twisting and zeroing in on their prey. Emboldened by the arrival of the three sinister-looking creatures, the other ones in the hall left their shadows and started coming for Strobe.

Okay, come and get me. I'm gonna take out as many of you as I can before you do.

Sliding the crossbow from his back, Strobe brought it up and started pulling the trigger as fast as his less-flexible left finger would allow. But instead of the weapon responding to Strobe's trigger pull, all that happened was . . .

Nothing.

Strobe immediately locked onto a possible reason. The disgusting gelatinous ooze that had paralyzed his hand might have done the same thing to his crossbow. Some of the stuff could have found its way into the casing and jammed the mechanism.

I'm a dead man, for sure!

Strobe's fatal thought was pushed aside by the sound of whirling blades. The helicopter! In the frenzy of the past few minutes Strobe had totally forgotten all about it.

When Strobe turned and charged for the stage at the

end of the hall, a hopeful plan was already forming in his head. He had to get up to the roof of the hall. The pilot could meet him there and whisk him off to safety.

But how to get up there? As Strobe approached the dark stage, the huge serpent statue slowly became visible to him. As soon as he saw the statue, Strobe knew that he could use it as a ladder to the ceiling.

Slinging the crossbow back over his shoulder, Strobe leaped up onto the stage and hit the statue at a run. He quickly scaled the larger-than-life serpent to the top, where he found himself face-to-face with the wooden idol's gaping mouth and long sharp teeth.

In the hall behind and below him, Strobe could hear the snapping-sucking sounds of dekayi feet. Holding tightly on to one of the statue's teeth, Strobe shot a look over his shoulder. A half dozen of the dekayi were on the walls and fanning out toward the ceiling, trying to cut off his escape route. Several more of the creatures had slithered onto the stage and were about to crawl up the statue.

Now what?

A thought hit Strobe like a punch, slamming him into action. He yanked off his backpack and hung it on the statue's long, curving tongue. Found the flares in the pack. Started setting them off, one after the other.

The first few he threw to the floor far below, aiming

for the rows of cushions that faced the stage. Some feeling was coming back into Strobe's right hand, but he still had to use his left, making things—such as accuracy—more difficult.

But Strobe was humming now. He thought he had a slim chance to get out of this. When one of the dekayi suddenly curled around a wooden hump of the statue's twisting shape and leaped for him, Strobe was ready. He jammed a flare into the thing's mouth, instantly turning hisses to screams when the white-hot magnesium flame scorched the creature. Writhing backward from Strobe's attack, the dekayi lost contact with the statue, fell to the stage below, and hit it with a hollow thud.

All the other dekayi immediately halted their progress toward their prey. The flares had added a dangerous new component to the fight. The floor of the hall was already ablaze, the cushions acting like brittle tinder, feeding the fire, and causing it to expand rapidly.

Strobe pulled down his cell mouthpiece, told the pilot of the helicopter to meet him on the roof, then tried to figure out how to get *up* to the roof. It was then that Strobe noticed a circular stained-glass window—black with a jagged red slash through the middle—on the wall above and behind the statue, near the apex of the roof.

That was it, Strobe knew. His escape route. All he needed to do was get to that window. As fast as possible. The flames below had already worked their way to the stage, leaping higher with every second. They looked like living things that wanted to eat Strobe alive.

Just like the serpents. Fortunately, most of the creatures were retreating, getting out of the building before they burned to a crisp. But a few die-hard dekayi were still coming for Strobe. One was on the wall behind Strobe. Another was upside down on the ceiling, crawling toward him.

HISSSSSSSS!!!

The dekayi on the wall had suddenly leaped to the wooden statue and was slithering upward toward its prey. Strobe set off another flare, and held it out toward the serpent. The creature immediately retreated a short ways down the statue.

"Not far enough, you giant maggot."

Strobe started down the statue toward the dekayi, jabbing the flare toward the creature as he went. That seemed to do it. The serpent twisted and leaped back to the wall, where its grotesque, suctioned feet took hold of the wood and stuck.

"Not as dumb an ugly slimeball as I thought you were."

Strobe was definitely feeling it now, his body humming with energy, his thoughts sharp and focused. He was even trash-talking a dekayi! But Strobe still had several more obstacles to deal with. The other dekayi had crawled across the ceiling and was now blocking the window that Strobe had targeted as his escape route.

"Bad idea, dude."

Reaching into his backpack, Strobe pulled out a flare launcher. Typically used to fire a flare in the air to indicate a person's position or to put out a distress call, Strobe was about to improvise. He kept a wary eye on the dekayi nearest him as he delicately loaded his burning flare, then . . .

BAMMM!!!

The flare flew upward in a spectacular flaming arc and hit the dekayi with such force that the device impaled the leathery skin of the creature. The thing reacted violently, screaming as it tried to keep its grip on the wooden wall. But it couldn't. Falling to the floor below, the creature disappeared into the flames, which had racheted the temperature in the hall up to an almost unbearable level.

The other dekayi was now retreating back down the wall. Strobe's only enemy at this point was the fire. He wiped the sweat from his eyes as he reached into his backpack and pulled out an odd-looking contraption, long and slim.

"James Bond time," Strobe said with a tense smile, mentally thanking the other MCOs, who had been very thorough putting together his pack before they had left New York.

After a quick and delicate maneuver up and onto the very top of the serpent statue—vertigo territory—Strobe aimed his James Bond contraption at the ceiling just above the stained-glass window and pulled a trigger. A sharp hook attached to a long synthetic rope shot upward and stuck into the ceiling. Strobe gave the rope a hard pull to test it. If it didn't hold his weight, he was a dead man. Simple as that.

The flames had crawled up the statue and were licking at Strobe's feet as he pulled on his backpack. After testing the rope a final time, Strobe swung out into the space above the out-of-control fire.

Just as he began to climb toward the ceiling, Strobe went into a freefall! He looked wildly up at the ceiling. The hook at the end of the rope had lost its grip! Strobe was a mere second away from being engulfed in flames when the hook mercifully snagged on the edge of the jutting window frame that surrounded the window . . . and held.

Strobe jolted to a bone-jarring halt. A quick sigh of relief was followed by a difficult climb to the ceiling. Swinging precariously back and forth on the rope, Strobe finally reached the window.

He slid the crossbow from his shoulder, reached back, and slammed the butt of the weapon into the glass. It shattered outward, creating a large, jagged hole. After clearing the larger shards of glass away from the border of the window, Strobe carefully crawled through the opening. Using the bottom frame of the window as a foothold, he eased himself into a standing position outside the building. He steadied himself, then reached up, grabbed hold of the edge of the roof and pulled himself up and away from the window.

The helicopter was waiting for him. As Strobe made his way carefully toward the copter, all was chaos below. A crowd of dekayi—in their human form—had gathered and were quickly forming several lines from a large water trough at the edge of the square to the burning meeting hall. They were furiously passing buckets of water down the lines to the source of the fire when Strobe reached the helicopter. As soon as he was safely inside, the chopper took off.

But Strobe wasn't leaving unnoticed. The dekayi might have been blindly focused on the out-of-control blaze, but on the other side of the square . . .

The Tall Man slowly emerged from the shadows. His

cadaverous face glowed red from the fire as he looked up at the departing helicopter, his alert, cruel eyes tracing its path until it could no longer be seen. Then, the dekayi did something unexpected.

He smiled. It was a smile that could send a chill down the spine of the devil himself.

22

Walking through the dark woods near Annabel's
house, Toby was about to jump a small stream when he
noticed something . . . the faint impression of a bare
foot in the damp ground next to the stream. The foot
outline pointed out a new direction for Toby, which he
immediately followed.

Toby had ridden his bike over to Annabel's immediately after getting the ghastly news about Calanthe's Altering. He had urged Annabel to stay home while he
searched for Calanthe. In spite of the fact that she could
barely speak—the result of her throat still feeling like it
was on fire—Annabel wouldn't hear of it. The two had
decided that Calanthe had taken to the woods, an easy
call, and had split up to look for her.

After discovering the bare footprint, Toby walked farther and farther into the increasingly dense woodland.
His NVGs allowed him to pick up additional cues in the

pitch-black night that someone had blazed a path through this part of the forest.

A couple of fern plants flattened by a passerby.

A chest-high tree branch freshly snapped off near the trunk.

Another impression in the ground, this one sharper, the heel of someone's bare foot, indicating run . . . not stroll.

Toby suddenly stopped. He was standing at the juncture of two streams. The brook he had been following ran into a larger one, which curved off between the trees and disappeared into the darkness. Staring at the stream with a thoughtful frown, Toby activated his cell and pulled down his mouthpiece.

"Annabel. I think I know where Calanthe went."

■ ■ ■

It took them almost half an hour to reach the railroad bridge. They followed the stream the entire way and approached the bridge from the opposite direction that Toby and Calanthe had come the previous night. There was a bend in the stream just before the bridge. As soon as the trestle came into sight, Toby stopped Annabel and indicated they should head away from the stream and approach the bridge from another angle.

Annabel nodded. She followed Toby into the woods

and up a steep hill, toward the train tracks that bridged the stream. When the two emerged from the woods and were standing on the tracks, Toby conveyed to Annabel that he would approach the tunnel under the bridge from the left, she from the right.

He waited until Annabel had disappeared into the woods before making his approach. He went slowly, scouring the trees and underbrush, looking for any movement, any sign of Calanthe. Halfway down the hill, Toby stopped. He closed his eyes and allowed the forest sounds to sink in.

Crickets . . .

The distant hum of something electric . . .

The leaves above, whispering and rustling in the nighttime breeze . . .

Hearing nothing to indicate that Calanthe was anywhere nearby, Toby continued down the steep hill, walking sideways for traction and balance. He stopped just before the opening of the tunnel and pressed his back up against the stone base of the bridge. He listened for a moment, then took a quick peek around the corner.

Nothing.

The gurgles of the stream echoed off the sides of the tunnel, an oddly peaceful, reassuring sound. When Toby saw Annabel appear on the other side of the tunnel, the two walked toward each other and met at just about the same spot Toby had been with Calanthe.

"Anything?" Toby asked in a whisper.

Annabel shook her head.

"Looks like I was wrong."

"Not necessarily. She might have heard us. Taken off."

And just like that, there was Calanthe, right in front of Toby's and Annabel's faces, freezing them in place.

The duo's statue-like reaction was provoked by the fact that they weren't looking at Calanthe, but rather her monstrous alter ego, hanging by a long tail from a girder overhead!

The creature's reptilian head, easily twice the size of Calanthe's human head, moved slowly back and forth in front of Annabel and Toby. Its leathery eyelids blinked up and down over its piercing, emotionless black eyes.

Toby and Annabel were so freaked, it wasn't difficult for them to stand completely still. They didn't want to chance so much as taking a breath. Any movement and who knew how the creature Calanthe had become might react?

The ghastly, diamond-shaped head suddenly focused on Annabel. The creature's reptilian tongue darted in and out, looking as though it couldn't wait to taste something. The lethal teeth glinted in the darkness. The head moved toward Annabel and stopped a mere inch from her face.

The serpent sniffed audibly, checking Annabel out, then started to move slowly down the length of her body. Its oily, leathery skin issued a strange creaking sound as it stretched farther out from the girder above. In spite of the cold night, Annabel could feel herself sweating. She wasn't sure how much of this she could take!

The creature's head was now at Annabel's feet. After a moment, it traveled back up her body and once again stopped a whisper away from her face. This time Annabel looked the serpent right in the eye. If there was any vestige of Calanthe left in her hideous alter ego, Annabel wanted to communicate with her. Silently, with just her eyes. Telling Calanthe to please come back to them.

Suddenly, the horrendous thing moved away from Annabel. It was Toby's turn. Like Annabel, it wasn't long before Toby started to sweat from the incredible tension of being given an intimate once-over from a ten-foot-long serpent. He could feel the sweat running down the back of his neck, causing an itch that took every ounce of willpower not to scratch.

Unlike Annabel, Toby couldn't bring himself to look the thing in the eye. It was difficult for him to believe there was any part of Calanthe left in such an astoundingly ugly creature.

And then, just like that, the creature disappeared as suddenly as it had appeared. One second it was so close to Toby he could feel a breeze from the flickering tongue, then it was gone, up into the pitch darkness under the train trestle.

Even then, Toby and Annabel didn't dare move. They stayed right where they were, listening to the sound of the serpent's huge, muscular body as it slithered in and out of the girders overhead, up and around to the top of the bridge, then finally into the underbrush that lined the tracks.

Only when he could no longer hear Calanthe did Toby allow himself to move. He breathed in deeply and slowly stretched his neck from side to side, trying to unlock it from its frozen state. Annabel had slid down the rock wall next to him and was sitting on her haunches.

Moments passed in silence. Neither said anything. Toby wasn't sure what to say anyway, how he could even begin to express how he felt about what had just happened.

Annabel didn't have to say anything. Everything she was feeling was right there, in her eyes. When Toby looked down at Annabel . . .

He could see the tears, sparkling in the darkness, threatening to overflow and fall down her cheeks.

23

Staring grimly out of the Cessna's window as it taxied
along the runway, Strobe saw Harvey standing on the
tarmac when the plane took a sudden turn and headed
toward the terminal. Harvey's expression mirrored
Strobe's. He stood very still, waiting for the plane to come
to a stop. When it did, he boarded immediately.

Strobe stayed seated as Harvey entered the plane,
walked down the aisle, and sat across from him. Harvey
had a laptop with him, which he now opened. He took
out a small digital recorder, turned it on, and placed it on
the floor between them. No words were spoken during
all this. Strobe knew what was about to take place. An
intensive debriefing of the events that had occurred in
the dekayi village.

When Harvey was ready, he looked at Strobe and nodded. Strobe collected his thoughts, then began his story.

It took over an hour. After telling the basic facts,

Strobe was subjected to one question after another from Harvey, until the head of Killer Pizza's MCO operations was satisfied that he had all the information he needed.

Strobe's initial euphoria after escaping from the dekayi village had quickly given way to depression, the images of the helpless MCOs hovering in his mind's eye the entire way back to Montreal. Strobe felt he should have done more to help them. But what else could he have done? After the debriefing, he waited for Harvey to weigh in with his opinion.

"Since there are no other parties to interview about this situation, no one to corroborate your story, I have to take what you just told me at face value. And I do. All considered, I believe that if you had tried to help Holt, Dixon, or Harris, the result would have been me losing four of my crew instead of three."

An inward sigh of relief from Strobe. It's what he had wanted to hear. It didn't make it any less of a burden, leaving Holt and Dixon and Harris behind, but at least he hadn't been branded a deserter by Harvey.

"Are you sending a crew up there?"

"Yes. This is priority now."

"Can I—"

"No. You need to get back to Hidden Hills. Chances

are the dekayi will be even more determined to track down Calanthe, considering what's happened."

Strobe nodded, started to collect his things. He needed to go to the main terminal, where he would book a commercial flight back to Ohio.

"Chief?"

"Yes."

"Something I can't get out of my head. I just have this weird feeling about it."

"What?"

"It seems to me they could have had me, as well. If they'd wanted to."

That got Harvey's attention.

"Think about it. Holt, Dixon, Harris. All more experienced than me. I didn't hear anything in the village while I was keeping lookout. Not one of them managed to get a shot off. Which means they had to have been taken completely by surprise. Why not me? The dekayi had their chances. Out in the woods. When I stopped to help Dixon."

"What could be the reason for that?"

"Like you say, they're bent on tracking down Calanthe. I'm thinking the tall dude was part of that group. He recognizes me from New York, figures there's a chance I might lead him to Calanthe."

Harvey was thinking about this when Strobe added, "I'm not sure how they'd be able to follow me, though. No computers, cars, electricity, phones. I doubt they have a GPS system."

Harvey nodded. "Just the same, take a roundabout way back to Hidden Hills. Make it as difficult as possible for them to track you. If you have any sense they're on to you when you get close to Hidden Hills . . ."

"I'll pull out," Strobe said, finishing Harvey's sentence for him. Just then Strobe's cell sounded inside his pocket, an old-fashioned ring like the one from a 1950s cradle phone. Strobe took out the cell, had a brief conversation, then signed off.

"Annabel. It appears Calanthe's a big girl now. She went through her Altering a couple of hours ago. Annabel and Toby have no idea where she is. She just took off. But not before almost killing Annabel."

Harvey was silent. He sat still for a moment, then said, "I trust Calanthe is not lost for good. Do what you can on your end. I'll do the same on mine."

"You got it."

"Good luck."

"You, too."

When Strobe descended the short ladder to the tarmac, he walked to the terminal, turned, and watched the

Cessna taxi back out onto the runway. As the plane moved farther away from him, Strobe found himself wishing the dekayi would follow him home. After his disastrous trip to the Canadian wilds, there were people to avenge now.

But there was also a life to protect, assuming that Calanthe wasn't lost to them forever. With that important assignment to tend to, Strobe now had to figure out how he was going to get back to Hidden Hills.

Without leaving any tracks.

24

After his harrowing late-night adventure, Toby cer-
tainly didn't feel like doing the weekly brunch with his
dad. He especially wanted to cancel after he and Annabel
had come back empty-handed from an early morning
search for Calanthe. Wherever Calanthe was, she apparently wanted to stay hidden.

Toby couldn't believe how quickly everything had
fallen apart over the past twelve hours. Calanthe's Altering and its violent and still-unfolding aftermath. Strobe's
horrible trip to the dekayi village, which Annabel had
told Toby about after she received a call from their MCO
partner first thing in the morning.

In spite of these worries, Toby decided to go ahead
with the brunch. There wasn't anything he and Annabel
could do at this point, anyway, as far as Calanthe and
Strobe were concerned. Strobe would eventually arrive
back in Hidden Hills. Calanthe would either come back

to them, or she wouldn't. All they could do in the mean-time was wait. Helplessly.

So Toby was in the kitchen when his dad came pattering in shortly after noon, still in his pajamas. Mr. Magill sat down at the table, opened the Sunday paper, then took a sip of coffee from his favorite mug, which Toby had placed in his hand as he walked past on the way to his chair. Mr. Magill was the picture of content-ment as he waited for brunch to be served.

Not so, Toby. Moving quickly about the kitchen, jug-gling three dishes at once, he was intense and focused. For today's brunch, Toby was having another go at his Sweet Tooth Pizza. The first version, which he had served up a two Sundays before, had fallen short of his usual high standards. So the chef had gone back under the hood, made a few radical adjustments, and was about to present his latest—and hopefully, much improved—version of STP.

Pulling the pizza out of the oven after the timing bell went off, Toby placed it on the counter. He felt the famil-iar quiver of excitement as he took off his oven mitt. Taste testing one of his latest recipes just never got old. After ceremoniously cutting the pizza precisely into eight slices, Toby picked out a slice and tasted it.

"Well?"

Toby jumped when his dad asked the all-important question.

"Dad! Don't do that."

"What'd I do?"

"I didn't know you were watching me, that's all."

"Well, I was. What's the verdict?"

"I need another taste before I render a verdict." Toby closed his eyes in order to better concentrate on what his taste buds conveyed about the various nuances of the dish. He took a second bite of the pizza. When he finally opened his eyes . . .

"And?" Mr. Magill asked urgently.

"And . . ." Toby put several slices of pizza onto a plate, added grits and a half dozen turkey-and-cranberry sausages, another Toby Magill original, and delivered the savory dish to his father. "This is a very . . . tasty . . . dish!"

Mr. Magill's eyes lit up at Toby's assessment of the Sweet Tooth Pizza. For his son to give one of his own creations the okay meant that it had to be something really special.

Toby stood back and waited for his dad's reaction. He didn't have to wait long. "Oh . . . *oh!* This is absolutely wonderful, Toby. Wow! This is your best so far. Hands down!"

"You say that every time I serve you something new."

"And I always mean it."

Smiling at his dad's reaction, Toby went to get himself a few slices of pizza. Before he could return to the table, however, his cell buzzed on the kitchen counter.

"Hello?"

Mr. Magill was so engrossed in his pizza that he didn't see his son's expression when he answered the phone. Good thing, too. Whatever it was he had just heard, Toby looked shocked. He turned away from his dad, listened for a few more moments, then said—in a tone that sounded like a parody of a calm voice—"Yes, I can."

That was the extent of the conversation. As he pocketed his cell, Toby was already heading out of the kitchen. "Gotta check something out, Dad."

"What? What is it?"

"Oh, you know. Work. Always something goin' on down there."

"Is it that urgent? You haven't even had your pizza yet."

"Just means there's that much more for you."

Mr. Magill didn't seem to mind that part of Toby having to take off. "Take a slice, at least."

"Don't mind if I do."

"This is really, *really* excellent."

"Thanks, Dad. You're my number-one fan."

"That I am. Yes, sirree, *that* . . . I definitely am."

■ ■ ■

It was Calanthe who had called Toby, the absolute last person's voice he was expecting to hear when he answered his cell. Toby couldn't remember Calanthe even having a cell phone, let alone receiving any instruction on how to use one.

She was behind his house in the woods. Making a show for his dad that he was leaving for Killer Pizza, he yelled "so long" as he exited through the front door, then circled around to his backyard. But Toby didn't enter the woods right away. Having no idea what to expect from Calanthe, he was concerned about seeing her. She had sounded very scared on the phone. And exhausted. Before signing off, she had asked Toby not to call Annabel. Not yet, anyway. She wanted to talk to him first.

So Toby entered the woods cautiously, squinting as he scanned the trees and moved deeper into the forest. A large cloud suddenly blanketed the sun overhead, plunging the woods into a convincing version of an eerie moonlit evening.

"Please, don't come too close."

Toby froze. A moment later, Calanthe emerged into view and stopped about ten yards away from him. She was wearing the same sleeveless tee and baggy pajama bottoms she had worn the previous night, when she had run away from the Oshiro house. She was barefoot. Her clothes were dirty and muddy, a testament to the horrendous night she had just spent out in the cold woods.

"You must be freezing, Calanthe. Here, take my jacket."

But as Toby took a step toward Calanthe, she held up her hands. "No. Stay right there. I'm not sure if I can control this yet."

Toby instantly took a step back. "The turning, you mean?"

Calanthe nodded. "I don't remember much about what happened last night. But I do know the Altering occurred."

Toby waited for Calanthe to tell him what she did remember.

"I vaguely remember when it began. Then, what I did to Annabel. I remember running away. After that, not much. When I woke up this morning, I was lying in the bushes, near that railroad bridge? I was naked. That's when I knew—"

"We found you, Calanthe. Last night. At the railroad bridge."

Calanthe looked startled at this news. "Had I already turned?"

Toby nodded. "Yeah. You must have been ten feet long, maybe more. Sniffed us up and down. You were *this close* to us."

Calanthe looked horrified at the thought of what her monstrous alter ego must have put her friends through. "Then?"

"You left."

Calanthe suddenly sat down on the ground. She looked like she didn't have the strength to stand any longer. When Toby made an instinctual move toward her, Calanthe once again motioned for him to stay where he was. Her dark hair fell around her face, obscuring her features, as she stared at the ground. After what felt like an eternity of silence, Calanthe said, "Annabel must hate me."

"What? No . . . no, Calanthe. Annabel doesn't hate you. Are you kidding? The only thing on Annabel's mind right now is getting you back. Making sure you're safe."

When Calanthe glanced up at Toby, her expression was one of complete and utter surprise. "Why? Why would she feel that way? I almost killed her. It's not the proper response."

"Maybe not in your culture. But here, Annabel will do anything to help you. She's not mad at you, she doesn't have any bad feelings about you whatsoever."

"But that's just so totally random."

Toby couldn't help but smile. Seeing his reaction, Calanthe said, "This is not an amusing situation, Toby."

"I know, I know. It's just . . ."

The two fell silent. Toby tried to figure out where to go from here. What to do.

"What is it we can do for you, Calanthe? What do you need right now?"

Calanthe thought about that. "I need time. Not much, I don't think. But I can't go back to Annabel's. Not yet. Not until I'm positive I can control what I've become."

"So you're saying you're going to stay? Here, in Hidden Hills? With us?"

"Of course. Where else would I go?"

Toby was relieved, hearing this. He thought Calanthe might have been considering taking off—which was the last thing Toby wanted. Calanthe, on her own, somewhere *out there*, with the dekayi tracking her down.

"You can't stay out here in the woods, though."

"Where else is there?"

Toby quickly thought through what it would entail if he hid Calanthe in his basement. He didn't like the risk factor of that arrangement. Then it came to him.

"I know." When Calanthe gave him a questioning look, Toby nodded. "I know the perfect place."

Toby used the back alley entrance to get to the secret underground training center in the Killer Pizza building. It was too risky to take Calanthe through the kitchen, down the hall, and into the storage room, where there was a concealed shelf/door, that served as a second entrance to the basement area.

Toby showed Calanthe the locker room first. The showers. Where the towels were. The clothes closet, with the stacks of T-shirts, sweatpants, and socks. After finding a pair of sneakers in Annabel's locker and giving them to Calanthe, Toby led her through the exercise room and out into the hall.

It was when Toby got the roll-away bed out of the storage room off the hallway and rolled it into the classroom that he realized the KP basement maybe wasn't the *perfect* place for Calanthe to live until she was more comfortable with her new powers.

Entering the classroom, Calanthe's eyes immediately went to the illustrations of monsters that lined the walls. Toby didn't say anything as he set up Calanthe's makeshift bed. He was hoping that she would just—

"I'm one of these, aren't I?"

Toby winced. Exactly what he didn't want to hear. He straightened up after tucking in the top sheet on the bed, turned, and looked at Calanthe. She was staring up at an illustration of a werewolf.

"Technically—"

"I am what you would call a monster. I don't really belong here. In your world." It sounded as though it was the first time this had occurred to Calanthe.

"Yes, you absolutely do belong here."

"What do you call my people? I don't see them here."

Toby hesitated, then said, "Dekayi. That's the . . . term we use."

Calanthe nodded, thinking about that.

"Calanthe. Please listen to me. Just because you're now able to turn into something like . . . the things in these pictures? That doesn't mean you're a monster, okay?"

Stepping away from the illustration of the werewolf, Calanthe looked across the room at Toby and crossed her arms. It was a prove-it-to-me kind of gesture.

"I mean, look at last night. You could have eaten Annabel and me right up, right there under the bridge. We had no way to defend ourselves. But you didn't."

Calanthe's face was a mask, her not-giving-anything-away expression.

"What I'm trying to say is . . . there are people, humans, who are total monsters without being able to change into anything. It's just who they are. And that's not who you are. You're so far from that you're just . . . well, you're one of the coolest people I've ever met."

Calanthe was silent. Finally, she said, "Thank you for that, Toby. That is helpful to know."

A look of exhaustion suddenly came over Calanthe. She walked to her bed and sat down.

"Are you hungry, Calanthe? It's been a long time since you've eaten."

"Yes, I am a bit hungry."

"I'll go upstairs and get you something. Be right back."

"Toby?"

Toby stopped at the door.

"A Fangtastic Hawaiian would be nice."

"You got it."

As Toby stepped out of the room and into the hallway, Calanthe once again called him back. "Are you certain this is going to be okay with Annabel? That she will forgive me for what I did to her last night?"

"Yes, I'm totally certain." Calanthe looked very vulnerable to Toby, sitting on her cot in her dirty tee and pajama bottoms. "Matter of fact, you know what Annabel told me?"

Calanthe shook her head no.

"She said that even though she's only known you for a couple of weeks, she already loves you like a sister."

Hearing that, Calanthe frowned. "I don't know what a sister is. Or love, for that matter. They're just words I've learned recently."

Toby thought for a moment. "I think the best way to describe love is . . . it's the vibe you're getting from Annabel. And from me. And Strobe, in his own way. It means we'll do anything for you. Whatever it takes, we'll protect you, make sure your people don't take you away from us."

How to protect Calanthe, if and when her people came for her, that was the question Toby couldn't answer right then.

25

Strobe lay on the bed, staring up at the ceiling. Hav-
ing had practically no sleep for the past forty-eight hours,
he was so tired that he was having trouble keeping his
eyes open. But Strobe wanted to keep his eyes open.
Every time he closed them, the terrifying images from his
trip to the dekayi village would run through his mind's
eye like a nightmare dream.

Strobe had taken a plane from Montreal to Buffalo,
New York, then backtracked—away from Ohio—by taking a bus to Scranton, Pennsylvania. He was now in a
sleeper compartment on a train bound for Cleveland.
From there . . . well, Strobe wasn't sure how he was getting from Cleveland, in the northern part of Ohio, to
Hidden Hills, in the southern part. He'd figure that out
when he got there.

Which is what Strobe had been doing all day long
and into the night. Improvising his route as he went.

Would all this zigzagging on trains, planes, and buses work? Would it result in Strobe shaking off the dekayi? If, indeed, they were actually following him? The only way to know that would be . . .

Strobe suddenly sat up in bed and stared at his compartment door. He was sure he'd heard something out in the corridor. He sat still for a moment, then eased out of bed, and moved silently across the room.

Staring at the slight crack between the door and floor, Strobe's pulse jumped when a shadow appeared just outside the door. The dark outline of the shadow intruded a few inches into the room, making Strobe think that the shadow might be able to enter under the door and materialize into whoever was casting it. Not the most outrageous of scenarios, considering what Strobe had witnessed up at the dekayi village.

Eyes locked on the shadow, Strobe held his breath. Whoever—or whatever—was just outside his door was standing perfectly still. Then the shadow moved slowly from one side of the door to the other. Strobe glanced at his backpack, lying on the floor by his bed, was considering grabbing the knife he had concealed in a secret inside pocket when . . .

CLACK-CLACK-CLACK-CLACK-CLACK-CLACK-CLACK!!!

Strobe jumped when a train blasted past the window,

heading in the opposite direction from the one Strobe's was traveling. The close proximity of the two trains caused the loud ricocheting of sound and clatter, which disappeared as soon as the trains had concluded their nighttime passing.

When Strobe looked back at the door, the shadow was gone. He immediately snapped back the bolt lock, yanked the door open, and stuck his head out into corridor. He was just in time to see the sliding door at one end of the train car closing, the silhouette of a head visible on the other side of the door window.

Strobe took off down the passageway and entered the dark, swaying interior area where his train car was connected to the next. A quick look around to make sure no one was lurking in shadows, then Strobe opened the door opposite the one that had just whooshed shut and entered the next car.

Again, Strobe saw the door at the opposite end of the car slide shut. The etched silhouette of a head appeared briefly on the other side of the door's window before disappearing into the darkness of the connecting compartment.

Strobe arrived at the next train car within fifteen seconds. As soon as he entered he stopped dead in his tracks. He had arrived in the dining car. It was half filled, the people sitting in booths that lined each side of the aisle. Couples, families, a few solo passengers. It was past the dinner hour, and the people were playing games, talking, reading.

Strobe studied the solo people in the booths, trying to determine if any of them had just sat down. But very quickly Strobe was the one being scrutinized. In his haste to go after his mysterious nighttime visitor, he had charged out of his room in T-shirt and boxers. Returning everyone's sudden stares, Strobe smiled.

"Good evening, all. Did anyone just come here? Run through the car? Sit down?"

A few older people turned away from Strobe in disgust. Others shook their heads no. A young girl with her parents was laughing with her brother, the two of them clearly delighted at this surprising late-night diversion.

"Okay . . . well, thank you all very much. And good night." Strobe backed toward the door, nodded to the laughing girl and her brother, then turned and went back to the connecting compartment between the two cars.

He inspected it carefully. There was nowhere for a person to hide. There were two doors, one on each side of the connecting compartment. The dekayi—if that's what had been sneaking around outside Strobe's room—might have escaped outside.

Strobe was about to leave the compartment when he suddenly felt a sudden stinging sensation in his leg. At first, he thought he'd been bitten, but no . . . it wasn't that. Strobe was alone in the compartment. Staring at his bare leg, Strobe couldn't make out anything in the dim light. He quickly returned to his room to get a better look, only to find that his door had automatically locked behind him when he left his room.

"Great, my evening is turning into a slapstick comedy," Strobe muttered under his breath.

After finding a porter and explaining his situation, a pantless Strobe was let back into his room. He immediately grabbed a powerful pocket flashlight from his backpack and sat on the bed to examine his leg. The odd sensation in his thigh had been coming and going and Strobe was starting to feel a bit nauseous.

"Holy crap!"

Strobe dropped his flashlight, leaped off the bed, and flattened himself against the wall. It was an instinctive—and pointless—reaction, as though getting away from the bed would distance Strobe from what he had just seen in his leg. Momentarily frozen, Strobe picked up his flashlight and returned to the bed.

He hesitated, then trained the flashlight once again on his thigh. The thing that had caused Strobe to react so violently was still there. Just under his skin was the unmistakable outline of a miniature snake!

"I can't believe it," Strobe said in amazement. "They snaked me."

Had the snake been there since the dekayi village? This is what Strobe wondered as he stared at the disgusting thing lodged under his skin. In all the excitement, a tiny little bite before the snake invaded his body? Something like that could have escaped Strobe's attention.

But why? What was the thing doing there? A disturbing thought made Strobe wince in disgust. The snake was there to grow, larger and larger, eventually taking over his entire body! What a repulsive—

But no. That wasn't it, Strobe realized. *This is how they're tracking me,* he thought. *This thing is their supernatural GPS device!*

Another wave of nausea suddenly welled up in Strobe. When he doubled over in pain, Strobe knew he had to cut the thing out. The sooner, the better. Like, *right now.*

When the sick feeling had passed, Strobe grabbed his backpack. He needed his knife to perform the operation.

Shining his flashlight inside the backpack to locate

the knife, Strobe suddenly froze. Caught in the bright beam of the flashlight were several tiny black snakes, slithering over one another in an attempt to escape the bright glare.

They planted an entire nest of these things, Strobe thought feverishly. It really had been a ruse, allowing him to escape the dekayi village so they could follow him back home. Determined to undermine the dekayi's plan, Strobe slowly took out his knife, a jacket, a shirt, and his first aid travel kit from the backpack, taking care not to disturb the insidious snakes. Going into the bathroom, Strobe arranged everything he would need to cut the snake from his leg on the small counter. He sat down on the toilet seat cover and stared at the nauseating, squiggly snake contour under his skin. Then he bit his lip hard to distract himself from the pain of the knife cut and made the incision. . . .

■ ■ ■

Entering the dark, swaying connecting compartment, Strobe let the door slide shut behind him. After cutting the wriggling miniature snake neatly in half, Strobe had extracted the two pieces from under his skin and flushed them down the toilet, fighting back an impulse to throw up as he watched the "supernatural tracking device" disappear down the toilet bowl.

After stitching up his leg, Strobe had carefully inspected every pocket in his pants and shirt, several times each, before putting them on. The same thing with his jacket. Just before exiting his room, Strobe had placed his backpack in the small closet, hoping the dekayi wouldn't discover it until the train had arrived in Cleveland.

Picking one of the two doors in the connecting compartment, Strobe positioned himself in front of it. The train was traveling through a swath of forest, the outlines of the trees clearly visible against the moonlit sky. Strobe couldn't believe what he was about to do, but he didn't see any alternative. He had checked the train schedule before leaving his room. The next scheduled stop was Pittsburgh. That was too long to wait to get off the train. Besides, Strobe was concerned that his mysterious visitor might notice him slipping off the train if he exited in Pittsburgh. But here, in the middle of nowhere . . .

Strobe grabbed the handle and opened the door, bracing himself for a moment against the cold wind that whipped across his face and caused his jacket to flap loudly, like a flag.

Then, without giving it another thought, he jumped.

26

"Calanthe? We're here."

Reaching the bottom of the back steps that led to the Killer Pizza basement, Toby thought it was a good idea to give Calanthe a heads-up that he and Annabel had arrived. He didn't want to find out how Calanthe might react if they just walked in and surprised her.

Toby had contacted Annabel immediately after receiving a call from Calanthe an hour or so before. After spending the rest of Sunday and most of Monday alone in the Killer Pizza basement getting used to her post-Altering powers and abilities, Calanthe had requested a meeting with the two of them.

"In here!"

Calanthe's response had come from the exercise room. As Toby walked down the hall, he wondered what it must have been like for Calanthe, here, all alone, in the KP basement these past few days. Calanthe's situation reminded him of what some of the superheroes went through in his graphic novels, in the origin stories when they first discovered who and what they were. Never an easy transition.

When Toby and Annabel entered the exercise room, Calanthe was standing next to the punching bag. She was dressed in a Killer Pizza T-shirt. Sweatpants. No socks or shoes. She looked hyper, bursting with energy. She was sweating after what must have been an intense workout on the bag.

"We have gloves for that," Toby said.

Calanthe looked at her hands, still curled into fists. Her knuckles were bleeding. She shrugged. "I don't need them."

Toby nodded. He and Annabel stayed where they were, near the entrance to the room. Until Calanthe told them otherwise, it was probably best to keep their distance from her.

"Watch this," Calanthe said. Standing up straight, her arms immediately began to disappear into her body! Her skin turned reptilian!

"Oh, no. Okay, that's enough." Toby couldn't help but turn away from the gruesome sight.

Annabel winced, but kept watching.

Calanthe didn't do the full transformation. When her

arms were no longer visible, she caused them to grow right back out. Her scaly skin returned to normal. She smiled, looking like a child who has just mastered something very difficult, like riding a bicycle for the first time without any help from a parent.

"That's . . ." Annabel was at a loss for words.

"It was very difficult at first. And frustrating. But I discovered a trick that gave me control over it. A mental thing. I picture a whirlpool, with my human features disappearing into it."

"Whatever works," Toby said, relieved that Calanthe was back to normal.

"So it is okay. You don't need to stay so far away from me anymore."

Still, Toby and Annabel walked a bit cautiously across the room to where Calanthe was standing. As they approached, Calanthe suddenly looked uncomfortable. Annabel noticed that she was looking anywhere but right at her.

"Calanthe, what happened the other night? It's done. Over. I don't want you to even give it a second thought. I'm perfectly okay, see?" Annabel smiled and held out her hands to emphasize the point.

"You don't sound okay to me."

That much was true. Annabel still talked on the whispery side and sounded hoarse when she did. "My throat doesn't hurt anymore. It just sounds that way. But nothing's damaged. I'll be back to normal before you know it."

A frown suddenly distorted Calanthe's features. "In all that's happened these last few days, I forgot all about Strobe. How is *he* doing?"

Annabel looked over at Toby, her concerned expression asking, *Should we tell her?*

Toby thought about that, then nodded. Better that Calanthe know everything. She would eventually, anyway, so why not now?

■ ■ ■

Walking at the edge of the exercise room, Calanthe dragged her hand along the wall as she went. Her downcast expression signaled how bad she felt about what she had just heard.

In addition to the dekayi village fiasco, Annabel had also relayed to Calanthe the updated information she had received from Strobe that morning. His otherworldly tracking device. The jump from the train. His hours-long walk through the forest, which had taken most of the night, a trek that finally ended when he stumbled on a rest stop at the side of the Pennsylvania Turnpike. At that very moment, Strobe was on his way back to Ohio, courtesy of a trucker named Mustang.

Calanthe suddenly stopped her pacing and looked over at Toby and Annabel. "I'm ashamed of what my people did to Strobe. As for the others, I don't even know what to say—"

"They're not your people anymore, Calanthe," Annabel said. "We are. You're here. With us, now."

"Which is why they're coming for me," Calanthe said, her voice sounding flat, resolved to that fact.

"No, they're not," Toby said. "Didn't you hear what Annabel just told you? Strobe found out how they were following him. He took care of it."

"It doesn't matter what Strobe does. They will find me."

"How do you know that?" Toby followed his question with a short, nervous laugh.

Calanthe had a puzzled expression on her face. She looked as though she had just discovered—at that very moment—how it was she knew that her people would find her. "When I was picturing Strobe in my village, what happened to him, what happened to the others. All of a sudden, I just *knew*."

Toby was getting a really weird feeling about all this. When he glanced at Annabel, he could tell she was feeling the same way.

"It's because of the Altering," Calanthe explained. "I

feel completely different now. I feel like . . . I've grown up. I'm so much more sensitive to everything. My entire body is able to pick up sensations it wasn't able to before."

"But maybe you're wrong, about them coming after you," Annabel suggested, her whispery voice sounding a bit desperate to Toby. "I mean, everything you're feeling right now . . . it must be kind of like an *explosion* of feelings, right? It has to be hard to sort it all out. To get used to it."

Calanthe shook her head. "They will arrive here. Sometime before the Day of Days. Don't you see? The elders of my village will interpret these recent events as punishment."

"Punishment?"

"Yes. From our gods. My people have done something to upset them. This is what the elders will believe. Which means they *have* to find me now. I'm the one. The only one. They must sacrifice me, and only me, in order to win back our gods favor."

"This is totally crazy," Toby said. "You don't believe all that stuff, do you, Calanthe?"

When Calanthe didn't respond right away, it was clear that she was struggling with her answer. In that moment, Toby understood just how difficult it had been—and still was—for Calanthe to simply throw away everything she had learned in her first fourteen years. All of her customs, all of her beliefs.

Finally, Calanthe said, "No, I don't believe any of that any longer. But my people do, and that's all that matters. I can't tell you exactly when they'll be here. Or how many will come. But this much I know. . . ."

When Calanthe looked at Toby and Annabel, just before she told them what it was she knew, her dark eyes suddenly became luminous, the way they briefly were that morning in Annabel's room on her first day of school.

Seeing this, Toby felt a chill run right down his spine. He had always felt a strange kind of power emanating from Calanthe, right from the first time he had laid eyes on her. But now the power was more than just palpable. It was *there*, in full sight, in the luminous glow of her eyes. And Toby knew Calanthe was telling the truth when she said . . .

"They are definitely coming for me, and there is nothing we can do to stop them."

PART THREE:
THE STAND

1

"I swear . . . this time . . . I've really, *really* had it . . ."

Marching up the cracked walkway to the front door of
the dilapidated house, Mrs. Riley mumbled angrily to herself as she went. She lived right next door to the house
that had long been dubbed "haunted" by the kids of the
neighborhood. For well over twenty years, generations of
children had delighted in telling gruesome stories to one
another about what the mean old man who lived there—
rarely seen—had done to the unfortunate kids who had
strayed onto his property.

Ironically, with Halloween just days away, the haunted
house was the only one on the street that wasn't decorated for the holiday. But the local kids wouldn't want
it any other way. The creepy place—with its overgrown
trees and bushes and half-attached outdoor shutters hanging askew and the always curtained windows—was perfect just as it was.

Mrs. Riley wasn't thinking about the haunted house stuff as she knocked firmly on the door. (She knew from past visits the doorbell didn't work.) It was the incessant barking of the man's two dogs that was driving her crazy. She hated that the man kept the poor things outside all the time. Even in the winter! Who on earth would do such a thing, especially to such little dogs? Why have pets if you never allowed them inside, anyway? So, yes, Mrs. Riley definitely felt sorry for the dogs, but still . . . somehow or other, their barking had to stop.

Mrs. Riley suddenly stopped pounding on the door. The old man hadn't answered, no surprise, but that wasn't the thing that had provoked her to stop knocking. It was the sound of the dogs, *inside* the house. They would be outside for a few moments, then inside. Outside, inside. Going absolutely crazy with their barking, even more so than usual.

Mrs. Riley had never heard the dogs inside, so that was definitely odd. She peeked through a cracked window in the front door, couldn't see anything except a deserted hall and a stairway to the right. The place really did have a haunted look, what with the visible layers of dust in the hallway and on the stairway bannister and the overall feeling of . . . well, the place truly was spooky. And so was the old man who lived inside.

Just the same, Mrs. Riley stepped off the small square

concrete porch and walked around to the side yard. She needed to have it out with Mr. Stull. This couldn't wait any longer. When she arrived at the gate at the back of the house, she tried the latch . . . and the gate swung open.

Mrs. Riley paused. Should she really go back there? What about the dogs? They might attack her. But Mrs. Riley didn't think so. She was a dog person herself and knew the adage about a dog's bark being worse than its bite was true, more often than not.

So Mrs. Riley took a confident step into the overgrown and cluttered backyard. Immediately, two ugly little mutts popped through a hole in the glass sliding door at the back of the house. They charged at Mrs. Riley, barking shrilly, but stopped before they reached her. Mrs. Riley had the feeling they were trying to tell her something, not scare her away. When she looked over at the sliding door, Mrs. Riley gasped. Someone had smashed a huge hole in the glass door!

The atmosphere in the backyard suddenly felt charged to Mrs. Riley. Dangerous. She felt the hair at the back of her neck stand on end.

"Mister Stull?" she called out, loud and clear.

No answer.

Call the police. Now. Tell them about the break-in. Mrs. Riley knew that's what she should do, but instead . . . she took a step toward the door. Then another one.

Yes, just go back home and call the police. That's what any sane person would do.

But before she knew it, Mrs. Riley was stepping through the large jagged hole in the sliding glass door, pushing aside the dirty curtains as she went, and . . .

She was inside the house.

What on earth do you think you're doing?! Mrs. Riley felt scared and thrilled at the same time. She squinted to try to see better in the dark room. It looked like a den of some sort, with way too much furniture, randomly placed around the room. Sitting on a stand was a very old-fashioned television that looked like it was from the 1970s. The TV was on, playing a game show.

Very, very creepy. As though sensing that something was very wrong inside the house, the dogs had stayed outside. Barking.

"Mister Stull?"

Still no response. Mrs. Riley focused on a plaid stuffed lounge chair on the other side of the room. The chair was facing away from her and toward the TV. An arm was draped over the side of the chair.

Mrs. Riley's heart was really racing now. She knew she had gone far enough. She should get out, right now. But there was that part of her, the "I shouldn't open the door, but I have to open the door!" part that caused her to slowly circle around the chair, kicking aside bits of glass from the shattered sliding door as she went.

Getting closer to the chair, Mrs. Riley noticed a silver-dollar-size hole in the back of it, near the top, with some stuffing popping out. After a few more steps, Mrs. Riley stopped when she had reached a spot where she could see Mr. Stull.

"What on earth!"

Mrs. Riley felt her breath catch. The figure sitting stiffly in the chair looked like a *mummy*, one that was wearing clothes instead of wrappings. The skin looked like parchment paper. This person, this thing, couldn't possibly be Mr. Stull. He was old, but he wasn't *that* old!

Mrs. Riley had a sudden thought that this must be a prank of some sort, something cooked up by the kids in the neighborhood. Taking another step, she put herself between the TV and the stuffed chair. From her new angle, with the flickering blue light of the television behind her, she was now able to clearly see the figure's ghastly face.

And Mrs. Riley knew this was no Halloween prank. The decrepit figure in the chair was definitely Mr. Stull, the distinctive, massive black mole on his forehead being a dead giveaway. But the horrifying thing about the obviously dead man was . . . he had no eyes!

There was a split second for this to register with Mrs. Riley, then she threw her hands up in front of her face, stumbled backward and . . .

"EEEEEEEYYYYYYYYYIIIIIIAAAAAAAAAA!!!"

■ ■ ■

Energized from its detour to the small town of Beaver Falls, Pennsylvania, north of Pittsburgh, the rukh smashed through the dark woods in a kind of gleeful, demented rage. As with its trip to the Central Park Zoo, the creature had just left something more in its wake than its distinctive scent, a scent that spooked any animal it crossed paths with. It had left an urban legend-size mystery.

Yes, the kids on Mrs. Riley's street would now have fresh fuel for their haunted-house stories. A new, amped-up version. Mr. Stull, the mummified, ghostly avenger!

The creature had been making steady progress since it began its tristate journey, charging nightly through the heavily forested Pennsylvania landscape, slowly but surely zeroing in on its prey. Unfortunately for Calanthe, the hideous demon was showing no aftereffects from its fall from the New York rooftop. Matter of fact, it looked stronger—and deadlier—than ever. Mr. Stull could certainly attest to that.

If the mean old man in the haunted house were still alive, that is.

2

Strobe winced as he got out of bed. He was still sore in places he'd never felt sore before. Going into the bathroom, he checked himself out in the mirror. Black-and-blue marks all over his body, numerous cuts and scrapes, the result of his wild-and-tumble ride down the gravel incline and into the woods after he had jumped from the train. At least no bones were broken. It was just a matter of bandaging up the cuts, taking an Advil or two, and Strobe figured he'd be good to go.

Where Strobe was going was to the basement of Killer Pizza. He had arrived in Hidden Hills earlier in the day, had gone home after he was sure his mother was off to work, and slept away most of the day while Toby and Annabel were at school. The plan was to meet to figure out how to deal with the impending arrival of the dekayi. When Strobe had heard from Annabel about Calanthe's new powers, and her declaration that her people were definitely coming for her, he was less certain that he had given the dekayi the slip.

The meeting was happening in an hour or so, so Strobe applied some ointment to his cuts, put on the bandages, and went gingerly to look for the Advil.

■ ■ ■

Unfortunately, over at Annabel's house, something was underway that threatened not only to derail the group's important meeting, but also lift the mask of Calanthe's identity disguise. Annabel was sitting on the living room sofa. Her father, too angry to sit still, paced back and forth on the carpet. Mrs. Oshiro was perched on an ornate stuffed chair opposite Annabel.

"You're hiding something from us," Mr. Oshiro said as he passed in front of his daughter. "We know this, and we want to know what it is."

Annabel was doing her best to look composed and unconcerned, even though she was anything but. Calanthe had not returned to the Oshiro household for several days now—and Annabel was desperately trying to figure how to explain why she wasn't around.

Annabel had told her parents that Calanthe was staying at a newfound friend's house while she recuperated in the Killer Pizza basement. That was over the weekend, however, and it was now Tuesday and her parents weren't buying that Calanthe was still with this new phantom friend of hers.

That wasn't the only thing that was making Mr. and Mrs. Oshiro suspicious of their daughter and their foreign-exchange-student houseguest. Try as she might, Annabel hadn't been able to submerge her concern about what had occurred over the past few days, and her parents had picked up on her anxiety. They knew something was off with her. And they wanted to know what it was, having surprised her when she had come home from school.

"Well, you see . . ." Annabel hesitated, not having a clue how to finish her sentence. She was in the midst of a real crisis, and she had no idea how to get out of it.

"Hello, Mr. and Mrs. Oshiro."

Jolted by the sound of Calanthe's voice, everyone turned toward the entrance to the living room. Calanthe stood in the archway, an innocent smile on her face. She was dressed in the outfit Annabel had taken over to the KP basement the day before.

"Calanthe," Mrs. Oshiro said, surprised by her sudden appearance. Mr. Oshiro's eyes narrowed suspiciously. He didn't trust this young woman.

Calanthe didn't appear intimidated by Mr. Oshiro's scrutiny as she walked across the room and sat next to

Annabel. "I have a feeling that you're discussing where I've been."

That's exactly what we're doing! Annabel thought, more concerned than relieved that Calanthe had returned to the Oshiro household. After all, what was Calanthe going to say about where she'd been?

"I have a confession to make. Annabel has not been telling you the truth about this particular topic."

What?! Annabel tried to not appear blindsided at Calanthe's statement.

"It's not her fault. I insisted that she not tell you the truth. I didn't want you to worry about me, or burden you in any way."

Annabel nodded slowly, as though she knew what Calanthe was talking about.

"I have been in the hospital. I had a diabetic attack."

This is getting more interesting all the time, Annabel thought.

"Calanthe, of course we should have known that." Mrs. Oshiro looked profoundly concerned about her houseguest's revelation. Mr. Oshiro still looked suspicious.

"It's all under control now. I'm feeling much better. My parents have been informed, everything's been taken care of. They paid the bill, dealt with all of that." Calanthe nodded at Annabel's parents, a soldiering-on expression on her face. "I do apologize for this, however. But as I said, I didn't want to worry you. You have both been so gracious to me. And you're both very busy, I know, so I didn't want to trouble you with this."

Annabel was amazed at Calanthe's story. Where had she come up with it? Whatever the answer, Calanthe had pulled off the neat trick of completely silencing her parents. Even her Dad wasn't sure what to say.

Calanthe suddenly stood up. "I'm sorry, but if you'll excuse me. I do still feel a bit weak."

"By all means, Calanthe." Mrs. Oshiro stood and indicated the foyer, and the stairway beyond. "Is there anything we can get for you?"

"No, thank you. I just need some rest."

And with that, Calanthe exited the room and went up the stairs to her bedroom. Annabel looked contritely at her parents. "I'm sorry, Mom and Dad. I know I shouldn't have lied to you about this."

"No, you shouldn't have." Mr. Oshiro was stern in his reply, but his tone wasn't as harsh as it had been, before Calanthe's appearance.

"Is it okay if I go make sure Calanthe has everything she needs? I know she wouldn't tell you, even if she did need anything. She's been so insistent to not burden you with any of this."

A look between Mr. and Mrs. Oshiro, then Annabel's

dad gave her a grudging nod. Annabel tried not to look too relieved. She was almost out of the room when Mr. Oshiro said, "No more lying, though, Annabel, understand? I won't have that."

When Annabel turned toward her parents, one hand was behind her back, fingers crossed. "I promise. No more lying."

■ ■ ■

Calanthe had gone to the Hidden Hills Library to do research for her make-believe story about her illness. This is what Annabel discovered right after going upstairs to Calanthe's bedroom.

"I was so amazed, Annabel, what I found there. Why didn't you tell me about this place? It was like . . . the entire world within four walls, for anyone to discover!"

Annabel smiled at Calanthe's childlike enthusiasm over her discovery of the local library. "I guess you didn't have a library in your village, huh?"

"That is what you would call an understatement, yes? No, we didn't have a library. The elders wanted our world to be as *small* as possible. But here . . . all those books! I think I like them even more than your computers. Holding them, looking through them, the smell of them. It was wonderful."

"I'm really proud of you, Calanthe. You just . . . went

and did this. What gave you the idea to go to the library, anyway?"

"It was my bedroom in the Killer Pizza basement. Surrounded by all the books there. But they were only about one thing. Monsters. So when I sensed your concern about how long I was staying away from your house, I knew I needed to go somewhere else to get some ideas for my make-believe story."

"And you came up with the perfect one. Just in time, too. My parents were about to bust me good."

"Yes, I knew that."

Annabel looked at Calanthe. Could she really sense all these things?

"Anyway, it's good that's out of the way. Now we can go to Killer Pizza for our meeting."

"Let's wait until my parents have left. They have some kind of business dinner tonight, so it shouldn't be too long."

Calanthe had gotten up from her bed and was walking slowly around the room.

"I'm really happy you're feeling better, Calanthe. You look great. You really do."

Calanthe smiled, but something in her expression signaled that she hadn't really heard what Annabel just said. Her mind was obviously somewhere else. "I wasn't gone for long, Annabel, but I really missed being here. This is like home to me now."

Annabel felt a warm glow, hearing Calanthe say that.

"Which is why I will do anything to stay here. Let them come for me. That's what I say. They will feel my wrath if they do."

The archaic term for "violent rage and fury" sounded just right, somehow, coming from Calanthe. But as much as Annabel loved that Calanthe was embracing Hidden Hills as her new home, she had deep concerns that the girl's "wrath" wasn't going to be enough to deal with the forces that Calanthe claimed were closing in on their sub-urban community.

Which meant they had to come up with something more than that. Much more, and fast.

3

Calanthe wanted to speak first at the meeting, so an hour later, when everyone had gathered in the KP classroom, she had the floor.

"First, I would like to say to you, Strobe, that I am very sorry for what happened to you, and the others, at my village."

"We knew the dangers."

"Just the same . . . I wanted you to know how sorry I am."

Strobe nodded.

Calanthe took a moment before moving on to her other topic. It appeared to the trio that she was . . . praying? Everyone looked at one another. They'd never seen Calanthe do this before. After a moment of silence, Calanthe's solemn expression was replaced by a more animated one.

"The next thing I wanted to say was . . . I discovered something important today when I was at the library, besides my make-believe illness." Calanthe pulled some sheets of paper from her pocket. "The best that I can figure, from studying calendars and maps of the sky, and reading some historical books, is that the Day of Days will be occurring tomorrow night."

"Halloween," Toby said. "Perfect."

"It is perfect," Calanthe replied, a serious look on her face. "Considering the origins of this holiday you call Halloween. Listen to this . . ." Looking down at her paper, Calanthe started to read.

"Halloween's origins date back to an ancient Celtic festival that marked the end of summer and the beginning of the dark, cold winter, a time of year often associated with human death. The Celts believed that on the night of the festival, the boundary between the worlds of the living and dead became blurred."

Calanthe looked up from her notes to emphasize the importance of what she was reading. "It was on this night that the ghosts of the dead were able to return to earth, to cause trouble and damage crops. The Celts believed that the presence of these ghosts made it easier for the Celtic priests to make prophecies about the future. For a people entirely dependent on the volatile natural world, these prophecies were an important source of comfort and direction during the long, dark winter."

Calanthe paused. She looked like she was getting to

the good part. "To commemorate this yearly festival, known as Samhain, the Celtic priests built huge sacred bonfires, where the people gathered to burn crops and animals as sacrifices to the Celtic deities."

Calanthe looked at everyone, her dark eyes flashing with excitement.

"Is that all they sacrificed?" Toby asked warily. "Animals?"

"That's what it said in the book. It was amazing to me, reading this, how much the Celts were like my people. The Celtic priests. Our village elders. The festival, celebrated at the same time of year. The crops, of supreme importance in both of our worlds. And the sacrifices, of course."

"Yours . . . much more intense," Toby observed.

"But think about this. The Celts . . ." Calanthe checked her notes. "They lived over two thousand years ago. My people live now, in the modern world." Calanthe shook her head in amazement at this.

"History lesson aside," Strobe said, "The bottom line is you're pretty sure the Day of Days is tomorrow."

Calanthe gave Strobe a nod.

"I don't believe my people will arrive, during the day, however. Even if they did, it is likely they will wait for the cover of darkness to come for me."

"Okay, so check it out." Strobe got up gingerly from his chair. Annabel watched with concern.

As he walked slowly around the room. Strobe had obviously taken a beating on his trip to Canada. The fact that he was even up and about was a testament to his strength and stamina. And craziness. "I thought for sure I'd given the dekayi the slip, but clearly Calanthe doesn't think I did. If a battle is going down sometime tomorrow night, we need to pick the place for it."

"What do you mean?" Toby asked.

"When we fought the alpha dude? We were scrambling, man, running for our lives. I don't want to do that again, if we can help it. So what I'm saying is we pick out a place, somewhere nearby, but isolated. When the dekayi arrive, we lure them to this place, which we've rigged with, you know, various deadly devices. This way we do battle on our own turf. That should give us an advantage, at least for starters."

"I like it," Toby said.

"I do, too." Annabel had a pensive look on her face. "And I think I might know a place. I heard my dad talking the other day about an abandoned steel mill over on Blake Street. He's going in with a group of business associates to put together an offer to buy the land."

"Blake Street . . ." Strobe frowned, trying to picture it. "That's not too far away, right? What's it like around there?"

"Everything's overgrown. The steel mill, ware-houses . . . they're just rusting away."

"There are houses, though, and a few stores right down the road from the place," Toby pointed out.

"Yeah, there are."

"That could be a problem. In which case, I have a backup." Toby went to the front of the classroom, picked up a piece of chalk, and wrote "Shock Corridor" on the blackboard.

Strobe leaned up against the wall and gave Toby a "go on" look.

"That was the name of our local haunted house at-traction, the kind you have to pay to get in? It was in an old building that used to be a hospital. *You can check in—*"

"*But you can't check out!*" Annabel said with a grin, finishing the Shock Corridor tagline for Toby.

"You went, too, Annabel?"

"Of course. The Deadly Doctor?"

"The Ambulance to Hell?"

Toby and Annabel laughed.

"Okay, that's enough, you two."

"Point being, this could be just what we're looking for. It's a brick building. Two stories."

"It is a bit out there, though," Annabel said.

"It's farther than the steel mill, yeah, but if we're after something more isolated—"

"I don't understand what you're talking about," Calanthe interrupted. "What are these . . . attractions?"

"They're fun places to go on Halloween," Toby explained. "The people that put on the attraction hire a bunch of people, make them up to look like zombies, vampires, characters in popular horror movies. Then they put together these really creepy rooms and places that you have to go through? To get to the end of the attraction? The whole idea is to scare everyone who comes to the place out of their wits."

"And you have to pay money for this?" Calanthe asked.

Annabel laughed. "Sounds even stranger than people getting dressed up in costumes and going trick-or-treating around the neighborhood, huh."

"It's confusing more than anything. You said these are fun places to go on Halloween. Why would anyone want to be scared like that? What is the point?"

"You know what?" Strobe said. "I'm sure there are many interesting psychological answers to that question, but now's not the time to get into it. Tobe, you said this attraction *was* in the old hospital. As in, no longer?"

"Right. Some people started a newer, bigger one over in Moon Township a few years back. Put Shock Corridor right out of business. Easy to see why. Maniac Maze is *awesome*, let me tell you. If we weren't doing this tomorrow, I'd definitely be there." Toby frowned. Had he actually just said that?

"An old hospital." Strobe thought about that. "Sounds pretty good, actually. Lots of interesting spaces."

"You bet," Toby said. "Hospital rooms. A cafeteria. Basement tunnels. A boiler room."

"You want to go there just 'cause it used to be a Halloween attraction."

"There's that, too."

"I have to say, a theme is definitely developing here."

"Theme?" Calanthe asked.

"Yeah, something that . . . ties everything together. In this case? No matter where we turn, no matter where we look, there it is."

Calanthe frowned. She didn't know what Strobe was talking about.

"Halloween, baby. Halloween."

4

"This feels..."

Toby and Annabel looked at Calanthe, wondering how the former hospital felt to her. To them it felt dank and creepy. Smashed-out windows at the opposite ends of the corridor and a partially caved-in roof let in enough light to illuminate the decrepit hallway, which ran the length of what had been a patient wing. When day turned to night, however, the place would be pitch-black. So if it felt creepy now . . .

"Like a very good place," Calanthe concluded. "To make what Strobe called 'Our Stand.'"

Just then Strobe came up from a nearby stairwell. "You were totally right about this place, Tobe. It's perfect. And the basement?" Strobe indicated where he'd just been with a thumbs-up. "Might be the best place of all. Plenty of corridors and cul-de-sacs to booby-trap."

Not for the first time, Toby was amazed at how much

Strobe seemed to relish an impending fight with anything that could be labeled "monster." Even his horrendous trip to Calanthe's village hadn't seemed to dampen his enthusiasm.

"Calanthe happens to agree with you, Strobe," Annabel said.

"Yeah?"

Calanthe gave Strobe a nod.

"So that makes four of us?"

Nods all around.

"Time to get our hands dirty, then."

■ ■ ■

Standing on a stepladder in a dark tunnel, Strobe twisted the rest of a line of wire around an overhead pipe, then tied an extra knot in the wire to make certain it was secure. The wire drooped from the pipe to the concrete floor and off into the darkness of the tunnel.

"Okay. Pull it tight!"

It took a few moments, but then the wire rose toward the ceiling as someone pulled from the opposite end of the passageway.

"Looks good!" Strobe yelled as he jumped from the stepladder to the floor. It was Toby he met halfway down the tunnel, both of them using their high-powered flashlights to see where they were going.

After working nonstop on three booby traps for more than four hours, the two were drenched in sweat. They'd sent Annabel and Calanthe home a short while before. Even though there were just the two of them, they were determined to do as much work on the traps as possible before calling it a night.

Fact was, this was fun for Strobe and Toby. Constructing elaborate, deadly snares for their enemy in a creepy, old deserted hospital? It was like a video game, for real.

Calanthe had been fascinated by the work. The planning of the traps, what they were for, the construction of them. She'd been a great help, too, especially with some of the heavy lifting, seeing as she was even stronger physically now than when the trio had first met her, thanks to the Altering.

But when Strobe had suggested that he take her and Annabel back to the Oshiro residence in the truck he'd borrowed from a nameless, shady-sounding "contact," Annabel had instantly taken him up on his offer. She didn't think it was a good idea for her and Calanthe to stay out too late. The last thing she wanted was to make her parents even more suspicious than they already were. Which meant that Annabel and Calanthe were going to school in the morning. It had been decided that it was important for the two girls to continue to pretend that all was well in Hidden Hills-land. At least until all hell broke loose.

"Excellent work, man," Strobe said as he and Toby leaned up against the wall, then slid down into a sitting position on the cool concrete floor.

"Yeah, we're doin' okay. I wish we were going a little faster, but better to have a few less traps that we're positive actually work than throwing up a bunch more and crossing our fingers."

"Agreed." Strobe held out a clenched fist. Toby tapped it with his own clenched fist, then pulled a couple of sodas from a padded cooler he was carrying with him, gave one to Strobe, and kept one for himself. The two popped open their cans and took long, thirsty gulps.

"I can't believe how good you are at planning and putting these traps together," Strobe said. "This is some pretty elaborate stuff we're building here."

"Yeah, well, I've had practice."

"You have?"

"In miniature. I used to build these really intricate mazes in my bedroom when I was a kid. This was during my *Star Wars* phase. It was always the same setup. Luke and Leia being chased by the rancor, the Gorax, the krayt dragon. I built the traps in the mazes. Or rather, Luke and Leia built them. Guess who won, every time?"

"Wow, you really were a geek, weren't you?"

"Always and forever."

"At least all that playtime is paying off."

"Yeah. Who knew?" After a couple of monster-size carbonated burps, Toby leaned his head up against the wall and closed his eyes. "I'm thinking I should head home around midnight. Get scolded, maybe grounded for being out too late on a school night. Then I'm up bright and early, get ready for school, and I'll come here instead for some more trap making."

"Sounds like a plan."

"How 'bout you? Calling it quits when you take me home tonight?"

"Nope. Stayin' here."

"Really?"

"Yeah, my mom's not expecting me back until the weekend. No sense going home till then. So this place is gonna be my hotel for the night."

"Lovely."

Toby and Strobe fell silent as they drank their sodas and chomped on a bag of chips Toby had pulled out of his backpack.

"So . . ."

Strobe glanced over at Toby, who was staring at his soda can as if there was something wrong with it. "So . . . what?"

Toby looked hesitant to follow up his one-syllable conversation starter. "It was pretty bad up there, huh?"

Strobe looked like he didn't want to deal with Toby's

question. He'd already gone over all that with Annabel when they talked on the phone, and she had relayed everything to Toby and Calanthe. But then Strobe exhaled a small sigh and nodded, a rare display of vulnerability for the guy.

"Yeah, it was bad."

"I'm really glad you made it out of there, man."

"Well, I would hope so."

A slight smile from Toby, then he was serious again. "So what do you think? Are the other MCOs dead?" The way Toby asked the question, it sounded like he wasn't sure if he wanted to know the answer.

"I don't know. Last I heard from Harvey, the troops he sent up there reported that the village is totally deserted. No sign of Holt, Dixon, or Harris."

"Everyone just cleared out?"

"Yeah. A hundred, hundred-fifty people, gone. No tracks. The best Harvey can figure, they went underground."

"Maybe Calanthe . . ." Toby stopped, didn't finish his thought.

"That's what Harvey's thinking. Once we get done with whatever we have to deal with here, maybe Calanthe can help locate her former clan. But first things first, right?"

Strobe finished off his soda, grabbed one last handful

of chips, and hopped up with an ease that suggested he was feeling better, physically. "Did you see that room around the corner? With the padlock on it?"

Toby shook his head no.

"Well, the suspense is killing me."

Strobe walked back down the tunnel to where he had left the ladder. A large canvas sack resembling a baseball equipment bag was propped up against the wall. Strobe rummaged around inside the bag and pulled out a heavy-duty industrial-size metal cutter. The cutter, along with some of the other tools the group had been using to construct the traps, had been supplied by Strobe's mysterious contact. Between the contact Strobe wouldn't say who the guy was, which concerned Toby and Annabel—KP headquarters, and the local dump, they had managed to find just about everything they'd needed for their booby-trapping work.

"This should do the trick, don't you think?" Strobe said, holding up the cutter.

Toby followed Strobe down the tunnel and around the corner. At the end of a cul-de-sac was the door with the padlock. It took Strobe a couple of tries to cut through the lock, but he finally did it, the sweat dripping from his face from the strain of the effort and the airless, musty atmosphere of the tunnel.

"Okay, let's see what we got," Strobe said, tossing the cutter to the concrete floor.

"Probably just a bunch of old hospital equipment."

"Which we might be able to use, dude."

When Strobe pulled the heavy door open, the creaking of the rusty hinges sounded exactly like a haunted house door. Toby and Strobe looked at each other and smiled. The squeaking door was perfect, an apt punctuation point to four hours of working in Shock Corridor. But it turned out to be just a warm-up for what was inside the room.

When Strobe and Toby scanned the dark area with their flashlights, they laughed at what they saw. The group that had staged the yearly Halloween attraction had left behind some of their props and mannequins.

"I can't believe they didn't take this."

"Me neither." Strobe moved farther into the room, examining the contents. "Then again, this stuff is total crap."

Taking a different path around the room than Strobe, Toby saw that Strobe was right. The Dracula, Frankenstein, and zombie mannequins had seen much better days. Or Halloweens. So had the assortment of grave markers, skeletons, and felt-stuffed bats.

"I'll tell you one thing, though. All this is pretty irresistible, don't you think?"

Strobe nodded as he shone his flashlight around the room. "We just might be able to find a place for it."

Toby and Strobe looked at each other, then smacked a high five. They might very well be facing a life-and-death situation within the next twenty-four hours, but that didn't mean they couldn't have a little fun in the meantime.

5

At midnight, Strobe took Toby home, then returned to the hospital.

At two in the morning, Strobe was still up, working on one of the traps in the hospital's former cafeteria. He had already set off the thing numerous times. Just the same, Strobe felt compelled to trigger the trap one more time. After the hair-raising misfire of his crossbow up in the dekayi village, Strobe was determined there would be no misfires in this battle.

After a final run-through on the cafeteria trap, Strobe finally dragged himself down to the basement to catch a few hours of sleep. He would have liked to have started right in on the next monster snare, but knew he needed to shut down his brain, at least for a little while. So Strobe set his watch for five A.M. and lay down on the concrete floor, using his backpack for a pillow.

Strobe didn't mind the harsh conditions of his sleeping

quarters. After his wildly dangerous and over-the-top misadventures on the road, he was home. That's all that really mattered right now. And Strobe couldn't deny how good it felt, being reunited with his team.

Strobe had sensed that Toby and Annabel felt the same way when they met earlier in the evening, in KP's underground training center. Nobody had said anything about what they were feeling. They didn't really need to. It was just there, the comfortable vibes bouncing back and forth between them when they had entered the classroom and taken their seats.

So as Strobe drifted off to sleep, that's what he was thinking about. Not the impending battle with the dekayi. Not the next trap he was going to construct. But how good it felt to be back in a place that he was more and more beginning to think of as a home.

Which made Strobe suddenly think of Calanthe. For the first time in her life, that's what she must be feeling. That she was in a place she could actually call home. That she had friends.

That she wasn't an orphan, any longer.

■ ■ ■

Toby was wide awake. He had tried to get to sleep earlier, but there was too much on his mind. So he had gotten out his *Monsters of the World* textbook, which he was now scanning with his flashlight. He was looking for anything that might be helpful in the upcoming "Monster Mash-up" with the dekayi. Tomorrow night. Halloween night. Definitely a different kind of trick or treat.

Thumbing through the "Attacks and Counterattacks" section, Toby discovered that he knew most of this stuff already. Still, it was good to brush up on the key points presented in pages 103 to 157. It was like studying for a test. Only this test promised to be a little more intense than the classroom kind. Toby wouldn't be getting a grade for it, either, of course. This was the pass-or-fail kind.

Pass . . . you live.

Fail . . . you die.

Now that was a test worth studying for.

■ ■ ■

At the Oshiro household, all lights were out, including Annabel's bed table lamp. Like Toby, Annabel initially had trouble falling asleep. But sleep had finally come for her.

Just down the hall from Annabel, Calanthe was sitting in a chair by her bedroom window, staring outside. Calanthe knew there would be no sleep for her tonight. Ever since the Altering, she'd been so pumped up that she didn't know what to do with all the energy.

For now, she was putting it into worrying. Not the most constructive way to use her newfound zest, but

Calanthe couldn't help it. Strobe had been right, when he thought about what Calanthe must be feeling about her new home in Hidden Hills. Since her arrival in the suburban community, only a few weeks before, Calanthe had come to treasure so much. And now she was afraid of losing it.

Staring outside, Calanthe watched the wind whipping through the trees. She was seeing the trees, their silhouettes dancing in the dark, but not really seeing them. They were just background to what Calanthe was actually doing, which was picturing everything she had experienced so far in her new world. Going through the moments, over and over, like a visual mantra.

Calanthe wanted to imprint her Hidden Hills memories in her mind. That way, if the impending Day of Days was her *last* day, she would be able take everything with her. Her strange new customs. The vivid intensity of Triple H. The slang. And Annabel, Toby, and Strobe, of course. The memory of them Calanthe would hold closest.

What Calanthe didn't realize—as she sat in her chair, going through all this in her mind—was that she really wasn't all that different from a typical teenager. The way she was feeling right now her fears, her longing to belong, the *intensity* of her feelings—made her very much like the young people she had felt so distanced from just a week earlier.

Please let me survive tomorrow night! Calanthe suddenly thought.

Outside, the trees continued to sway back and forth in the night wind. Something suddenly flew past the window. A nearby streetlamp blinked a couple of times, then went out.

And that's when Calanthe felt it.

6

"Annabel . . . *Annabel*!"

Annabel woke with a start. She blinked as she looked around her room. The digital clock read 3:35. Calanthe was standing over her, hand still on her arm where she had shaken her awake.

"Calanthe?" Annabel replied groggily.

"They're here!" Calanthe whispered.

Annabel immediately threw off her covers, jumped out of bed, and started for her closet. She stopped before getting there and looked back at Calanthe. "Wait . . . what?"

"They're here. They have arrived!"

"But you said . . ."

"I know. I misjudged when they would come for me."

Annabel didn't ask any more questions about Calanthe's miscalculation on the dekayi's arrival time in Hidden Hills. There wasn't any time. Fortunately, the two had already gone over what they would do when the dekayi arrived. So they were able to snap into concentrated action as soon as Annabel had called Strobe to tell him to come get them.

They dressed quickly in their black jeans, T-shirts, and black hooded sweatshirts—their official "battle attire"—then tiptoed down the stairs to the first floor. After making their way silently to the kitchen, they snuck out the back door, then waited in the shadows of the side yard for Strobe to arrive.

■ ■ ■

As soon as Annabel and Calanthe hopped into the backseat of the battered Ford pickup Strobe had borrowed from his unknown contact, Strobe gunned it down the quiet street. He had picked up Toby before heading over to the Oshiro house.

"Take it easy, Strobe," Annabel urged. "You don't want to wake up the entire neighborhood."

"The sooner we get back to Shock Corridor, the better. Do you know where they are, Calanthe? Can you pick that up with your super-antennae?"

"No."

"We won't even get to the hospital if you're pulled over by the police," Annabel pointed out. "A fifteen year old? Driving without a license?"

"Hey, you gotta do what you gotta do sometimes to defeat the forces of evil," Strobe countered. But he did let up a bit on the gas pedal. "So, you were a tad off on when these dudes were gonna show up, huh, Calanthe?"

"Yes, I'm sorry about that." Calanthe sounded genuinely contrite.

"Actually, you weren't really off," Toby said. "You said they were coming on Halloween. And that they'd come at night. Well, Halloween began at midnight, and it's definitely night out there. We just assumed it would be the night part of Halloween when everyone was out trick-or-treating and partying and getting into trouble."

"Good point," Annabel said.

Twenty minutes later, Strobe turned off Streets Run and gunned it up a steep two-lane road that was boxed in on both sides by tall, bare-limbed trees. They hadn't gone very far when, from the backseat, Calanthe suddenly said . . .

"They're here."

Everyone looked at Calanthe. She was staring intently through the front windshield, her body tense.

"Where?" Strobe asked.

"Nearby."

"How nearby?"

"Close enough so that it will be a race to the hospital."

Strobe was no longer easing up on the pedal. "Okay, listen up, everyone. As soon as we get there, immediately head to your positions. Calanthe, you to the basement—"

"I do not wish to go to the basement," Calanthe interrupted. "I want to be with all of you, fighting with you. This is what I have decided."

"No, Calanthe," Annabel said. "Toby and Strobe and I have a little experience with this type of thing. The fighting, I mean. You don't. Above all else, we want to protect you. Not put you in more danger."

"I fought the rukh in the lake," Calanthe reminded everyone.

"Yeah, and you were in a coma for more than a week after that," Strobe pointed out. "The best way you can help us is by going to the basement. That way they'll have to pass the traps we've set in order to get to you. See?"

Calanthe nodded, reluctantly.

Everyone's eyes were now on the woods surrounding the car, watching for any movement.

"One last thing before we get to the hospital," Annabel said. "I did some research on snakes."

"Research on snakes," Strobe said with a frown.

"I thought it might be useful. Seeing as we have no idea what the dekayi's weaknesses are."

"What'd you find out?" Toby asked. "Better make it snappy."

"We're assuming we have to hit a dekayi's heart in order to kill it, right?"

"Right," Strobe agreed.

"Okay, well, a snake's heart is located just before the bronchi, which is about a sixth of the way down their body from the head."

"That barely gives us even a general idea where it is," Strobe said.

"Well, it's something, anyway. But get this. A snake's heart is able to move around."

"Move around?" Toby replied.

"Yes. Snakes don't have a diaphragm, which is why their heart is able to do that. That doesn't mean the dekayi have the same capability. But I'm thinking they might. Which means we're either going to have to get lucky or find another way to stop them other than a direct hit to the heart."

"Good thing we have the traps," Toby said.

"Just remember the dekayi can paralyze you with their black, jelly-like spit," Strobe said. "I know we've prepared for that, but always beware of that neat little trick."

Just then Strobe drove over a rise in the road, and the hulking silhouette of the abandoned hospital came into view. The group reflexively sat up straighter in their seats and stared at the forlorn-looking two-story structure, which was completely surrounded by a high chain-link fence.

Overhead, an almost full moon was playing peek-a-boo with the dark clouds that scudded across a black sky. Glancing up at the moon, Toby didn't think he would have been surprised if a witch had suddenly appeared from behind one of the clouds and streaked across the heavens on her broomstick. The night definitely had that kind of black-magic feel to it.

Strobe was really pushing the old Ford at this point. Its engine whined in protest as the chain-link fence loomed closer and closer. Suddenly . . .

BAMMMMM!!!

Startled screams. Screeching tires. Strobe yanked on the steering wheel in an attempt to get the spinning truck under control. The truck did a spectacular 360, threatened to tip over, then skidded to a stop at the side of the road.

"What was *that*?" Strobe asked, scanning the area to see what they had just collided with.

"The rukh," Calanthe said.

Dazed from the impact, Toby was holding the side of his head, where it had slammed up against the window.

He squinted to see through the rear window. Sure enough, there were the creature's huge footprints, smashing heavily into view in the dirt at the side of the road and coming right for them.

"Go, Strobe!" Annabel yelled.

Strobe was already flooring it. There was a high-pitched whine from under the truck. The tires, struggling to get traction. When they did, the truck leaped forward.

There was no time to stop and open the gate. So Strobe barreled right into it and blasted it off its hinges. Flying upward, the bottom metal tubing of the gate was snagged by the front grill of the truck.

CRASSSHHHHH!!!

Swinging heavily down onto the hood, the gate smashed into the windshield, cracking it. Strobe now had a distorted broken-glass/chain-link view of the hospital as he sped toward it over the uneven road.

"We lose it?" Strobe shouted, trying to be heard over the loud clattering of the gate as it bounced up and down on the hood.

"Can't tell!" Annabel called back.

"Just go, man!" Toby urged.

When he was almost to the hospital, Strobe spun the steering wheel. Raced past the front entrance. Headed for the side of the building. Fishtailing around the corner,

Strobe gunned it past a long row of busted-out, boarded-over windows.

Arriving at the back of the hospital, the group leaped out of the truck before it had even come to a complete stop. They took a quick look at the huge imprint of the rukh's shoulder at the back of the truck as they ran toward a rear double-door entrance that was boarded over with plywood. Over the door was a faded sign.

EMERGENCY

7

Coming around a corner in the hallway, Annabel—who was leading the group—suddenly froze in place. There, standing behind what had once been the nurses' station, was a very tall man! Annabel quickly leveled her crossbow at the figure.

"No, Annabel! It's okay."

Strobe pulled Annabel's weapon down before she got off a shot. Confused at Strobe's interference, Annabel approached the man and saw that it was . . .

Dracula?

Annabel's angry expression showed exactly how she felt about Toby and Strobe planting the vampire king in the main wing of the hospital. "What is wrong with you two?" she hissed. "That is so incredibly juvenile!"

"Sorry, we forgot to warn you." Toby offered Annabel a contrite look. "We didn't do it just for fun, though. We put Drac here as a possible distraction. The Wolfman is over in the—"

"*Stifle it!*" Strobe frowned, listening hard for a repeat of the sound.

"What is it?" Annabel whispered.

Nothing but an eerie silence hung in the dark hospital corridors. The calm before the battle.

"Let's get to our places," Strobe ordered. "Now."

The quartet headed off in different directions, fanning across the lobby in front of the nurses' station.

"Hey. Everyone?" Toby had stopped at the entrance to a nearby hallway. The rest of the group looked back at him. "Good luck."

Staring across the dark lobby at his friends, considering what they were all about to do, and why they were doing it, Toby felt an intense connection to Annabel, Strobe, and Calanthe. But then a chill swept through him. Before he could banish the thought, there it was, front and center.

Would they ever see each other again?

Yes, Toby immediately decided. They would. They had to.

■ ■ ■

Strobe had the lookout position, at the front of the hospital, in a former patient room on the second floor. The window in the room—smashed long ago, with just the jagged glass edges remaining—was boarded over. Earlier, however, while scoping out the place, Strobe had pulled away part of the covering to be able to see outside.

He had just hunkered down by the window when he saw them. Two men, walking slowly toward the hospital. Strobe's pulse leaped at the sight of the duo. One was definitely the Tall Man. The other, Strobe couldn't make out his features.

"How'd you two manage to track me to Hidden Hills?" Strobe asked with a frown.

Actually, it had been the rukh. The Tall Man had hit a dead end in Pittsburgh, which is where he had discovered that Strobe was no longer on the train. Even though the creature was more than a hundred miles away at the time—as it crashed through the woods north of Pittsburgh—it had been able to sense its master. After a necessary detour to the Pittsburgh train station, the rukh had then led the Tall Man and his battle companion to Hidden Hills. Divine intervention, this chance meeting between demon and master, is how the Tall Man interpreted it.

Strobe found his infrared binoculars in his backpack and trained them on the two figures. Pulling them into focus, Strobe was startled to see that the Tall Man's companion was a woman, not a man. With her heavily tattooed face, blank but fierce expression, and overly muscular body, she looked like a warrior from an ancient time. She looked even more sinister and deadly than the Tall Man.

Strobe pulled down his cell mouthpiece and relayed to everyone what he was seeing as the two continued toward the hospital. Their gait was unhurried, confident. Arriving at the center of the circular driveway, which curved around in the front of the building, they suddenly stopped. And looked right up at Strobe.

Strobe froze in place. He hadn't thought he was visible to the duo as he studied them from his darkened-room vantage point, but obviously he had been. Strobe stayed right where he was and waited for whatever came next.

The two figures stood silently. The Tall Man continued to look up at Strobe. The woman warrior scanned the building, looking for a way in. When the Tall Man held his arms out wide, a conciliatory gesture that signaled to Strobe that he wanted to talk, the gesture caught Strobe off guard. And it made him very suspicious.

"I would like to speak to whoever is in charge of your group."

"What?" Strobe had found it difficult to understand Calanthe when she first arrived in Hidden Hills, but the Tall Man's accent was so strong Strobe hadn't been able to make out a single word.

The Tall Man repeated his request.

"You know what? You gotta slow it down, dude. I can't understand you!"

"What?"

Strobe almost laughed. The group's deadly predicament certainly wasn't funny, but Strobe and the Tall Man not being able to understand each other? Definitely some humor in that, Strobe had to admit.

"Slower. Understand? Talk slowwwwwwer." Strobe slowed things down himself, demonstrating for the Tall Man what he meant.

The third time was the charm. Strobe understood that the Tall Man wanted to speak to the group's leader. "Before you speak to anyone," Strobe replied, "I want to see that invisible freak, in full view, standing right next to you."

The Tall Man hesitated, as though he was deciphering what Strobe had just said, then smiled a cold smile. When he glanced toward the front of the building, Strobe saw him nod slightly. Moments later, the rukh appeared. Standing slightly behind and to the side of the Tall Man, the huge, ghastly creature looked like the perfect pet from hell.

What a trio! Strobe thought. Then, the conversation continued.

"The person in charge. If you please."

"I'll do."

"In that case, you have the power to make this unpleasant situation very quick. And painless. You give us Calanthe, and we walk away. Within a few days, the three men you left behind in the village will appear in Montreal. None the worse for wear."

So they were alive. Strobe felt a wave of relief, hearing this. But then he instantly realized the spot the Tall Man had put him in.

"Can't do that."

The Tall Man appeared to be surprised at Strobe's response. "So would you rather die? Because this is what will happen if you do not give us what is rightfully ours. You will be sentencing your friends to death, as well. So many deaths, which simply does not have to be."

"They're not my friends. They're soldiers. They knew the risks."

"And so do you, if you do not give me what I want."

Strobe studied the trio as he fingered his crossbow, propped up against the wall next to him. "My final word on the subject is . . . Calanthe is not rightfully yours. Which means no go on us handing her over. You're gonna have to come get her."

"Oh, that we will. That we definitely—"

In a lightning move, Strobe grabbed his crossbow, thrust it out the window, and started firing. He was shocked at how quickly the Tall Man and the woman moved. And how fast the rukh instantly disappeared.

"It's on, everyone!" Strobe yelled into his mouthpiece. "They're coming!"

8

Annabel had the left wing. Toby, the right. First floor. From his second-floor lookout position, Strobe was right in the middle of the long front hospital wing.

In the basement, in a former operating room, stood Calanthe. She jumped—a startled reaction—when she heard Strobe over her cell earpiece, conveying to everyone that the Tall Man and his companions were coming. She immediately went to the door, opened it, and looked out into the dark hallway. Calanthe didn't know how long she would be able to stay in the basement before going up and joining her friends. The plan was, if anyone got into trouble, they'd send out word via cell.

Calanthe suddenly sensed—more so than heard—a commotion upstairs. And she knew that the hospital had been invaded. As Strobe had warned, *it was on*. The Tall Man was coming for her.

Which meant that the Slice, the gruesome name for the Day of Days ritual, was at hand.

■ ■ ■

The rukh—supernatural battering ram that it was—had crashed right through the boarded-up front entrance to the hospital. Strobe relayed this information to Toby and Annabel, then tried to find the Tall Man and the woman.

The Tall Man was to his right, walking closely along the front of the building. The woman was heading in the opposite direction. They weren't following the rukh into the hospital, that much was clear. Strobe gave Annabel and Toby the heads-up on this, then charged out of the room and down the hall.

Hitting the stairwell at a run, Strobe bounded down the stairs and came out on the first floor, at the spot where Toby had told everyone good luck. He sprinted across the lobby, leaped over the counter of the nurse's station, and brought up his crossbow into a shooting position.

From his spot behind the counter, Strobe had a direct view down the hall that led to the front entrance of the hospital. He wasn't able to see the invisible rukh, but he could definitely see the path the thing was taking, which happened to be right in his direction!

The group had scattered gravel up and down the hallways of the hospital for just this purpose. So Strobe was able to witness the hallway gravel exploding into pieces as it was pulverized by the rukh's feet. And he knew where to aim his crossbow.

When he did, Strobe started firing as fast as he could press the trigger. The rukh flashed in and out of view as it was struck by the arrows. Strobe knew the arrows wouldn't stop the creature, but their impact did slow the charging beast from a thunderous run to a flinching jog.

Just what Strobe hoped would happen. He tossed aside his crossbow and grabbed another weapon that he had stored under the nurse's station counter. Nicknamed the Ghost Buster (by Strobe), the weapon—which emitted an unlawfully potent taser—actually did somewhat resemble the weapons used by the ghost busters in the iconic comedy.

When Strobe aimed the Ghost Buster down the hall . . . he paused. He needed to hit the rukh at just the right moment. The creature had gone invisible again, but its steadily advancing path was betrayed by the erupting gravel. When the rukh was almost to the lobby area in front of the nurses' station . . .

Strobe fired.

A taser burst from the weapon and slammed into the creature, the powerful electrical charge stopping the thing in its tracks. The weapon rendered the rukh immediately visible, its body shuddering from the powerful current coursing through its body.

Strobe had to act quickly. He didn't know how long the taser would freeze the rukh in one spot. He dumped the Ghost Buster, slid down the counter, and grabbed a crudely constructed lever that was located just in front of the Dracula mannequin.

When Strobe pulled the lever, he set off the first of the monster booby traps. Dubbed Hammer Down by Toby, it was tripped by a wire that ran up a post at the end of the nurses' station, across the ceiling of the lobby and a short way into the hallway. Exactly where the rukh was frozen in place by the Ghost Buster's taser.

AAAAARRRRGGGGGGGHHHHHH!!!

The creature reared back and screamed when a heavy sharp-tipped metal shaft—the object that had been released when Strobe pulled the lever—swung down from the ceiling and impaled the rukh's chest.

The creature frantically tried to pull the shaft from its body. But the taser was still sending a powerful stream of electricity through the beast's massive frame. Between that and the Hammer Down, it wasn't long before the rukh slowly slumped to the floor. . . .

And was still.

Strobe couldn't believe how well their first trap had

worked. "One down!" he yelled into his mouthpiece. "Talk to me, you guys!"

From Toby: "I have the tall guy in my sights."

"Annabel?"

Nothing from Annabel.

Toby: "Go help her, Strobe."

"I'm on it. Be careful, man."

Strobe jumped over the counter and took off down the hallway to his left, which is where Annabel had taken up her position.

Aside from the obvious reason that the Tall Man was incredibly dangerous, Strobe had told Toby to be careful because they hadn't had time to booby-trap Toby's location. It was the final thing they had planned to deal with, while Annabel and Calanthe were at school and they were all waiting for daylight to turn to night and the dekayi to arrive. But the dekayi's early arrival had squashed those plans.

So Toby was the only obstacle between the Tall Man and the stairway to the basement, where Calanthe was waiting as bait in the former operating room. Toby's defensive position was behind a five-foot-tall barrier that he and Strobe had constructed only hours before. The jagged wall of discarded tables, chairs, two-by-fours, and other junk they'd found in the basement stretched from one side of the hall to the other. It was the only thing protecting Toby from the Tall Man, who was striding down the center of the hallway in his direction.

Lying on the floor of the hallway behind the barrier, Toby made sure the tall, gaunt figure was dead center in his crossbow sight, then started firing. In a flash, the Tall Man disappeared. Simply took off into a nearby room, crashing through the door as though it were made of paper. Toby hesitated, shocked at the sudden retreat of the Tall Man, then crawled through a small opening in the barrier. He stood and quickly moved up against the side of the hall.

Heart thumping wildly, Toby inched his way toward the tattered door, pieces of which littered the hallway. He stopped just outside the room and listened intently. Couldn't hear a thing to indicate that the dekayi was in the room. No breathing. No scrape of a shoe against the floor.

But it could be a trap. Toby knew the Tall Man just might be waiting for him to enter before springing it. So he made sure all of his body armor was firmly in place. The armor included a face shield, an added component to their gear to guard against a numbing slimeball attack. Satisfied that he was as ready as he could possibly be, Toby slid quickly into the room.

Nothing. Toby swung his crossbow back and forth,

scrutinizing every corner. A cold breeze was blowing into the room through a gaping, smashed window. Toby warily approached the window and glanced outside. There were a pair of heavy footprints where the Tall Man had landed. Toby leaned slightly out of the window to get a better look outside the building. No sign of the guy.

Toby pulled down his mouthpiece. "The tall dude has left the building. I'm heading to the nurses' station."

■ ■ ■

The woman warrior—who had entered the left wing of the hospital through a window—hadn't left the building when Annabel had discovered her and started pumping arrows in her direction. Instead, the intimidating figure had turned into her serpent alter ego and slithered/crawled right at Annabel!

So Annabel had turned and ran. Just as the plan called for her to do. It was a tricky thing Annabel was attempting to pull off. She needed to stay out of the deadly range of the slithering creature, yet remain close enough to lead it to the booby trap they had constructed in the cafeteria. So as Strobe was leaping over the nurses' station counter to come to her aid, Annabel was blasting through the double doors of the cafeteria and sprinting across the empty space where tables and chairs used to be.

The serpent was trailing by a mere second at this point, the hissing and slithering and suction-crawling sounds getting louder and louder as it closed in on Annabel. The monster the warrior woman had turned into was bigger and stronger-looking than the ones Strobe had faced in the dekayi village. Or the one Calanthe had turned into. To Annabel, this serpent looked like something that had been groomed for one thing and one thing only. . . .

War.

As she ran toward the cafeteria serving counter at the far end of the room, Annabel suddenly felt something heavy strike her back, the impact almost dropping her to her knees. Annabel was certain she'd been hit by a blast of the black, numbing ooze Strobe had warned them about. And which Annabel's back body armor had fortunately prevented from making contact with her skin.

Annabel managed to stay upright after the hit, but stumbled just as she was about to go over the serving counter. Instead of a clearing leap, Annabel's foot hit the counter when she jumped, resulting in a head-over-heels tumble to the other side. She hit the floor hard, the painful collision stunning her and bringing her forward momentum to a dead stop.

Just then the deadly serpent reared up on the other side of the counter. Temporarily incapacitated by her painful fall, Annabel felt frozen in place. Besides the numbing pain, Annabel had the very odd sensation that the serpent's heavy-lidded eyes were somehow hypnotizing her!

Suddenly, the serpent's sinister head swiveled away and focused on something in the deep darkness a few yards away.

Following the serpent's gaze, Annabel could just make out . . . yes, it was the mummy mannequin that Toby and Strobe had planted behind the counter! A couple of gravestones had been arranged around the figure as a macabre accent.

Sorry, guys! And thanks!

Taking quick advantage of the mummy distraction, Annabel desperately crab-crawled—her back toward the floor—away from the counter.

The serpent's head immediately snapped back and focused front and center on Annabel.

That's right! Come get me!

The creature complied, its massive body crashing onto the counter and slithering across it.

Annabel frantically propelled her body toward the rear of the kitchen area, still moving in her awkward crab-crawl to be able to see the serpent as it came for her.

The thing slithered/crawled toward her like a coiling, propulsive, unstoppable machine.

Annabel took a quick look behind her and saw that she was almost to the place she needed to be.

The serpent's head suddenly shot up toward the ceiling. The long poisonous fangs slid into view from under its thin, leathery lips. It was preparing for a lethal strike!

Annabel had to act. Now.

She whirled and desperately launched herself toward the lever that would trigger the monster trap.

Her fingers found the lever . . .

Curled around the wood . . .

And pulled.

SWWWWISSSHHH!!!

A sheet of sharpened steel immediately plunged downward from the ceiling and . . .

CRRRRACKK!

Caught the mammoth serpent dead center in the middle of its thick, slippery body, slicing the thing neatly in half!

Annabel pulled herself to her feet and backed away across the kitchen until she was up against the rear wall. She wanted as much distance between her and the two writhing halves of the serpent as possible. Even in its death throes, Annabel knew the serpent could be deadly.

"Annabel!"

"In here!"

When Strobe threw open the double doors of the cafeteria, Annabel was maneuvering around the perimeter of the kitchen to get back to the dining area. When she did, she leaned up against the serving counter with a relieved sigh.

"Annabel! Down!"

Annabel was confused. Why was Strobe telling her to get down? But there was no time for questions. Strobe already had his crossbow up and aimed right at her!

Annabel threw herself to the floor as the cafeteria was filled with the sharp, hissing sounds of one arrow after another as they burst from Strobe's crossbow. Turning to look through the foot-wide opening between the stainless steel front of the counter and the floor, she was shocked by what she saw.

The serpent wasn't in its death throes. It was mutating! Becoming two serpents instead of one!

"Annabel! Let's go!"

Strobe's arrows had backed one half of the serpent away from Annabel as it was coming over the counter for her. The half that already had a head.

Annabel leaped to her feet. Charging across the cafeteria in Strobe's direction, all Annabel could think was . . .

Now *how are we going to kill this thing?*

9

After outflanking Toby, the Tall Man had reentered the hospital from the rear and quickly made his way to the lobby area in front of the nurses' station. The dekayi knew this is where he needed to be to get to Calanthe. He could sense it.

But as he was about to open the door that led to the basement stairway, the Tall Man suddenly hesitated. He looked around the lobby, spotted the Ghost Buster on the nurses' station counter. In one fluid movement, the Tall Man walked across the lobby, grabbed the large weapon, and threw it with awesome force at the stairway door.

BLAMMMMM!!!

The Tall Man had smelled the Rock-a-Monster trap, the explosion that Toby and Strobe had rigged to go off by the inward movement of the door. Instead of being blown to pieces as he entered the stairwell, the blast only caused the Tall Man to take a few steps back and wait for the falling rubble to settle. Then he walked through the gaping hole where the door used to be and went down the stairs to find Calanthe.

■ ■ ■

Just as he was crawling back under the hallway barrier to get to the nurse's station Toby heard the doorway explosion.

Strobe: "Tobe!"

"Yeah, I heard it, too."

Strobe: "We got a little snake problem here! Be there as soon as we can."

"I'm on it. Good luck!"

Toby leaped to his feet and ran down the hall. The dust from the explosion was billowing around a corner at the end of the hall and forming a solid white smoke screen between Toby and the lobby. When Toby pushed through it and entered the lobby, he started coughing from the heavy dust particles that hung in the air.

Leveling his crossbow as he slowly approached the stairway, Toby scoured the immediate area for any sign of the Tall Man. But all Toby was able to find was the warped remains of the Ghost Buster on the floor of the stairwell. That's when Toby knew. The Tall Man had sensed the trap. Had passed through the doorway, unharmed. And was now in the basement, going after Calanthe!

Just as Toby was about to run through the doorway to the basement, he felt something grab his ankle from behind. In an instant, he was slammed to the floor and pulled roughly across the lobby.

Toby tossed aside his crossbow and reached out wildly for something, anything, to grab on to, to stop himself from being pulled . . .

Where? What *was* this thing that had grabbed hold of him? Glancing down at his foot, Toby saw something wrapped around his ankle. When he realized what he was looking at, Toby recoiled at the disgusting sight. The thing was the rukh's incredibly long, fleshy black tongue!

The creature was up and standing in the spot where Strobe's taser had stopped it cold and the monster trap had finished it off. Or so Strobe had thought. The rukh looked unsteady, but also ready, willing, and able to turn Toby into dinner for one. As Toby struggled in the creature's long-range grip, the thing took another wobbly step toward its prey, at the same time opening its mouth even wider in anticipation of his arrival.

Toby frantically reached for the knife sheath on his forearm plate and undid the strap that held the knife in place.

As though sensing what Toby was about to do, the

rukh's writhing, snake-like tongue reeled him in even faster!

Toby yanked the knife from its sheath. Just as he was about to try to free himself from the rukh's grip . . .

The attack was over as quickly as it had begun. The creature teetered from one side to the other. . . .

Then toppled over and hit the floor with a resounding thud. The creature was finally dead.

But was it? Toby wasn't completely sure about that. That's because the thing's black tongue was still wrapped around his ankle and still pulling him down the hall! Toby sliced right through the tongue with his knife, then watched as the remaining part moved slower and slower down the hall . . . until it finally came to a complete stop.

Toby immediately pulled down his mouthpiece. "Strobe."

No answer.

"Strobe! You there?"

Nothing. Toby could hear the sounds of an intense battle down the hall. Yells back and forth between Strobe and Annabel. The pop of a flare followed by a red glow that illuminated darting shapes and shadows. Toby's first impulse was to help his friends.

But he knew what came first. Above all else, they

were here to protect Calanthe. He took a final look down the hall in Strobe and Annabel's direction, then ran across the lobby and retrieved his crossbow.

Heading down the stairs, Toby arrived at the basement corridor and jogged down the wide passageway toward Calanthe's operating-room hideout. On his way, he passed the fourth and final trap—another Hammer Down—that he and Strobe had constructed in the corridor.

The trap had been sprung. And it had done some damage. Toby immediately locked in on a path of blood that led away from the Hammer Down and followed it to the operating room. He hesitated a brief moment before entering, then went in, combat ready.

Toby felt the creepy sensation of déjà vu wash over him as he burst into the room. The place had been one of the "visiting hours" destinations in the Shock Corridor attraction, where the Deadly Doctor had done his foul deeds every night for the several weeks leading up to Halloween. Leaping flames and hellish demon faces painted on the walls still remained, which had jump-started a recall of the delighted screams Toby had heard years before in this very room.

But the fun scares of Shock Corridor were obviously bush league compared to this! Taking in the length and breadth of the room through his NVGs and discovering that the room was empty, Toby's déjà vu feeling was quickly replaced by dread.

Calanthe was gone.

The Tall Man had obviously tripped Hammer Down, but the trap hadn't been able to finish him. The person who was determined to offer up Calanthe as a sacrifice to his gods was still on his feet.

And he had his offering.

Toby backtracked to the corridor, his eyes immediately locking on the Tall Man's blood trail, which continued down the hall. Toby was about to head down the passageway when he heard sounds behind him, coming down the stairs. Not knowing if it was Strobe and Annabel, or something else, Toby turned toward the stairway and brought up his crossbow.

Fortunately, it was Strobe and Annabel, who emerged from the cloud of dust that still hung in the air from the explosion on the first floor. The two looked like they'd just been through the worst fight of their young MCO careers. Their body armor was scratched, gouged, and covered with the dekayi's black-tinged ooze. Their expressions were alert to the current situation, but still carried the shock and intensity of what they'd just been through.

"Those dudes *were* able to move their hearts around," Strobe said as he and Annabel approached. "Totally hit-and-miss time. We finally hit."

"Where's Calanthe?" Annabel asked.

"Gone. She's been taken this way, down the hall."

The trio immediately headed down the corridor. Several turns in the passageway led them to a ladder set in the concrete wall, the metal rungs leading upward to an opening in the ceiling. When the group had checked out the hospital earlier to decide where to put their traps, they had discovered the ladder, which led to a separate utility building about fifty yards away from the hospital.

The three quickly scaled the ladder to the building, then followed the trail of blood—barely visible now—outside. The utility building was behind the hospital, which is where the trail suddenly went cold. The Tall Man's wound had apparently stopped bleeding. Which meant he could be anywhere.

"I'll go around this side of the hospital, check out the front," Strobe said.

"I'll take the other side, head back into the building. Could be he's in there, thinking we'll just search outside." This from Annabel.

"Okay. I'll take the rear of the hospital," Toby said.

"Keep in touch." Strobe was immediately off, jogging toward the side of the hospital.

Annabel and Toby exchanged a worried look, gave each other hopeful nods, then headed in separate directions to try to find Calanthe before the Tall Man could accomplish what he had come all this way to do.

10

The Tall Man looked down at Calanthe. His eyes were hard, unyielding. "It saddens me that you do not realize what an honor this is for you, Calanthe, to have been chosen for this."

Calanthe wasn't even trying to struggle anymore. The Tall Man had her in a grip that prevented her from doing much of anything, except what her captor wanted her to do. Calanthe had been about to turn into her serpent alter ego back in the operating room to defend herself, but the Tall Man had descended on her too quickly. Even with his traumatic injury—the Hammer Down had sliced through his shoulder—the Tall Man had been able to apply a firm grip to Calanthe's wrist that had paralyzed her. Frozen her in place.

As it turned out, the Tall Man didn't need to turn into his alter ego to paralyze people with the black numbing ooze. He could impart paralysis with one hand.

So Calanthe had meekly allowed the Tall Man to lead her out of the hospital and into the woods, their final destination being a clearing by a cliff overlooking a river. This is where they were now. This is the place the Tall Man had chosen to perform the ritual that would take Calanthe's life.

"You are such a tool," Calanthe suddenly said. The Tall Man glared at Calanthe, then he smiled a cold smile. "An expression you learned in your wonderful new world, no doubt."

"You have no idea how much I have learned in the little time I've been in this world. It eclipses the so-called wisdom you claim to possess."

"Yet still you don't understand that this is your destiny."

"No. Just because you say it doesn't make it so. Everyone has a right to make his or her own destiny. And it is in our power to do so. This is one of the important things I have learned."

The Tall Man listened to Calanthe's blasphemous words, then he shrugged. "Ah, but I'm the one with the knife, Calanthe." In a sudden movement, the Tall Man raised his knife high over his head. The knife had a long, curved shaft and a simple wooden handle. The knife appeared to be very old. Its shaft had foreign markings etched in the metal along its length. Its handle was speckled with dark stains. Just as the arc of the knife reached its zenith . . .

Zzzzzwwwwwwwwaaaaakkkkk!!!

The Tall Man cried out in alarm as the knife blade was suddenly struck by a flashing arrow, the two connecting metals causing an intense fiery spark in the darkness. The impact of the arrow blasted the knife from the Tall Man's hand. It twirled end over end and landed in the dirt at the edge of the cliff.

Before the Tall Man could react, Toby charged out of the darkness. His expression was set. Fierce. Just like he had in Central Park, Toby was about to take on the Tall Man in hand-to-hand combat. But he knew this time there would be no retreat. This time he was taking the fight all the way to its conclusion.

The surprise attack gave Toby quick advantage over the Tall Man. A bruising tackle. Several well-placed martial arts moves that elicited gasps of pain from his enemy. But the Tall Man was simply too powerful and was able to quickly gain the upper hand in the struggle. Turning his defensive mode into an awesome offensive assault, the dekayi slapped aside one of Toby's moves, grabbed his smaller opponent, and slammed him onto his back near the edge of the cliff. Before Toby could even catch his breath, he found himself instantly paralyzed by the Tall Man's wristlock.

Toby couldn't believe it. Just like that, he was completely powerless. He couldn't do a thing to defend himself. But Toby had done the important thing. He had freed Calanthe to do what she needed to do.

The Tall Man was reaching for his knife where it had fallen near the cliff's edge when Toby heard a hissing sound. And then . . . the dekayi's neck was suddenly in the grip of a serpent's tail. The powerful serpent muscles lifted the Tall Man up and away from Toby, shook him like a rag doll—snapping his neck in the process—and threw him far out over the cliff!

Toby was stunned at how fast all that had happened. He rolled onto his stomach and watched as the Tall Man's lifeless body fell to the river far below. When it hit the water, there was a distance-delayed split second before the sound came to Toby. By then the body had already disappeared underwater and was being swept away downriver by the strong current.

Toby still felt numb from the Tall Man's wristlock, so it was a bit of a struggle to get to his feet. He took a moment to steady himself, then pulled down his mouthpiece and said, "Guys. I'm with Calanthe. The woods. Back of the hospital."

When Toby turned to Calanthe, she was transforming back into her human self. Toby kept his distance, allowed Calanthe to do what she needed to do. By the time Strobe and Annabel arrived in the clearing at the edge of the cliff, Calanthe was herself again.

Standing together in the clearing, the foursome looked barely able to stand upright. But they were able to manage a collective smile, happy and relieved that the battle was over.

Just then the first light of day made its appearance across the river. Toby, Annabel, Strobe, and Calanthe instinctively turned toward the light. The tops of the trees suddenly looked aflame, sparked by an unseen sun.

After such a brutal fight, a perfect, peaceful moment.

And a beautiful Halloween day had begun.

EPILOGUE:
GOOD-BYE

Toby, Annabel, Strobe, and Calanthe stood in the back alley of Killer Pizza. A street lamp shone down on them, circling them in a pool of light. It was as though they were on a dark stage, a single overhead spotlight highlighting them for an unseen audience. Steve Rogers stood a respectful distance away, near the black sedan he just driven in from New York.

I can't believe this is happening, Annabel thought.

What was happening was that Calanthe's bags were packed and already in the trunk of Steve's car. A week after Calanthe's prayer to survive the Day of Days had been answered, she realized that she could not stay in Hidden Hills. Living with Annabel, hanging out with Toby and Strobe, going to school, and acting as though nothing had happened? No, Calanthe knew it was her duty to go back to New York. And help Harvey in any way that she could to locate the missing MCOs. It was the least she could do, after everything the KP crew had done for her.

"I will be coming back," Calanthe said.

Annabel nodded. She felt terrible about Calanthe leaving. She felt like a part of her was going away. *Whatever you do, don't cry*, Annabel urged herself.

It's all reversed, now, Toby thought as he looked at Calanthe. *It's like she's the grownup, telling us everything's gonna be okay.*

Toby was right about that. Since the group's epic battle at Shock Corridor, Calanthe did look much more grown-up. And, for the first time, really, very much relaxed in her new world.

What Calanthe didn't look like anymore was the doomed heroine Annabel had once compared her to. It was in her eyes. Calanthe's haunted look, the one Toby had tried to capture in his drawing . . . it was no longer there.

Calanthe suddenly approached Annabel and gave her a hug. Annabel was surprised and touched by the gesture. In spite of her insistence to herself not to cry, Annabel couldn't help it. A stifled sniffle gave her away.

Now Calanthe walked to Toby and Strobe and held up her hand for a high five. Strobe slapped Calanthe's hand, then said, "You're cool, girl."

"So are you, Strobe. And you, Toby."

Toby smiled, completed the high five, then stepped away. Before getting into the car, Calanthe turned back to the trio. "I don't know the proper thing to say now. It feels like there should be something, something final, before I leave."

"You've already said it, Calanthe," Annabel replied.

"Take care of yourself," Strobe said.

"And come back," Toby added. "To Hidden Hills, as soon as possible, okay?"

Calanthe held up a hand in farewell, then got into the car.

"See you all," Steve said as he came around the car. "And need I say it? You did a great job. Again."

"Thanks, Steve." Toby and Annabel and Strobe waved to Steve as he got into the car and started it up. The car's windows were tinted, so the trio weren't able to see Calanthe as the car moved off down the alley. Then, just before the car disappeared around the corner, the passenger-side window opened and Calanthe reached out a hand for a final good-bye.

The trio stayed in the middle of the alley after Calanthe had gone. A light drizzle had begun to fall.

"I didn't see it ending like this," Toby said.

"I'm not sure I did, either," Strobe said.

"It's not ending, you guys. Calanthe's coming back."

"Yeah."

Everyone knew the dangers Calanthe would be facing up in the wilds of Canada.

"Well, as much as I'd love to stay here and commiserate about all this, Toby and I have a pizza shift that's about to start." Strobe turned and headed for the narrow alley that ran between the Killer Pizza building and the dog-obedience school next door.

"Hey, wait for me," Annabel said.

"What do you mean, wait for you?" Toby had joined Strobe and was walking toward the front of the building.

"I'm back on the payroll."

"Since when?"

"Since right now. The only reason I quit was because I had to, remember? Now that Calanthe's gone, my agreement with my dad no longer applies."

The excuse Annabel had come up with to explain Calanthe's sudden departure was a complication in her diabetic condition. Annabel had told her parents that Calanthe felt it was best to return home, until she was better.

"Let me ask you something, Annabel," Strobe said.

"Yeah?"

"Your dad doesn't like you hanging with us, does he?

That's the main reason he doesn't want you to work here. He doesn't think we're good enough for you. That's what I think, anyway."

When Annabel didn't respond right away . . .

"Yeah, that's what I thought."

"Listen, Strobe. You and Toby are my friends. My best friends. And nobody's going to tell me who my friends can or cannot be. Okay?"

Strobe looked at Annabel. He was pleased by Annabel's declaration of independence. "Okay."

The trio had reached the front of the KP building. A small crowd was gathered there for the final Monster Mash-up of the season. For this important event, Toby had chosen *Tremors*, one of his favorite creature features.

Unfortunately, it had started to rain harder and the crowd was quickly dispersing. Instead of following Strobe and Toby into Killer Pizza. Annabel stopped under the small awning that stretched across the length of the shop.

Annabel wasn't sure how long she had been standing there before Toby came back outside and joined her. A group of kids who had been watching the movie were retreating down the street, laughing crazily as they zigzagged through the rain. "I'm gonna miss her, too." Annabel nodded, then gave Toby a bittersweet smile.

Just then Strobe opened the front door. "Hey, c'mon,

you two. I just got two phone orders for the All-Nighter Horror Special."

Which meant a total of six specialty pizzas and eight side orders, to go along with a total of six horror DVD rentals that were stocked in a case by the ordering counter.

"Okay," Toby said.

"By the way, one of the orders was from your sister, Tobe."

"No way."

Strobe shrugged.

"Aw, man, I can't believe my mom is letting Stacey's little brat friends stay over. They're gonna keep me up the entire night!"

Annabel smiled at Toby's little rant, then hesitated by the front door after Toby had joined Strobe inside the shop. Even though the movie crowd was completely gone by now, the battle on the screen across the street continued between the humans and the underground monsters.

The *Tremors* "graboids" definitely bore some similarities to the dekayi serpents the KP crew had just dealt with. Watching the movie—alone now under the awning—Annabel found herself thinking about all of the incredible Calanthe moments that had been packed into such a short amount of time, from her arrival to her recent departure. Memories to last . . . well, a lifetime, really.

Annabel took a final look down the street. A sudden shiver swept through her. She turned, opened the door with the KP monster mascot stenciled on it, and went into Killer Pizza, the bright lights of the shop a warm, welcome beacon in the dark, rainy night.

RECIPE FOR
SWEET TOOTH PIZZA

INGREDIENTS:

(Recipe below or purchase already-made
   pizza crust):
¼ cup mascarpone (cheese)
¼ cup semisweet chocolate chips
1 large or 2 medium Granny Smith apples,
   peeled, cored, and thinly sliced
streusel topping (recipe below)

DIRECTIONS:

1. Prepare pizza base. Roll out dough on
   a lightly floured surface, then place on
   a baking sheet.

2. Spread a thin layer of mascarpone over
   the dough.

3. Sprinkle the chocolate chips evenly over
   the cheese.

4. Place the apple slices in a single layer
   over the cheese and chips.

5. Sprinkle the prepared streusel over the
   top.

6. Bake at 400° for 18–20 minutes.

7. Remove from oven and let it rest a few
   minutes before slicing.

PIZZA BASE:

INGREDIENTS:
2 cups flour
½ tsp salt
½ tsp fresh yeast
¾ cup lukewarm water
1 tbsp olive oil

DIRECTIONS FOR PIZZA BASE:

1. In a large bowl, mix flour and salt
   together, dissolve yeast in water, and
   slowly add to the flour. Mix well until it
   forms a dough. If too sticky, add flour.

2. Knead the dough into a ball, place on a
   tray with a light sprinkling of flour, and
   cover with a damp cloth. Leave to rise
   in a warm place.

3. After 30 minutes, divide dough in half,
   roll out each dough ball on a lightly
   floured surface into a circle until ¼ inch
   thick. Continue with recipe.

STREUSEL TOPPING:

INGREDIENTS:
½ cup packed brown sugar
3 tbsp flour
½ tsp cinnamon
2 tbsp cold butter or margarine
¼ cup coarsely chopped pecans

DIRECTIONS FOR STREUSEL:
In a small bowl, mix sugar, flour, and
cinnamon. Add the butter or margarine and
cut in with a pastry blender or two butter
knives. Add the pecans last.

Can't find mascarpone? Simply brush
pizza dough with melted butter or
margarine in place of the cheese. Or, for
a *really* sweet Sweet Tooth Pizza, use a
chocolate hazelnut spread instead of the
mascarpone.

ENJOY!

ACKNOWLEDGMENTS

Thanks to: Jean Feiwel and everyone at Feiwel and Friends, for their help and support on the first two *Killer Pizza* books. They're a terrific group, and I feel fortunate to be a part of it.

Kathryn McKeon, my editor, for her assistance and encouragement throughout the rewriting process.

Fellow author Lewis Buzbee, for his wise counsel and friendship.

Finally, my wife, for coming up with the recipe for Sweet Tooth Pizza. We taste-tested various versions before settling on this one. It's one sweet dish. Bon appétit, Jo!

GO FISH

GREG TAYLOR

What did you want to be when you grew up?
A musician or anything that had to do with the movie business.

When did you realize you wanted to be a writer?
In college, where I had a good experience in a screenwriting class. It was the first time I thought of screenwriting as a possible career. It took me many years to develop the discipline to actually become a professional writer, but the first positive step in that long journey was my Theater Arts 290 class, taught by Joe Adamson. To whom I say, many thanks.

What's your most embarrassing childhood memory?
That would have to be the time I was hit by a milk truck. (To readers who have never seen a milk truck, they still delivered milk and other dairy products to homes when I was a kid.) I was around nine years old, playing with some friends outside. One of my friends grabbed my bike and took off with it. When I ran into the street to reclaim my bike—not looking to see if any vehicles were coming, one of the all-time "never do that" rules—I was hit by the truck. After twirling around and

falling to the ground from the impact, my right leg (or was it my left?) was run over by the truck's back tire.

I'm sure I was in shock at the time, but it was an embarrassing moment, just the same. There I was, sitting in the street, my leg flattened into the asphalt, the center of open-mouthed stares from my friends and—very quickly—surrounded by my hysterical mother and my friends' mothers. A nasty experience, to be sure, but one with a positive payoff. After coming back from the hospital with my leg encased in a gleaming white cast, I was the MAN on my street. At least for a little while.

As a young person, who did you look up to most?

Carl Bennett, a neighbor who was two years older than me. Carl was tall, athletic, and very cool. Here is a lasting image I have of him. . . .

My neighborhood friends and I occasionally engaged in a "King of the Hill" battle on an empty lot with the kids who lived on the street below us. It was a simple contest. Fight your way to the top of the hill and stay there by shoving enemy interlopers off of the summit.

I always struggled to make it even halfway up the hill, but that was OK. Because, always, there was Carl, at the very top, heroically slinging our opponents every which way and sending them back down the steep slope. A true-life "king of the hill." That was Carl.

What was your worst subject in school?

I can't remember what my worst subject was, grade-wise, but I do remember the subjects I didn't like, which was anything having to do with mathematics. In college, my worst subject was Symbolic Logic. I failed that class in miserable fashion.

What was your best subject in school?

In high school, art and music classes. In college, screenwriting and Symbolic Logic.

Symbolic Logic? Explanation. After failing, I had to retake the class because I needed it as a requirement. As before, I struggled, but eventually I unraveled the mystery of the subject and was rewarded with an "A." It was an important lesson. Sometimes it's possible to turn things around, even difficult things you don't want to do, if you force yourself to focus and spend the time needed to overcome the problem.

What was your first job?

In high school I worked at a fast-food takeout place called Mr. Chicken. I was alone during my shift, taking phone orders, making the chicken and cole slaw and french fries, and ringing up the orders on the old-fashioned cash register, where I had to figure out the return change in my head. (Not always an easy task, especially during dinner rush hours.) I really hated that job, but on the upside, I was able to draw on the experience for *Killer Pizza.*

How did you celebrate publishing your first book?

I went to dinner with my wife, Joanne, and Jessica and Stuart, my daughter and son-in-law. We ate at a really cool place called Ludo Bites, a "temporary" restaurant in Los Angeles that served numerous small, interesting and—to me—exotic dishes. I was up most of the night with an epic stomachache, but that was one tasty dinner.

Where do you find inspiration for your writing?

Just about everywhere. My personal life, other people's personal lives, the newspaper, music, books, movies, the culture at large.

Which of your characters is most like you?

Toby, in *Killer Pizza*. I don't have a weight problem like Toby, but I did struggle with self-confidence as a kid. Also, like Toby, I'm kind of shy. I'm sure that's why I made him *Killer Pizza*'s main character. I understood "Tobe" in a way that made him real to me.

Are you a morning person or a night owl?

Definitely a morning person. I love sitting down with that first cup of coffee and feeling the caffeine kick in as I start work on my latest book or script.

Which do you like better: cats or dogs?

I grew up with dogs. My family always had one. So I've continued that tradition over the years. My family hit the jackpot with our current canine, Cleo. A German shepherd/border collie mix—that's our best guess, anyway—she's the smartest, most playful and affectionate dog we've ever had. She also has the most varied and interesting dialogue. I never tire of listening to her.

Where do you go for peace and quiet?

My office, which is in my backyard and separate from the house. One of the reasons I appreciate my office so much is that I worked for many, many years in a converted bedroom in the house. It could get very loud in there, especially when my children were younger.

What makes you laugh out loud?

What comes immediately to mind are three scenes in two of my favorite movies, the "Puttin' on the Ritz" and Frankenstein/Blind Man scenes in *Young Frankenstein*, and the moment in *A Christmas Story* when the father chases the pack of dogs out of his house and swears at them in that incredibly high falsetto voice of his. I lose it every time.

What's your favorite song?

I love too many songs to pick an absolute favorite, but if I were forced to, I'd go with "In My Life" by The Beatles.

Who is your favorite fictional character?

Again, a tough one. Huck Finn is certainly one of my favorites. I also love Tex, the title character of S.E. Hinton's book. To complete my top three . . . David Copperfield.

What are you most afraid of?

I'm not sure I'm most afraid of black mold, but it's something that really creeps me out. It's just so insidious, like something in a horror movie.

What time of year do you like best?

When I lived in Pennsylvania, fall and spring. The special thing about those two seasons is how relatively brief they are, so you have to enjoy them while they last. Now that I live in California, the beautiful winters are my favorite time of year.

What's your favorite TV show?

I'm going to answer this question in three parts. When I was younger, *The Avengers* and *The Wild Wild West*.

In the 1990s, *Northern Exposure*.

Currently, *Mad Men*. I would love it if that show ran forever, like one of those endless soap operas, but I know it won't.

If you could travel in time, where would you go?

I feel like I should pick an era I've never experienced—the 1940s, for example, an exciting and turbulent time in world history that I love reading about—but I'd probably go back to the mid-1960s.

Having lived through a number of decades since, I can appreciate how creative, lively, and colorful that time really was. I know some of my feelings about the '60s are simple nostalgia, but all you have to do is look at our current culture—fashion, design, neo-soul and pop music, graphic novels, superhero movies—to see how influential the early and mid-'60s truly were. Mostly in a good way, I think.

What's the best advice you have ever received about writing?

I really struggled as a writer early on, a frustrating time when I was unable to finish what I started. The thing that unlocked it for me was the book *Screenplay*, by Syd Field. He explained in a simple and very specific way about the three-act structure and how it pertains to scripts.

I've used that advice ever since, adapting it to books when I recently became an author. My advice to young authors is to keep going, keep reading, keep writing—even if you're struggling—because you never know when things will click for you, which I believe they will if you don't give up.

What would you do if you ever stopped writing?

I honestly don't know. At this point I don't feel equipped to do anything else, so I'm hoping to continue writing for a very long time.

What are some of the things you love most about being a writer?

Coming up with that new, exciting idea. Starting in on a new script or book, when everything is fresh and untrampled and the sky's still the limit. Being able to make my own hours. Also, reading books anytime during the day without feeling guilty about it because it falls into the category of "working."

What do you wish you could do better?
Write. I've never been completely satisfied with any of my scripts or books. Which I actually see as a good thing. There's always room for improvement, so writing has been a job that has never gotten old, never descended into boredom.

Where in the world do you feel most at home?
In my own home, especially during the holidays. Jessica and Ian, my daughter and son, are grown and no longer live with Jo and me, so it's always wonderful when we're back together, even for just a little while. That's when I'm truly the happiest.

Beatles super-fan Regina Bloomsbury and her band, the
Caverns, are determined to shake things up. When her
bandmates unexpectedly bail on her, Regina makes
a wish that alters her entire universe.

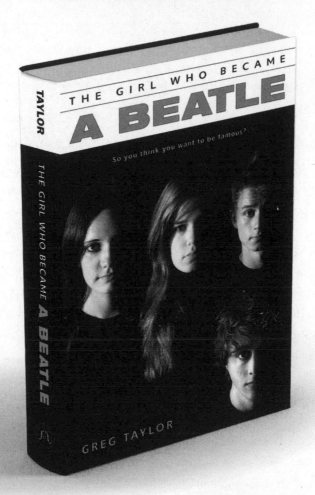

Turn the page to find out what happens in Greg Taylor's

THE GIRL WHO BECAME **A BEATLE**.

1

A lot of winter days in Twin Oaks are like some of the black-and-white movies I've seen. Dreary, colorless, a total drag. (*A Hard Day's Night* does not fall into this category, of course.)

The morning of the day that I made my wish . . . was not like that. As my eyes fluttered open, I could tell it was going to be bright and sunny. Unfortunately, that did nothing to soothe my anxious state.

My uptightness was not unusual. Most mornings I wake up with the same feeling in my gut. Kind of queasy. Like I'm not on solid ground. Like something is unresolved in my life.

So what was it that morning? Did I neglect to study for a test? Was someone mad at me at school for some reason? When I stumbled into the bathroom, I got to the bottom of this mystery.

There it was, staring back at me from the mirror. No, not my *face*. Well, come to think of it, that's a good place to start. I'm not all that confident about how I look. But I don't want to get into that right now.

So no, actually, it was the words on the mirror that cracked this little puzzle for me. Sometimes I write reminders on the mirror in lipstick. And what was there this morning was this:

BE FIRM. DO NOT TAKE NO FOR AN ANSWER.

Explanation . . .

I play guitar and sing lead vocals for a band called the Caverns. We're a pop band, I'm proud to say. Mostly retro. Sixties British Invasion covers (more than a few Beatles songs, of course), a smattering of tunes from some of the smarter, newer pop groups, and—to keep things interesting—a few originals thrown in here and there. (None of mine, however. I'm kind of shy about playing my own stuff for people.)

I formed the Caverns during the summer. So far, we've only played a handful of gigs. A couple of times at the local coffee shop, a Battle of the Bands at our high school. A street fair near my house. So, we're kind of a new band, which makes me a bit uptight sometimes about the whole enterprise. It's like when you've just started dating someone and you're not sure where things are headed.

Anyway, back to that message on the mirror. As it turns out, my anxiety about the band was justified. Julian, our lead guitarist, had told me just the previous day that the Circuit Club—a hugely popular band at my school and one that has played a lot more gigs than the Caverns—was interested in Danny, our drummer, and Lorna, our bass player. As if that wasn't bad enough, it seemed that D and L were seriously thinking of accepting the evil band's offer!

So *that's* what my mirror-mirror-on-the-wall lipstick

message was all about. "Be firm. Do not take no for an answer" referred to my begging Mrs. Densby, head of the Entertainment Committee at T.J. High, to let the Caverns play at the Back to School dance, which would be happening right after Christmas break. I figured if I could get the gig—which would not only be the biggest one we'd played so far, but would actually pay us something—it might prevent my fidgety bandmates from bolting for Circuit Club. One gig, that is what I was desperate for. Then I'd take it from there.

"Regina! Breakfast!"

That's my dad. The human clock. He yells those same two words at exactly 6:30 a.m. every school day. I kid you not. Another annoying thing about him is that he's a morning person. Which is something I'm certainly not.

Unfortunately, I can't avoid Dad in the a.m. He teaches music at my school. So not only do I have to listen to him chatter away as we eat breakfast (he insists we eat together every morning) but on the way to school, too.

I have to admit, Dad and I have a complicated relationship. Mom left us years ago. As a result, Dad is . . . overly protective, I guess you could say. I'm sixteen years old and trying to spread my wings a bit, right? Not untypical. Meanwhile, Dad is doing his best to keep them clipped. Also not untypical. The point is, our diametrically opposed viewpoints on this particular issue leads to more than a little tension between us.

Don't get me wrong. I love Mister B, as the students call him. For one thing, Dad's the reason I'm such a Beatles nerd. He gave me *Meet the Beatles!* (on vinyl) for my twelfth birthday, and I've been hooked on them ever since. So I owe him. But *still*, a girl needs her space. Especially in the morning. But my space, as usual, was about to be invaded.

"What's the cryptic lipstick message all about, kiddo?" Dad looked at me over the glasses he needs to read the morning paper.

"Nothing," I replied, instantly defensive.

"Anything I can help you with?"

"No."

Dad got that wary look in his eyes. I had been shutting him out more and more lately.

"Look, Dad, sometimes a girl needs to figure things out on her own. OK?" Dad looked concerned. But he gave me a reluctant nod.

He was uncharacteristically quiet on the way to school. Which was fine with me. It gave me time to figure out what I was going to say to Mrs. Densby. I didn't want to improvise this very important conversation. It had to be totally worked out.

So work it out I did as Dad drove silently through the peaceful, eternally slumbering suburban streets of Twin Oaks. By the time I entered the teeming halls of Thomas Jefferson High, I had my pitch memorized. That made me feel a little better, but there was still one very important thing I had to do before talking to Mrs. Densby.

Avoid my bandmates. That way they couldn't even broach the subject of breaking up the Caverns. Ducking Danny and Lorna wouldn't be difficult. They're a grade below me, so I didn't have any classes with them. But Julian was a different matter. We have the same math class and share the same home-room. Most days, that's good. Because, well, I guess it's time to tell you about Julian and me.

I'm in love with him. He's not in love with me.

Sorry. I know that's so . . . typical. Unrequited love and all. At least I'm pretty sure it's unrequited. Julian and I really get along, is the thing. We have a similar sense of humor. Kind of *off*, if you know what I mean. We like the same kinds of songs, of course. We sometimes finish each other's sentences. I like it when that happens because that tells me we're totally on the same wavelength.

All that said, what Julian and I have between us feels like a friends kind of vibe. So I've always been afraid to let Julian know how I really feel about him, because that might spoil what we already have.

Now you know one of the main reasons why I was so intent on preventing the Caverns from breaking up. I'm not sure if Julian and I would even see each other very much anymore. It could be the only reason we were friends was because we were in a band together. Take away the band . . . there goes Julian. And any chance for me to ever get up the nerve to tell him how I really feel about him.

Speaking of the boy, here he was. As soon as I entered my homeroom and sat down at my desk, he was standing right next to me.

"We gotta talk, Gina." Julian wore his hair in a classic Beatles cut and dressed '60s-style. Which made him all that more irresistible to me.

"I wouldn't get too close, Julian. I'm . . . getting sick."

"You're the worst liar in the world. All I have to do is look in your eyes."

I didn't want to look in his. He has really terrific blue-green eyes. Soulful eyes. You could get lost in those eyes. As for mine, I put sunglasses on. (I always have a pair on hand, even in winter, just in case I want to look mysterious. Or *inscrutable*, I believe is the word.)

"I have to study," I said.

"It's the last day before Christmas break. What do you have to study for?"

"SATs," I lied. Well, I was taking them sometime early in the New Year, but with my current crisis, I didn't really care about them.

"Danny and Lorna want to meet during lunch," Julian said.

"I can't. I have to—"

"If they're gonna quit, it's better to know sooner than later, don't you think?"

I didn't want to answer that question. So I didn't.

"C'mon, Gina, it's not the end of the world. There are plenty of musicians out there. You can put a new band together."

My heart sank. Because Julian had said "you," not "we."

"You sound like it's a done deal," I said. I wasn't looking at him when I said it. Julian slowly removed my sunglasses. I glanced sideways at him. He looked kind of sad. Which told me he knew it was a done deal. "I gotta get back to . . . this," I said lamely. And quickly put my sunglasses back on. Because I didn't want Julian to see me cry.

Can you believe it? Tears first thing in the a.m. I couldn't help it, however. The Caverns really did mean that much to me. Julian, Lorna, and Danny were my tribe, after all. The band was my identity. In the bizarre, surreal world called high school, the Caverns was my lifeline to sanity.

So that was one reason I started to lose it in homeroom class the morning of the day that I made my wish. The other reason was . . . I didn't think I was that great of a musician. Or singer. Or songwriter. And I figured that's why Danny and Lorna and Julian really wanted to break up the band. I wasn't good enough. Plain and simple.

Maybe everyone at my age has these kind of doubts. For those of you who don't, let me tell you, they can paralyze you. Just stop you in your tracks. Give you panic attacks.

My way of dealing with them was to keep moving. Like a shark. Keep practicing. Keep writing songs (even though nobody ever heard them). Keep trying to get gigs. That helped keep my insecurities at bay. But sometimes they took over.

This was one of those times. Julian, bless him, knew not to push it. He gave me a pat on the arm and said, "We'll talk later." I couldn't get any words out because of the lump in my throat. So I just nodded.

That's how my day started. And it would only get worse from there.

2

"Hi, Mrs. Densby."

I had managed to pull myself together and plaster a fake can-do smile across my face before approaching Mrs. Densby at the front of the auditorium. She had study hall second period, so I figured that was the best time to talk to her about the dance. The smile was meant to cover up the fact that my heart was beating like a hummingbird's.

"Hello, Regina. What can I do for you?"

"You can let the Caverns play at the Back to School dance."

Hmmm. That wasn't what I'd rehearsed, what I'd memorized on the way to school. I was going to break the ice with some small talk. Compliment her on her strange-looking outfit (she always wore weird ensembles that screamed, "Color-coordinated!"). But before I could stop myself, I had eliminated the preliminaries and cut right to the heart of the matter. It seemed to catch Mrs. Densby off guard. She took a moment to consider the question.

"Well, you see, I can't do that, Regina. DJ Jimmy already has the job."

DJs! Besides Circuit Club, the bane of my existence. What

was so special about DJs? Why did everyone want them instead of real, live music these days? At the school dances. At the pool parties in the summer. At the frat parties over at the college. Those were all places my dad had played with the Lost Souls, his high school band.

That was back in the day, that's for sure. The Golden Era, the Shangri-La, the Camelot for garage bands. I feel like I was born thirty years too late. Because today the DJs ruled. And they were strangling the Caverns. Taking all the gigs away from us.

"DJ Jimmy always gets the gigs," I said. "The ones he doesn't play, Circuit Club does. Why not do something different for a change?" I was aware that my voice went up a notch as I talked. Not a good sign. Another pitch and I'd be whining.

"Tell you what I'll do," Mrs. Densby said. "I'll put that suggestion before the committee."

"But that means the next dance. And that's not until next spring!" There it was. I had crossed the border into Whiny Burg with those last two words. I have terrible self-control.

"You kids are always in a hurry, aren't you?" Mrs. Densby leaned casually back in her chair. The look on her face seemed to say, *Wait until you get to my age. You'll learn to take life nice and easy.*

It was all I could do not to grab her by her purple lapels, shake her, and scream, *Yes! You betcha I'm in a hurry! My life depends on this!*

But I didn't. I took a deep breath, then, as calmly as possible, said, "I really wish you would reconsider about the upcoming Back to School dance, Mrs. Densby."

Mrs. Densby took off her glasses, which made my heart sink. 'Cause that's what my dad always did when we were about to have a heart-to-heart.

"Regina, I think it's wonderful that you are so devoted to your band." See, I knew it. "And you mustn't give up. I heard you play at that Battle of the Bands at the beginning of the school year." (The one we lost to Circuit Club.) "And I have to say, I thought you were really good. Especially those Beatles songs."

I gritted my teeth and said, "Thank you."

"Anything else, Regina?"

She'd already dismissed me. I could tell. Her mind was somewhere else. Where, I didn't want to know.

"No, that's it," I said meekly. (As my inner voice screamed, *"Hey, what happened to 'Be firm. Do not take no for an answer?' Huh? What happened?!!!"*)

Just then a paper airplane sailed over our heads and landed on the stage behind Mrs. Densby's desk. Giggles erupted behind me.

"Enough of that! This is *study hall*!" It was not a pretty sight to see Mrs. Densby morph from the Understanding Teacher into the Purple General. So I got out of there, fast. Besides, the bell was ringing, which meant I was going to be late for math class.

But really, at that point I didn't care. My one shot at keeping the band alive had been delivered a fatal blow. My Save the Band campaign was over.

Fortunately, as I dragged my carcass around a corner in the hallway, a ray of light streaming through a high window blasted me flush in the face. It was like being hit with divine inspiration.

I stopped suddenly and smiled up at the glorious light. *What on earth is wrong with you?* I scolded myself. This wasn't the only gig in town. Close to it, but not the *only* one.

There was the VFW, for instance, which sometimes hosted theme dances. True, no one my age would be caught dead in the place, but so what? I would go there right after school and tell them that what they absolutely *had to have* for the holidays was a Back to the '60s dance.

If that didn't work, I'd ask Dad to throw a Christmas party for all of his friends (I think he had some). The Caverns could entertain the guests, of course.

Then there was . . . well, I wasn't sure what else there was, but I'd think of something.

It ain't over till it's over, I thought. Then I practically skipped down the hall with renewed hope and energy.

(Are all teenagers like this? Ricocheting from despair to euphoria within one turn of the minute hand? If so, no wonder we're always so exhausted!)

Math, the class I was late for, was the one I had with Julian. I was bursting to tell him about all of my gig ideas but figured it might be best to just surprise him. Besides, when we made eye contact a couple of times, I got the impression he didn't really want to talk to me. Maybe because of my emo display in the morning. That kind of thing can make a guy uncomfortable. So we sidestepped each other after class, and I managed to avoid a confrontation with Lorna and Danny by not going to lunch.

As I stood at my locker at the end of the school day—with all the crazy energy swirling around me, that special energy that can only come from a rambunctious group of schoolkids just before a long vacation—I had convinced myself the Caverns (and hence, Julian and me) still had a chance. And I couldn't wait to get to the VFW and *make magic happen*!

"Regina?"

I froze. That unmistakable voice could come from only one person.

Lorna.

I pretended not to hear her. That way, maybe she'd just go away. Eventually. But she wasn't going away. I knew that. I just didn't want to believe it.

Lorna leaned against the locker next to mine. She's a cool-looking girl and a classic cynic. We hadn't known each other all that well before she tried out for the band. Still, like most kids in my school, I had certainly known *of* Lorna. That's because she'd always had a pretty wild rep. The whole punk, dressed-in-black thing? Lorna had blasted through that before she'd even hit her teenage years. Even though that wasn't her deal anymore, she still had a prickly personality and looked at the world through black-tinted glasses to a certain extent. She looked at me now, poker-faced.

"You've been a tough girl to find," she said.

"I've been busy."

"You've been avoiding me."

"And me," Danny piped in from behind.

I turned to face Danny. Normally, he's all smiles and high fives. He's like a human pinball. Talks a mile a minute and plays the drums like a madman. Think ADD ten-year-old in a fifteen-year-old body, and you've got the idea. Underneath all that hyper-energy, though, Danny's a really sweet guy and Lorna's opposite, personality-wise.

"Listen, guys, I've got some great ideas for gigs. I just need a little time. . . ."

"That's what you said last month," Lorna said. "*Two* months ago, you said that."

"All we ever do is practice," Danny added. It sounded rehearsed, what they were saying. And it really bugged me that Lorna was obviously the one who had been in charge of the rehearsal. Danny seemed like her puppet or something. Still, I had to be nice to Lorna. I needed her in the band. If she went, I had no doubt Danny would follow right behind her.

"Speaking of practicing, you guys are coming over tonight, right? It'll be fun. We'll kick off the holiday with some new tunes, and . . ."

"We're not coming over, Regina." Lorna didn't have a problem getting right to it. Danny looked at the linoleum floor. He wasn't big on confrontation.

"Why not?" I asked, as innocently as I could.

"C'mon, Regina. Julian must have told you."

"He said you might be joining Circuit Club. *Might* being the operative word here. I thought that meant I had a little time to get some gigs and—"

Interrupting my plea for patience, Lorna said in a bored, monotone voice, "You know what? I'm getting tired of the whole sixties thing, anyway."

Tired of '60s music! That was blasphemous, of course.

But I checked my anger and tried to channel it. "So you'd rather play with some techno . . . rap . . . heavy-metal band? Is that it?"

"At least they play for people once in a while. And get paid for it."

I was aware that a small group had gathered across the hallway and were staring at us. Someone whispered, "Catfight!"

"We'll talk about this tonight," I said in desperation.

"Didn't you hear anything we said?"

"I did, but I suggest you think it over a bit."

"We've been thinking about this for months. We're tired of thinking about it. We're tired of practicing all the time and never playing for anyone. It's a drag." Lorna looked at Danny for some backup. Danny glanced at me, helplessly, then went back to studying the pattern on the floor.

Before I knew what I was doing, I slammed my locker and walked off down the hallway.

"You can't just walk away like this, Regina," Lorna said in an angry, louder voice, drawing even more attention from the crowd.

I didn't respond. Tears were suddenly blinding my vision. The exit doors swam in a blur at the far end of the hall. If I could just get through those doors, I'd be OK. That's what I convinced myself.

"OK, we quit," Lorna yelled. "Is that what you needed to hear to make it official?"

It was. That single word was like a knife in my heart.

That's when I tripped. Maybe it was the fatal word, *quit*.

Maybe it was the blinding tears. Maybe both. But the rubber toe of my sneaker caught on the hallway floor at that precise moment, and I tumbled forward and hit the deck.

Picture that. With everyone watching . . . *splat*! Right on my face. Totally humiliated, I leaped to my feet and ran off down the hallway. I could hear some people laugh as I pushed through the doors and escaped outside.

I found a private spot on the other side of the football field before I gave in to a total breakdown. For the second time in the course of that misbegotten day, I lost it. But this one was a gusher compared to the one in homeroom.

I know what you're thinking. What a nutty gal. Or a case of overreacting hormones, at the very least. But the pain I felt was real, believe me. It was like I'd been hit in the gut and all the air had escaped from inside me. And as I sat behind the football field on the wet grass, I knew it was time to accept the inevitable.

The band was over. It really was. Just like that, my tribe had been reduced to a grand total of . . .

One.